PRAISE FOR AMANDA LAMB

"Amanda Lamb has crafted a cmopelling story... Maddie is definitely not dead last but out front, unearthing clues to the unfolding mystery. Keep digging, Maddie. Keep writing, Amanda!"
    –Scott Mason, author and Emmy-award-winning journalist

"Amanda has a gift of taking the reader on a journey of intrigue, laughter, and insight into what can be the wonderful and troubling world of journalism. She opens the mind with a laser beam shot of reality and we are better for it."
    –David Crabtree, award-winning television anchor and journalist.

"I love the way Amanda Lamb plunges into a powerful plot and takes readers for a riveting ride! The writing is crisp and clean. The story is compelling. There's an authenticity in Amanda's prose thanks, in part, to the author's background as a top-notch television journalist covering crime stories. What an awesome debut as a novelist!"
    –Bill Leslie, former news anchor for NBC affiliate WRAL-TV

"Amanda Lamb weaves together an intriguing mystery with a behind-the-scenes look at TV news. With 25 years of crime reporting, Lamb spins an authentic, compelling story about a reporter who finds herself in the midst of solving a murder. Readers will love the colorful characters & personal insights that make this mystery a must-read."
    –Sharon O'Donnell, author and award-winning columnist

LIES

THAT BIND

A MADDIE ARNETTE NOVEL

AMANDA LAMB

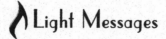 Light Messages

Durham, NC

Published 2021, by Light Messages
www.lightmessages.com
Durham, NC 27713 USA
SAN: 920-9298

Paperback ISBN: 978-1-61153-377-4
Ebook ISBN: 978-1-61153-378-1
Library of Congress Control Number: 2021930545

For my father, William Lamb.
Your career as a district attorney
inspired my interest in criminal law.
Your love and support
made me believe I could be anything.

PROLOGUE

That single sentence unraveled all the good in just a few seconds.

It wasn't really an admission. It was just four simple words. You couldn't help yourself. My questions put you on the defensive.

"What's it to you?"

They came on the heels of my inquiry, indirect, but subtle words with a subtext that we both understood to be an accusation. It wasn't what you did, it was about what it symbolized: the darkness of a person who I didn't know, didn't want to know.

"You know what you did," I said. To my surprise, I said it without anger, or even despair. It just came out in that moment. I hadn't planned to say it, but there it was, out in the open. And once it was out there, you only had two choices, lie or confess.

I'm pretty sure that you knew me well enough to know your admission changed everything. It undermined any positive narrative I had spun about you over the years. My naïve heart was officially broken, shattered under the weight of your ugly truth.

"What's it to you?"

The flippant way you said it, your inflection, made me realize that you were not the person I had fantasized about in my dreams. You were a stranger to me, a vain interloper preying on my vulnerable spirit. How could I be so wrong about a person? I've been beating myself up every single day since that moment wondering where I went off course.

No, you didn't do it to me. Frankly, it had little to do with me. But your admission finally made me see the real you. It also did something else, something brilliant. It set me free.

—Tilly

1

TRUTHSAYER

"MADDIE? MADDIE ARNETTE?" The unfamiliar woman said to me, tugging at my sleeve. I was used to people coming up to me in public places because I was a local television news reporter, but this was something different, this felt *personal*.

I scanned the grocery store and surveyed the dozens of people milling around the produce, carefully examining the tomatoes, avocados, and heads of lettuce for imperfections, and then putting them into their carts once they passed the eyeball test. I was safe. I was not alone. Nothing bad could happen to me here, at least that's what I told myself.

I had to be polite. That was a part of my job that I took seriously. No matter what happened in public, I couldn't lose my cool. I was a reflection of the Channel 8 News team, part of their brand, even when I wasn't working.

"Yes," I replied after a long pause, forcing a smile. "That's me."

"I've been trying to get in contact with you for a while. This is going to sound weird, but I have some important information for you. I know something that you need to know."

"I'm listening," I said, finally getting a firm grip on the thin plastic bag in my hands and delicately peeling it open to put a few bananas inside. It took me three tries to open the bag, one less than it usually

3

takes. I was silently applauding myself while at the same time quietly dreading what this woman was about to tell me.

People routinely approached me with story ideas. Most of the time their pitches were like the diverging roots of a tree—long and bending, curling down into the soil in a million different directions with no real focus. But I always listened. Once in a while someone would come to me with a true gem, a story that I knew *had* to be done and would make great television. But I had to listen to a lot of frog pitches to find that one prince story.

"It's about your father, Roger."

"What about Roger?" She had my full attention now. My heart started beating faster just hearing his name. I chose not to think about him most days, because when I did, I immediately remembered everything that I had lost in my life. We had been estranged for so long that it was easier for me not to think about him.

"I know this is going to sound crazy, but Roger didn't kill your mother."

The other shoppers in the brightly lit grocery store seemed to vanish, and it was just me and the woman in the red puffy down coat standing between the apples and the oranges. It suddenly struck me as odd that she was wearing such a heavy coat in the mild North Carolina climate. It was late February, and while the last remnants of what we called winter in the south seemed to be hanging around—slightly cold, gray mornings, occasional frost on the windshield—we all knew that spring was right around the corner. So, maybe she wasn't from here, this stranger overdressed in a heavy winter coat.

"How do you know that?" I whispered through gritted teeth as I leaned closer to her, trying to contain the potentially inflammatory conversation to our ears only. I could feel the panic rising in my throat, a tightness that strangled my words.

"Because my son is the one who killed your mother. The *wrong* man went to prison."

I couldn't hear anything the woman said after that because of the intense ringing in my ears. I looked right through her while her

4

lips continued to move quickly, her face animated, but there was no sound reaching me from her mouth, just the incessant roaring in my head that hijacked her words. Finally, she stopped talking and pressed a small piece of paper into my hand. She curled my fingers around it to make sure I didn't drop it.

"That's my number. Call me."

I reached out to grab the woman's arm, to keep her from leaving, but she was too fast. I needed to know more. I couldn't let her walk away. I felt a desperation that I hadn't felt in a long time. I flashed to a moment when I was a little girl, looking up at my mother, Patty, her red hair aglow with sunlight peeking through the strands, my small, chubby hand in hers. We were outside, walking somewhere, and I felt safe. Was it a real memory, or just something I made up? I couldn't really recall much about that time in my life. I was only three. I could never separate the true memories of my mother from the stories others told me over the years.

When I finally resurfaced from my daydream, the woman had slipped into the crowd of shoppers and disappeared. Suddenly, the people looked like they were in a video that was being fast-forwarded as they raced up and down the aisles. I stood motionless in the middle of the rush for a moment while I tried to process what the woman had just told me. Part of me wanted to run after her. The other part of me wanted to run away.

2

DEATH INVESTIGATION

I DROVE OUT OF THE GROCERY STORE PARKING LOT, my brain swirling around the bomb the woman had just dropped into my lap. I had left a full cart of groceries right there in the middle of the produce section and walked out. I knew it was the wrong thing to do—that someone else would now have to restock the shelves with my unpurchased pile of items—but I *had* to go. I felt like I was going to faint, right there under the fluorescent lights. Somehow, I made it to the safety of my car before tears came flooding down my face. I grabbed a handful of napkins from my glove compartment and wiped my cheeks. Why now? Why would this woman approach me with this information almost four decades after my mother's death? I had almost made peace with the fact that my father, Roger, was right where he was supposed to be—behind bars. I didn't need or want him in my life.

As the loop of contradicting facts ping-ponged around in my head, my phone rang. I hit the answer button on the screen and connected to my Bluetooth. My assignment editor's voice penetrated the sanctity of my car with her well-intentioned, but shrill tone. She always sounded breathless, like she was being chased or something was on fire right next to her.

"Maddie, I know you're off today, but I really need your help.

A few people called in sick and we're super short. Got a body call. Pretty sure it's a suicide, but still need a crew to check it out. Any way you could meet Buster there? I just need some boots on the ground."

Janie Page was an assignment editor for Channel 8 News who brainstormed story ideas every day and then assigned crews to cover them. Today, as usual, she sounded desperate. This was mostly because she never had enough people to get the job done. It was a shell game where she was constantly moving pieces around to see if she could get most of what she needed covered on any given day. It stressed me out just to think about her job. I didn't envy her.

Buster Patton was the television photographer I had worked with for many years. We finished each other's sentences, found the same bizarre things funny, and fought like a brother and sister. I called him my work-husband, and he called me his work-wife. Sometimes, we needed a break from each other. I joked that we desperately needed to go to marriage counseling. But deep down we loved and supported one other.

I pictured Janie twisting her blonde curls anxiously while she spoke to me, a large cup of lukewarm coffee by her hand, police scanners buzzing all around her in the background adding to her frenetic energy.

I knew this call on my day off wasn't Janie's fault. I was sure our boss, Dex Hughes, had told her to call me and ask me if I could come in. Dex was retired military and his directives often came across like orders on a battlefield. And, in a way, television news reporting was like being on a battlefield. With the constant deadlines, the pressure to be first, and the drive to scoop the competition, it was like throwing yourself into a fire and praying you would escape without too many burns. In addition, we now had to deal with constant criticism from viewers online, which only added to the battle fatigue.

I had stepped back from the crime beat two years ago after my husband, Adam, died from a brain tumor. Being a caregiver to him had exhausted me physically and emotionally in ways that I could never have imagined. Watching someone die stripped me of my desire to be part of other people's tragedies. Most importantly, I was now a single mother to twelve-year-old twins, and they needed my undivided attention, something I couldn't fully give them if my job sucked the life out of me.

Janie understood this, and, as a result, was always hesitant to ask me to fill in on these stories. But Dex had no such concerns about rerouting me to blood and guts on a semi-regular basis. He was a hardcore newsman, no-time-for-bullshit kind of guy. As much as I hated him for his Teflon exterior, I likewise admired him for the same set of character traits. You always knew where he stood, and I respected that. He knew that I was a workhorse with a healthy dose of martyrdom that made it hard for me to say no when they needed me.

My new beat after Adam's death was covering animal stories. Dex had jokingly dubbed it "Amazing Animal Tales," and the name had stuck. My producers often spelled it "Tails" as a joke. There were surprisingly plenty of these stories to go around—a bird that saved a baby from choking, a cat who could paint, monkeys who did complex math problems, and a bear that broke into a couple's house and fell asleep in their bed. But when real news broke, it was all-hands-on-deck, and my feature stories were shoved to the back burner. I accepted that. It was part of the job. Feel-good stories were something our audience wanted and enjoyed, but real news came first.

"Sure, Janie. I can do it. Just text me the address," I said, trying to hide the tears in my voice. That was the thing about news, just when you were wallowing in some personal crisis, *news happened*, and it wiped out everything else you were dealing with, at least for that moment. In some ways, this numbing effect was a welcome distraction from thinking my mother's murder. I knew that when the distraction was over, I would have to process what had just happened with the strange woman in the grocery store.

We didn't usually cover suicides, unless they somehow affected the public—like a person jumping off a bridge into rush hour traffic. But in the early stages of an any death investigation, the police usually didn't share with us whether or not the fatality was

8

suspicious. They simply labeled it a "death investigation" until they had enough information to classify it. The hope as a reporter was that someone you knew at the scene would tip you off that it was a suicide, so you could move on to another story and leave the grieving family in peace.

When I pulled up to 47 Conover Place, the crime scene tape stretched around the entire property. Investigators were concentrating on the driveway. They stood in a tight circle around what I presumed to be the body covered in a white sheet. Crime scene investigators from the Tirey County CSI unit walked around the driveway with blue sterile foot coverings, taking photographs and picking up items in their purple latex-gloved hands and putting them into plastic bags. Dusk was turning to dark, and a few investigators were rolling in large LED lights on tall metal stands to illuminate their work area.

I noticed Buster at the edge of the crime scene tape with his camera, shooting video of the plainclothes detectives as they consulted with one another in a tight circle around the mound with the white sheet covering it.

"What do we have?" I said, putting a gentle hand on Buster's back so as not to startle him.

"Look who the cat dragged in," he said with his trademark sarcasm, not looking up from the viewfinder. "Let me guess, Janie called you and made you feel guilty that someone called in sick. You were probably at the grocery store."

"Bingo, you're right on both counts. You know me so well, it's scary. But she made it sound like it was probably a suicide, at least that's what she thought after listening to the scanner traffic. And if we can confirm that, we can leave."

"I'm guessing she's probably right. There's a woman under the sheet. My guy inside the tape says they found a gun in the driveway next to the body. Looks like she lay out a towel first, sat on it and put a single bullet in her head. Not sure why someone would put down a towel first. It's odd. Maybe she didn't want to stain the driveway or something crazy like that. Who would care about the damn driveway when you're putting a bullet in your brain? I guess people aren't always thinking logically when they do stuff like this, or maybe they are, which is even weirder," Buster said, pulling away from the viewfinder and turning to face me. I could barely make him out in the fading light. "Problem is some family members found her, touched a bunch of stuff, tried to clean it up. Contaminated the scene. So, right now, it's hard to tell exactly what they have."

"What kind of towel?"

"What do you mean what kind of towel?"

"Like a bath towel, a beach towel?"

"I don't know, a beach towel I guess. I got here just before they covered her. It was a big towel, some kind of checkered pattern. I don't know, pink and white maybe. Why do you care?"

"You know me, I care about everything. Every little detail."

"That's what makes you *so crazy*," Buster snickered, and turned his attention back to the camera.

I saw two men off to the side who didn't look like investigators. One was middle-aged, and one older, maybe a father and a son. They looked tired and frazzled. Their dress-shirt sleeves were rolled up and they had their hands on their hips. Their shirts were wrinkled and unbuttoned at the neck making them look like they had lost their ties somewhere along the way. They looked like maybe they had come right from work. Their heads were close together and they were talking quietly, occasionally glancing over their shoulders at the officers.

"I'm guessing that's the family. Husband?"

"Nope, brother-in-law and nephew of the dead woman, so I'm told. They got here right after the cops. 911 got a call from a neighbor who heard a loud noise. Then she looked out the window and saw the dead lady in the driveway. Seems like it would be hard to see the driveway from the neighbors' houses through all those trees, but, apparently, this one neighbor has a bathroom window that has a partial view."

"So, where's the husband? Is there a husband?"

"Good question, one I would be asking if I were the cops. Name is Hubert Dawson, owns a popular chain of honky-tonk restaurants in the area. We've been there. I had a coupon, remember, two-for-one burgers? Called Hubert's Roadhouse. Dude is supposed to be a real prick according to my guy on the inside."

Buster loved to make me feel like he had better sources than I did; that's why he didn't want me to know who his "guy" was in the police department. But I really didn't care. I just wanted to confirm it was a suicide, so I could get on my way. I wanted to get home to my kids and relieve the babysitter, Candace. I had asked her to feed them dinner once again. This was a habit I was trying very hard to break. Since Adam died in 2016, I was trying to be both mother and father to Miranda and Blake. It wasn't easy.

I remembered eating at Hubert's Roadhouse one time. It was loud, filled with hokey, old-timey decorations, and peanut shells covered the floor. I also remembered that it was packed with customers and that the food was delicious.

Hubert had these corny commercials where he was equally as loud as the din in his restaurant, shouting at viewers to *Come on down to the Roadhouse!* I knew television advertising wasn't cheap, so I imagined he must be fairly successful if he could afford this type of platform.

I let Buster know I would be back in a few minutes. I needed to find someone who might tell me the cause of death off the record. It wasn't just about getting home to the kids. I couldn't stop thinking about the woman from the grocery store. I was still mired in our conversation, stuck in the heaviness of what she had told me and what it could mean. Her words kept coming back to me in flashes— *Roger didn't kill your mother. My son is the one. The wrong man went to prison.*

If she was telling the truth, my entire life had been built on a lie.

3

JUST TILLY

EVEN AS THE SUN DIPPED BENEATH THE HORIZON casting an orange glow over the scene, I could make out my old friend, Tommy Flick, a detective everyone called Kojak, standing beneath one of the LED crime scene lights to the side of the driveway. His bald head reflected the glow, and a toothpick dangled from his lips. I knew he had seen me. Our eyes locked briefly, but we both had reasons for wanting to keep our friendship quiet.

I felt my phone vibrate in my back pocket and looked down to see a text from him: "Walk down street. Meet at 41 Conover Place, near mailbox."

I turned away from the dead woman's house and started walking. Out of the corner of my eye, I saw Kojak duck beneath the crime scene tape and head in the same direction through the shadows. We reached the mailbox at about the same time. Kojak and I had been friends and colleagues since I started at Channel 8. In many ways, Kojak was always watching out for my best interests both professionally and personally.

"What are you doing out at night, kid?" he asked, giving me a playful slap on the back. He continued to call me "kid" even though we were maybe just about ten years apart in age. Although, he would never tell me his age, so I really didn't know for sure how much older he was. The nickname was an homage to my naivete when we first met many years prior. I was a young cub reporter with a lot to learn. He helped season me by showing me how things worked in the underbelly of the criminal justice system. I earned his trust and respect, and likewise, he earned mine.

"You know, Janie, *guilt trip*, same story," I rattled off.

"Got it. Some things never change, do they? Well, officially, but way off the record, think they're going to call this a suicide."

"Something in the way you're saying 'call' isn't convincing me that you're convinced."

"There's a note," Kojak said as he pulled a lollipop out of his pocket, unwrapped it, and replaced his toothpick with the candy, throwing the toothpick onto the ground. I was tempted to scold him for littering, but I stopped myself. I was just thankful he had traded cigarettes for lollipops, a habit that earned him the nickname of his namesake from the 1970s detective show. But now, even lollipops were a forbidden fruit because his wife, Marion, or "the drill sergeant" as he so often called her, was trying to get him to quit sugar. His secret was safe with me.

"So, that's it. There's a note. Must be a suicide then," I said, feeling relieved for me and sad for the dead woman at the same time.

"Sure, that's what they're saying. But it's a weird note. Was found it on her computer."

"What do you mean 'weird?'"

"I don't know how to explain it. It's like she's talking directly to someone she has a beef with, someone she was in a relationship with. Could be an intimate partner, family member. Hard to tell. I don't know. It's just weird. She's calling the person out. Like she caught him or her doing something real bad, and she's done with the fool for good. But it doesn't sound like a goodbye-to-the-world note to me. She comes across as strong, kind of a pistol, not like someone who is wallowing in self-pity. Someone to be reckoned with. Broads like that don't tend to take their own lives. I know, I'm married to one," he said referring to Marion.

"You have a name?" I asked, itching to do the online research that I always did when I got the name of anyone connected to a case I was covering. When you knew where to look, you could learn *a lot* about a person with just a few quick keystrokes.

"Tilly, Tilly Dawson. She's married to that redneck restaurant guy, you know the one who yells at you on TV? Tells you to *Come on down to the Roadhouse!* Ads give me a frigging headache, but they actually make damn good ribs. Cops love the place. He gives us twenty percent off."

"Does he know what happened? Have you called him yet?"

"He knows. We sent one of the guys over to his office. Apparently, he fell apart. Real torn up. He might have been a pretty shitty husband from what I'm hearing, but he certainly didn't want his wife to off herself. No one would want that. He gave us her laptop and password, gave us permission to look at it. That's how we found the note. Didn't act like he was hiding anything. Real straight up."

"Kids?"

"One girl, grown. Twenty-year-old named Delilah. Father called her right away. Officer who was there said she works as a waitress at one of his restaurants and she rushed over to her dad's office in her uniform and then literally fell to her knees in front of him, sobbing. Real sad stuff. I hate it for that young officer who had to break the news. But it's part of the job. I've had to do it myself many times. And it sucks."

"Really sad. Any bad blood between her and the daughter? Mothers and daughters can have complicated relationships."

"True, nothing so far. We're looking into everything."

"Tilly is an unusual name by the way. Is it short for something?"

"I don't know. That's what everyone calls her. Just Tilly."

As I stood there in the descending cloak of darkness I couldn't help but wonder what had been so bad in Tilly's life that she would want to end it. I also couldn't stop thinking about why a stranger would have wanted to end my mother's life.

4

ESTHER

I FOUND THE CRUMPLED PIECE OF PAPER from the woman in the grocery store on the floorboard of my car the next morning. It must have fallen from my pocket when I pulled out my phone. I couldn't decide if it was or a blessing or a curse that I hadn't lost the number. After some heated internal debate, I labeled it a sign, one that I needed to pay attention to as much as it pained me to think about reopening my childhood wounds. The woman had sought me out at this time in my life for *some* reason, and I owed it to myself to at least hear what she had to say, to find out what she thought she knew. It might be a trip down a rabbit hole with no reward, or it might be something I desperately needed to know.

Despite the prevailing belief that the woman's death from the previous night was a suicide, Dex still made me do a quick live report on the air in the eleven o'clock newscast saying there was a death investigation underway at 47 Conover Place. I felt very uncomfortable about putting this family's pain on blast into the public arena, but Dex rightfully pointed out that had she killed herself inside the house it would not have been a story. But, because she did it outside in a neighborhood where people could have seen her, it became a public incident, even though she was in her own driveway.

"Let's get on the record with it just in case it turns out to be something more," Dex said to me over the phone after I told him what I had learned about the suspected suicide note and the fact that the police didn't seem concerned that there was a killer on the loose. I practically begged him to let it go. I told him that if it did turn out to be a suicide, we would look awful for broadcasting this family's private tragedy, but my pleas had no impact on Dex's conscience. He told me to "buck up" and insisted that we do a live report, leaving no room for negotiation. So, I did what a good soldier does: I followed orders.

For my emotional well-being, I had intentionally deep-sixed the encounter in the grocery store until I saw the crumpled yellow sticky note on my black floor mat with a name and cell phone number written in red ink that weirdly matched the color of the woman's puffy winter coat. *Details, these were my forte.* The note read: "Call me! Esther."

I knew I would have to face this situation sooner or later, so I decided to go ahead and deal with it. I called Esther and left a message suggesting we meet for coffee at the Oak City Bistro. I hoped she couldn't detect the shakiness in my throat as I tried and failed to sound confident in my voicemail. On one hand, the logical part of my brain knew it was absurd to be talking about the outcome of a murder case from 1980 where a man was arrested, tried in a court of law and convicted by a jury of his peers. Yet, I had covered cases like this before. I knew it was possible for an innocent man to go to prison. Forensic science forty years ago wasn't even close to being as sophisticated as it is today. Back then, juries decided cases on a mountain of circumstantial evidence and science that was, at best, imperfect.

Maybe this woman, Esther, really did know *something*. But at the same time, I was afraid that whatever she knew could turn the story I had lived with for practically my entire life upside down. I didn't know what my world would look like if Roger was innocent. Plus, I had spent so many years hating Roger for what he did to my mother that I wasn't sure I could ever change my feelings even with new evidence to the contrary.

Like my visions of my mother, I had a few of Roger from the time I called "before"—Roger holding me in his big strong arms, my face nuzzling his shoulder, feeling safe. Like my visions of my mother, I was never sure if these were real, or just false images I made up to make myself feel better.

Along with my grandmother, Roger's mother, Belle, who raised me, I continued to visit Roger in prison after he was convicted. At the time, I didn't know why he was in prison, only that my mother was dead, and my father had been taken away from me. Deep down inside, I must have known there was some connection between the two, but I didn't want to admit it. I last visited him when I was twelve. After that, I told the judge I didn't want to see him anymore, and the judge told me I didn't have to see him if I didn't want to. I knew it made Belle sad, but I couldn't help it. Prison was a scary place, no place for a little girl. And I barely knew him anymore. What was the point?

It was moments like this when I longed for Adam's advice. He had been the only person other than Kojak and my best girlfriend Louise who knew the truth about my past. Adam was always my safe harbor, my best friend, my confidant, but when he died, all that changed. Suddenly, I had no safety net. My sad story now threatened to pull me back into a dark place, a place that Adam's love had rescued me from.

Only my love for my twins, Blake and Miranda, could pull me out of my self-pity after Adam's death and keep me going. If it weren't for them, I didn't know what cave I would be living in. So, while Esther's claims threatened to turn my world upside down again, knowing the truth was a risk I had to take. It was the only real path to freedom.

5

HOARDING

"GOT ANOTHER CAT LADY. Animal Control says she's got 93 cats in a two-bedroom townhouse. Completely toxic situation. Cat pee everywhere. You can smell the house a mile away. Officers are going there with a warrant now to take custody of them. Need you and Buster to get over there right away," Janie said with an inappropriate level of enthusiasm in her voice. I understood where she was coming from, though. We spent so many days prostrate to the news gods praying for something, *anything*, to happen, that when something finally did happen, it had the tendency to make us all giddy, even if this wasn't the most appropriate emotion to have.

"Got it," I replied, trying to match her glee with my measured neutrality. I knew we had something crazy like eleven hours of news to fill a day between all the shows, but inside, I refused to be happy about someone else's misfortune, even if it made good television. Publicly, I always put on a brave face and did my job. Most of my animal stories had happy endings, but every so often I got a curve ball like this one thrown at me where the animal beat and the crime beat intersected in a negative way.

When I pulled up to the cat lady's house, the door was wide open, and I could see inside the front hallway. It was piled high with brown cardboard boxes of overflowing stuff from the floor to the ceiling. On the grass, in front of the home, there were dozens of small metal cages that I presumed contained the cats the animal control officers had already rescued.

Being more than a bit on the obsessive-compulsive side myself, the concept of hoarding made me feel physically ill. I couldn't even leave dishes in the sink at night and go to bed. I couldn't leave my house in the morning if my bed was unmade. Peering into this woman's house was my worst nightmare realized. Yet, at the same time, I understood this woman had a mental illness and that she couldn't control her behavior without some help. It wasn't her fault.

Adam was always understanding of my need for order in the house. He attributed it to the fact that I didn't have control over my mother dying or Roger going to prison. This disruption in the order of my life at such a young age created a need for control, according to Adam, that manifested itself in big and small ways. It was the small ways that made me challenging to live with because I required a high level of organization in my house. Adam handled it well, ignoring my need to pick everything up off the floor or pile things on dressers and countertops. He quietly followed behind me and made sure I wasn't putting away something he didn't want to lose.

So, in a weird way I could relate to this woman. Her hoarding was not that different than my need for order; it was something neither of us could control.

I watched as the officers carried out skinny, unhealthy looking cats and placed them into the remaining empty metal carriers that lined the lawn. The animals' hair was patchy, their limbs scrawny, ears limp. They didn't even seem to protest, just dangled resolutely in the officers' meaty hands covered in blue latex gloves until they were gently placed into the waiting cages.

And then I saw the homeowner. She was probably my age, but with a visibly harder life under her weathered skin. She was leaning against a post on the front porch of the home that was covered in blue, crumbling paint, which contrasted sharply with her faded yellow, shapeless jumper. Her brown, curly hair was unkempt, but it was her face that caught my eye. It was more than just sadness buried in her eyes and sunken cheeks; *it was defeat*. It was as if this world she had created did have some kind of order to her; it was just order that no one else could understand. She watched with cool detachment as her beloved pets were carried out one by one to the small cages, averting her eyes only when a few let out tiny squeals as they passed by her.

As I watched the scene unfold, I kept feeling my phone vibrate in my pocket. I wanted to ignore it. I tried, but I couldn't resist the temptation. What if it was something important? What if it was one of the twins? When I finally gave in and clicked on the text message, I realized that Kojak had sent me a screenshot of Tilly's letter. It was probably the only thing that could keep me from thinking about my imminent meeting with Esther.

After a cursory scan I realized that Tilly Dawson was no wallflower, and in my opinion, after reading her powerful words, she didn't seem like someone who would take her own life.

6

PENNY

I WAS IN MY GRANDMOTHER'S GUEST ROOM when I heard the whispers coming from the adults in the other room. I could only catch tiny snippets of what they were saying, words drifting on the edge of my ability to hear them—dead, gun, driveway, blood, beach towel, suicide.

It sounded like my uncle and grandfather talking to my Grandma Trisha. They were talking about something that happened to my great aunt. I didn't really know her, but I had met her a few times. They called her "Tilly." My cousin was next to me in the bed snoring away. We had spent the night together at my grandmother's, something we did about once a month. We always had fun. My grandmother let us stay up late and watch anything we wanted on Netflix. She didn't check to see if the show was what my mom called "age appropriate," whatever that really means. I feel like I'm always explaining to my mom that being eleven today isn't the same as being eleven when she was growing up. That kids today know a lot more and can handle a lot more. Sometimes, I think she thinks it's like the eighties, when she grew up, when kids didn't really know anything because they didn't have the Internet.

I traced the ornate white wood of the headboard with my fingers as I waited for someone to come and tell us what was going on. I knew enough to know that when adults whispered something was very wrong.

I heard the door creak open before I saw the silhouette of my grandmother in the doorway, framed by a halo of light coming from a lamp in the hallway. She sat down on the edge of the bed; the coils in the old mattress groaned. I didn't know what time it was, but it had to be really early because the sun wasn't even up yet. The sun was always up when I woke up, which was usually after 7.

"Penny, Matilda, wake up. I have something to tell you; something's happened," Grandma Trisha said.

She told us in a hushed voice that something very bad had happened to Aunt Tilly, that she had been shot and she was dead. Like most adults, she left out important details that she didn't think we could handle. Not only could I handle them, I needed them. My head was spinning with questions—where, how, who? I was pretty sure my questions would not be answered, so I sat quietly and listened with my head resting uncomfortably against the knotty wooden headboard. My grandmother brushed the bangs out of my eyes with one hand, and then squeezed my cousin's shoulder with her other hand before leaving the room and telling us to get up and get dressed. She said people would be coming to the house to "pay their respects," and we had to be ready.

I knew what the word "suicide" meant because I read a lot of books, books that were meant for teenagers, but I didn't know anyone who had ever done it. I knew it was something that people didn't like to talk about, a "taboo" subject, as my mother would call it. I guessed maybe people were embarrassed by it, which really didn't make sense to me. To me, it was just very sad thinking about how bad someone's life must be for them to want to end it. I wondered what was so bad for Aunt Tilly. I really didn't know her very well. I had only been around her a few times at family events like weddings and funerals. She was married to my grandmother's brother, mean old Uncle Hubert. I could never understand how he got Aunt Tilly to marry him.

Aunt Tilly was younger than Uncle Hubert, by at least eight years if I had to guess. She was beautiful, with dark hair, red lips, and skin so pale and perfect she looked like Snow White. I couldn't imagine what could be so bad when you looked like that.

The worst thing I could think about in Aunt Tilly's life was Uncle Hubert. He was mean as a pit bull in my opinion. He always gave me the creeps, the way he looked at you with his dark eyes and barked orders at Grandma Trisha, his sister, when they worked at the restaurant they used to own together. My mom said Uncle Hubert "bought my grandmother out" because she just couldn't be around him anymore. I wasn't exactly sure what that meant, but I knew Grandma Trisha seemed a lot happier these days since she retired, and I guess she got some money from Uncle Hubert to go away, because she starting doing lots of things to her house like adding a screened-in porch which she loved, and a hot tub, which Matilda and I loved.

No, Uncle Hubert was not a nice man. I felt that way about him deep in my bones. And my bones were usually right.

7

DREAMS

I HAD A DREAM LAST NIGHt that I was on a beach, digging in the sand, and I found several beautiful pieces of costume jewelry. One piece was a thick, gold ring with bits of gemstones adorning it. There was a wide, silver cuff bracelet with an intricate design delicately carved into the metal. There were single earrings, not pairs, peeking from beneath the grains of sand, twinkling at me, urging me to take them. I decided they must be left over from a party on the beach the night before, that they were mine to take because no one had claimed them. But then I noticed something else—it was a key on a ring with a silver nameplate attached to a leather band that dangled from the key. As I pulled the key from the sand and wiped off the band, I could make out a name. It was engraved with the name "Tilly" in bold black letters on a shiny silver background.

I sat up in bed and threw the covers off. I was burning up. What did it mean? The jewelry discarded, the personalized key in the sand? It meant something bad had happened to the woman in my dream. Someone had taken her and left her jewelry and keys behind. But what did this have to do with Tilly? She wasn't missing. She was dead, dead by her own hand according to police. I thought about the letter again. I had already read through it several times trying to decipher what it meant. I looked at each line like it was part of

24

a bigger puzzle. If only I could put the pieces together, I would understand what she was trying to say.

I looked at my watch and suddenly realized I had to get the kids to school so that I wouldn't be late for my meeting with Esther, a meeting I was dreading. But I knew that I needed to go to satisfy my own curiosity. She had returned my call with a message of her own, agreeing to meet her at the nearby coffee shop I had suggested. I convinced myself that she was well-meaning, but simply misguided. But I had to find out for sure what she knew, or at the very least, *what she believed she knew.*

"Blake, Miranda, chop-chop. Everyone up. We need to get rolling," I yelled down the hallway in the direction of their bedrooms and was rewarded with their collective groans. "If you hurry up, I will take you to Chick-fil-A on the way to school," I said. I turned on the lights and opened the blinds in each bedroom as they groaned again, louder this time, and pulled the covers over their heads. Even as I busied myself with the mundane tasks of life, my strange dream and snippets of Tilly's letter kept coming back to me, like lines from a poem I had memorized for my middle school English class.

> *"You know what you did," I said. To my surprise, I said it without anger, or even despair. It just came out in that moment. I hadn't planned to say it, but there it was, out in the open. And once it was out there, you only had two choices: lie or confess.*

Finally, as I gathered a pile of laundry from the kids' rooms and headed for the washing machine downstairs, I heard their feet shuffling along the hardwood floors above me, drawers and closet doors opening and closing, the sound of water rushing from the tap in the bathroom. Chicken minis from their favorite fast-food drive-through had this kind of power, to move two twelve-year-olds in the direction of the car faster than any parent's threats ever could.

I always felt like mother of the year as I watched my kids excitedly unwrap their greasy fried food in the car, the smell of it prompting me to open the window and gasp for fresh air. But they loved it, and the smiles on their faces gave me the immediate gratification that every parent craves between the long list of complaints and the general whining of adolescence. By the time we got to school, they had crammed the wrappers back into the bag and handed it to me in the front seat of the car. They were ready to face the day, both even pausing to give me a quick peck on the cheek as they tumbled out of the car.

"I love you guys!" I yelled, waving overenthusiastically as they were swallowed by the crowd of kids on the sidewalk in front of the school. It was moments like this when I thought that parenting on my own might not be as hard as I thought it was going to be. Yet, I knew something else would come along to knock me off that fleeting pedestal. It always did.

Esther was waiting for me on a blue velvet couch in the corner of the Oak City Bistro. It was one part coffee shop and one part hipster restaurant with tons of gluten-free, cardboard-like, alternatives to real food. The salads looked like something I mowed up in the lawn last Saturday and the baked goods were so devoid of taste that the miniscule calories they contained were not worth the effort to chew them.

Esther sat ramrod straight, a cup of hot coffee perched on her stiff knees, held firmly by both hands tightly encircling the steaming mug. The red down coat I remembered from the grocery store was draped over the back of the couch next to her. Frankly, it was the coat that made me recognize her again. Her face that day had been a blur amidst the unbelievable, chilling words that were coming out of her mouth. Now, that I could really see her, I put her age somewhere in her mid-seventies. She was painfully thin; a faded green sweater hung limply from her bony shoulders over black leggings. Her bobbed, wispy white hair was unkempt, as if she had just removed a winter hat seconds before I walked in. Her large, dark eyes protruded from her impossibly lean face with its angular features that included a long, thin nose. She was someone I guessed had probably been beautiful in her younger years. I could still see it in her sharp features and the mesmerizing way the light played off her dark eyes.

"Thank you for coming," Esther said nervously as she gently placed her cup on the distressed wooden table in front of her. It looked like a piece of driftwood that someone had nailed to a tree stump. It probably was exactly that, I surmised. *Details.* I always seem to be distracted by them, especially during important moments like this one.

"Sure," I said, not really knowing what to say to this woman who might be about to rock my world or reveal just how nuts she really was.

"Where should I start?" She said to no one, glancing out the window.

"How about at the beginning?"

"So, Clifton—Clifton is my son. He had a drug problem. We didn't know how bad it was. As it turned out, it was *very bad.* He would do anything for money to buy drugs. Nothing got in his way. He even broke into our house on more than one occasion and stole from us, his own parents."

"Excuse me, but where was this? Where did Clifton grow up? Where did you live?"

"Pennsylvania, not far from your grandparents' house, the house where your mother was killed. We knew them, your family, not well, but we knew your grandparents, Rachel and Glen, and when your mother, Patty, returned home to stay with them, with you, you were so small, just a tiny little thing. I remember that time like it was yesterday. I always admired your mother's style. I would see her walking with you down that country road, holding your tiny hand, that long red hair of hers flowing so gracefully in the wind. I'll always remember how she wore those modern fitted dresses, stylish boots, and just a pair of gold hoops and her ring, that beautiful emerald-cut diamond, platinum engagement ring. It really stood out."

I tried to picture my mother like this. But most of the photographs I had seen of her came from Belle's newspaper clippings in the attic. They were family photos of all three of us in front of a Christmas tree, at a parade, celebrating my birthday. If pictures of my beautiful mother alone, or *just with me*, existed, I never saw them. My maternal grandparents didn't stay long in that house after the murder. They were already compromised with health issues, and they died not long after they left the house. I never knew what had become of the big old red farmhouse I saw in those newspaper clippings or the contents of the house. Had there been any memorabilia? My mother had two brothers, but they were both dead as well. Alcoholics. At least that's what I think Belle had told me.

Esther rocked back and forth, stroking her knees with both hands, like she was in a kind of a trance remembering the moment and was about to curl up in a ball right there on the couch in front of me. She freed one hand long enough to take a sip of her coffee.

Suddenly, without even realizing it, I was in the moment with Esther, picturing it for myself, my young mother happily walking slowly with me down the street, as if she had no other place she wanted or needed to be. I remembered that feeling so well because after she died all the adults around me always seemed so rushed, as if they had somewhere more important that they needed to be, and I was in the way. I felt certain my mother would never have made me feel that way.

I wondered if she talked to me or sang to me. She must have been sad, having left her husband, fleeing to her childhood home for shelter and her parents' support. Yet, Esther didn't mention her being sad.

Esther was growing on me. The details she was sharing gave her more credibility. As a journalist, I knew that the truth was in the details. This description of my mother could only have come from a real encounter between Esther and my mother. I decided Esther was telling the truth. At least about this. I was scared and thrilled all at once for what I might learn from her.

"You see, at that time, Clifton was always doing things for money, *bad things*, things to get money for drugs. He wasn't a bad person, really, just someone with demons, someone who couldn't control the demons, you know what I mean? The drugs got a hold of him and wouldn't let go."

I nodded on the outside but on the inside I was screaming for her to get to the damn point. What in the world did Clifton have to do with my mother's murder? But I knew I couldn't rush her. I might scare her away. I had to stay focused but appear relaxed and open. I told my brain to slow down, and I took a few deep breaths to calm myself.

"See, right after your mother's murder, we noticed that Clifton had come into some money. He put a down payment on a car in cash, a fancy Mustang, but he didn't have a job. It didn't make any sense. So, I just asked him where he got it. He told me he had fenced some jewelry that someone had given to him. So, I marched right down to the pawn shop and demanded they show me what he sold them. The man was so worried I was going to call the police, but when I finally convinced him that I wasn't, that I was just looking out for my troubled son, he showed them to me. It was a wedding ring and an engagement ring. They were your mother's. I knew them right away when I saw them. I froze for a minute. I felt like someone had reached into my chest and grabbed my heart and was squeezing it and wouldn't let go. I thanked him, gave him the rings back and walked away out of that store."

"Then, what did you do?" Suddenly, this little, frail woman had captured my complete attention.

"Nothing, I did absolutely nothing, *until now.*"

8

THE NOTE

I LEFT THE MEETING WITH ESTHER feeling more confused than ever. I couldn't decide if I was angry, devastated, or simply numb. Had my whole life been built on a lie? Was Clifton really the person who killed my mother? Was Roger innocent? Even more importantly, did an innocent man go to prison for a crime he didn't commit, losing thirty-nine years of his life? I pushed the questions away almost as soon as they popped into my head. I knew I didn't have the energy to handle what she had told me. I felt sick to my stomach. I felt like everyone in the restaurant could hear my heart pumping out of my chest. I had to get away.

Esther wanted to tell me more. She wanted to explain her reasons for not going to the police decades ago. She wanted to tell me what she called "the rest of the story," but I told her it would have to wait for another day, that I was so overwhelmed by what she had already said, that I needed time to process everything. I promised that I would meet with her again, although I didn't believe my own words even as they came out of my mouth. I just knew in that moment flight was my only option.

Tilly's alleged suicide note was a welcome distraction from my personal drama. After leaving the meeting with Esther, I pulled into the local park and rolled down the windows, preparing to read it again on my phone. It was unseasonably warm for late February. I breathed in the fresh air and thought I could feel the beginning of spring in the slightly balmy breeze. There was a subtle sweetness to it. I pulled up the screenshot of the note on my phone and read it again. I agreed with Kojak that it didn't seem like a traditional suicide note. It sounded more like a note you wrote when someone had severely disappointed you and you wanted that person out of your life.

> *The flippant way you said it, your inflection, made me realize that you were not the person I had fantasized about in my dreams. You were a stranger to me, a vain interloper preying on my vulnerable spirit. How could I be so wrong about a person?*

I still couldn't get over her decision to kill herself on the driveway in front of her home, an incredibly public place, and the fact that she took the time and care to put down a towel. For what reason? To be more comfortable? To prevent the blood from staining the pavement? It was a detail I couldn't shake. *The truth is in the details,* my mantra, kept playing in a loop in my head.

"I don't like it," I said to Kojak over the phone, after I got home and had reread the letter a few more times.

"Me neither, Kid, but they're dead set on closing this one. Pardon the pun. Husband was at work at the restaurant. He has a pretty tight alibi. He was in his office most of the time in the back, but lots of people saw him. Although, he does have a back entrance. Got some guys checking the surveillance video on that as we speak.

"Daughter was also at work at one of the restaurants; she had just finished her shift, so there's like an hour where she's not accounted for. But, I mean, she's a kid, just twenty. Hard to imagine a young woman doing something like this. She'd have to have a pretty big beef with her mom to knock her off like that.

"As far as the neighborhood where she shot herself, no one saw anything, except for the nosy neighbor who heard the shot and then ran to her bathroom window where she only had a partial view of the driveway. She saw the aftermath. Saw the lady in the driveway, no one else, no one running away, no cars. So, there's really nothing to say it's *not* a suicide. And because of this note, despite what *we* may think about it, I don't see anyone putting any time into this one. We got guys killing each other every other day on street corners. We don't have time for a maybe/maybe not suicide."

> *No, you didn't do it to me. Frankly, it had little to do with me. But your admission finally made me see the real you. It also did something else, something brilliant. It set me free.*

I had printed Tilly's note and it was sitting in front of me on my desk as I spoke with Kojak. I was perched on the edge of my chair in my home office doodling on the yellow slip of paper with Esther's name on it. I made a triangle at the top of the "E" and was drawing an intricate design in the space between the three lines. I was trying to come up with a stronger argument that would make Kojak fully agree with my point of view that more needed to be done on Tilly's case.

"Just because no one saw anything doesn't mean it wasn't a murder," I said.

"True," Kojak said after a few long seconds of silence. "But tell that to a group of homicide guys who have a bunch of gang bangers and drug dealers killing each other as we speak. They got their hands full. This one is easy to get rid of."

"Well, what can I do to try and disprove their theory?" I asked, knowing that I was once again jumping back into the world of crime, something I had purposely stepped away from so I could be a better parent to the twins and maintain my sanity. But it was there, right in front of me, a woman who was begging me from the grave to solve the mystery of her death.

"I don't know, kid. It seems like a done deal to me. But I promise you this, if you find something, something *credible*, I promise I'll take it to my guys."

And with that, I was off.

9

THE WRONG DIRT ROAD

"I KNOW IT SOUNDS GROSS, but it's really kind of cool, don't you think?" Janie said, trying to sell me on the idea of the man who found dead rats in the sewer and then stuffed them and put them on display. "Taxidermy is a real art. Frank has a big barn in Windle where he has them on display. He's got rats from cities all around the world. NPR has done several segments on him."

Nothing about this story was appealing to me, but it would take my mind off my meeting with Esther. After having had a little time to think about it, I knew she truly believed that Clifton—*not Roger*—killed my mother. It was too much for me to process, so my answer was not to process it all. If only Adam were alive, then I might have someone to talk through it with me. He had always been my first call in a crisis. Now, I had a list of people I could call, like my best friend, Louise, but they all ranked way below Adam.

Louise Chance was a former reporter who left television to stay home with her three boys, but then she got restless and decided to start an event-planning business. Between hosting weddings, birthday, and retirement parties, she was busier than ever. I didn't know how she juggled it all. But she always seemed to have time for me despite the fact that I had essentially fallen off the edge of the planet after Adam's death and shut everyone out for a very long time. Good friends stuck around even through the hard times. Louise was that kind of a friend.

When Buster and I started down the rutted, dirt road that our GPS led us to, we both felt uneasy. We had traveled down many dirt roads together before into remote areas for stories, but this road felt like a trap for some reason. My gut was telling me this wasn't a good idea, that we should turn around and forget the creepy taxidermist story.

"It says we stay on this road for three miles. Where in the hell does this guy live?" Buster said as he fiddled with the GPS on his phone, trying to make sure he had read it right.

"I'm not positive. But Janie researched him. She says he's legit," I said, with too much hesitation in my voice.

"And what makes you think Janie has any radar, especially over the phone, when it comes to creeps? Look at that boyfriend of hers."

"True," I said, thinking about Janie's boyfriend, Damien, who was always in trouble for something: a small amount of pot, not showing up to court, or failing to pay his child support. As smart as Janie was, she was always making excuses for him.

"He's really trying to get his life together. He's even taking night classes at the community college," she would say, or "Everyone has it out for him. That's why he can't hold on to a job. His bosses are always threatened by his talent."

I could never figure out what "talent" Janie was talking about, but I felt strongly that Damien was bad news, and I didn't want him to pull Janie down into his loser lifestyle. It was situations like this that made me think there was no possible way I could ever date again. Plus, with me being a forty-two-year-old widow, men weren't exactly banging down my door.

We bounced uncomfortably whenever the SUV dipped into one of the deep ruts. Buster's change rattled furiously in the armrest drink holder. Finally, we pulled up to a small white modular home with vinyl siding. Behind the house was a massive red barn.

"That's where he's got them," Buster said pointing to the barn.

"The stuffed rats?"

"No, the people he holds hostage and tortures, probably mostly women and children. Any unsuspecting victims her can lure down that sketchy road."

"Buster!" I screamed, playfully hitting him on the back of his head with my reporter's notebook.

I climbed the rickety wooden steps to the door and knocked. There was no bell. A small man with thinning brown hair and a bushy moustache opened it a crack and waved me around to the side door. He was peering at me through a sheet of plastic. I gestured for Buster to follow me. He was busy once again staring at his phone. I walked back to the car and knocked on the driver's side window of the SUV until I got his attention and he put down the window.

"Come on," I said with more than a hint of annoyance in my voice.

"I was waiting to make sure we were in the right place," he said with a grin.

"We are. And it's super sketchy. I'm not going in there alone. I'm waiting for you."

"What makes you think he's not going to kidnap both of us at gunpoint and torture us in the barn with the rest of the missing people?"

I shook my head and waited for Buster to unload his gear from the back of the car. This playful, sarcastic banter was part of our usual routine, a sideshow of sorts. But I wasn't feeling very playful at the moment. My gut was still telling me to leave this place and forget about the story.

Inside, we were surrounded by photos of an attractive Asian woman and several children that covered every inch of the wall space, including the ceiling beam that separated the kitchen from the den. They looked like glamour shots, or stock photos from advertisements, not like real pictures of real people he knew. The most disturbing thing was that there was no evidence of a woman and children living in the house—no toys, nothing feminine in the decorations—just colorful plastic bins everywhere stacked in neat towers. All the windows and doors were shrouded in heavy sheets of plastic. *To keep the blood off them when he kills people here,* I thought to myself, knowing Buster was thinking the exact same thing.

Clearly, I had spent too many years covering crime. It allowed me to imagine the most macabre scenarios even in seemingly benign situations.

"So, these photos, they're your family?" I asked cautiously.

"Yes," the little man replied, offering no elaboration. I knew we would eventually have to make our way to the barn and look at the stuffed rats. All I could think about was getting out of this situation alive. I looked down at my phone and realized I only had one bar. No one would even know we were here, no one but Janie. Chances were that she was already embroiled in the breaking news of the day and didn't even remember where she had sent us.

Frank told me in a quiet, almost monotone voice how he first got into taxidermy. He droned on, going over every minute detail of the process. I let the camera roll, even though I knew I only needed a small fraction of what he was saying to do my minute-and-a-half story.

"Let's go to the barn," the little man said abruptly, in midsentence, standing up and gesturing toward the back door of his house. I heard Buster exhale loudly behind me, and I silently wondered if we had finally gone down the wrong dirt road.

10

HUBERT

WE DID GET OUT ALIVE. Frank's barn contained just what he told us it did, dead rats. We saw no evidence of people being held hostage or tortured, although I did wonder where the "family" from the photographs in the house had gone. Or maybe there was not a real family, just a pretend family that Frank had made up using photos he found on the Internet because he longed for one. I wasn't sure which option made me sadder.

I was back in the newsroom scouring social media for an animal story instead of waiting for Janie to assign me another one that I didn't want to do. Esther had texted me twice, asking when we could get together again. She apologized in her texts for upsetting me, but she said it was something she felt like she had to do "before she left the earth," whatever that meant. I was angry that her catharsis had become my burden. The most frustrating part of the whole situation was that I had no idea what to do about it. So, I did nothing. I ignored her texts and kept searching for a new story.

When I couldn't find anything interesting, I turned my attention to Tilly's case. It had been more than twenty-four hours since I talked to Kojak, and I still had no idea how I was going to get the investigation reopened. My gut told me this case was not a suicide, and I didn't want it to be written off as one if someone had taken this woman's life. Someone had to stand up for justice. Someone had to stand up *for her*.

Even though it sounded like Tilly's husband, Hubert, had a strong alibi, I decided I needed to learn more about him. I looked him up on Facebook to see what kinds of things he posted. I found mostly photos of him posing in front of multiple locations of "Hubert's Roadhouse." I clicked on the link for the restaurant's page and learned that Hubert had opened his original restaurant featuring country cooking and blues music in Oak City in 2005 and then parlayed that success into nine other locations across the state. This man had struck serious professional gold no matter how hard he tried to come across as a country boy.

In Hubert's legendary commercials he was sitting at a barstool in his restaurant with a mug filled to the top with frothy beer in one hand and a fried turkey leg in the other hand. It wasn't hard to imagine by looking at his size that this was his usual diet.

"Tired of people telling you what to eat?" he screamed into the camera over a twangy blues ballad in the background. "Come on down to Hubert's Roadhouse. We'll serve you food just the way you like it, and it won't cost you an arm and a leg!"

With that, he took a big bite out of the turkey leg which looked like it had become rubbery after multiple takes of the commercial. So, rather than a clean bite, he had to gnaw on it like a wild animal to get it off the bone which only added to the depravity of the commercial. It was quite memorable and very disturbing at the same time.

Hubert was a large, middle-aged man with thinning hair and a Charlie Chaplin moustache. In his commercials, he always wore a business suit that looked to be a few sizes too small with a thin, leather bolo tie; the buttons of his jacket seemed to be straining to hold in his massive gut. Despite his almost comical appearance, it was clear from the fancy home I observed the night Tilly died that he was a successful businessman.

How he ended up with someone as attractive as her was mind-blowing. Tilly's Facebook page was mostly set to private, but there were a handful of profile pictures of her that I could see. She had porcelain skin, jet black hair, and red lips reminiscent of a 1950s movie star. There was one photo of her in a field, spinning in a white dress with direct sunlight obscuring most of her face. It was simply labeled "This is how I see you." Could that be from Hubert? I clicked on the text below the photo. There was no tag visible telling me who had posted it. But I didn't think it was Hubert. I didn't peg him as someone who used social media for personal reasons—just for business I assumed.

I scrolled through a few more photos that dated back a several years. One caught my eye—Tilly with her mini-me, her daughter, Delilah, as a teenager. She had both arms around the waist of the tall, gangly teen who had yet to grow into her body. But their likeness was uncanny. They both had the same jet black hair and fair skin. Tilly's face was beaming, and so was the daughter's awkward smile through her gleaming braces. It was clear the mother and daughter duo loved each other very much. Suddenly, I thought of my mother, Patty. Delilah and I had experienced the same loss, just at different ages. I knew in that moment it wasn't just about finding justice for Tilly; it was about finding justice for a little girl who lost her mother.

11

SETTING THE RECORD STRAIGHT

RELUCTANTLY, I FINALLY REPLIED to Esther's texts and agreed to meet with her again at the Oak City Bistro. A few days had passed, and I had experienced a wide range of emotions after first hearing her story—anger, disbelief, sadness. Now, I was confused about why she would bring up her version of my mother's murder after so many years of keeping such a dark secret. If she was telling the truth, surely she had broken some laws by protecting her son and allowing an innocent man to go to prison. Why wasn't she concerned about what could happen to *her* if she shared what she knew with me? I decided the only way to get my questions answered, to learn the truth once and for all, was to meet with her again.

"Maddie, I'm afraid I didn't approach this the right way," Esther said, placing a hand gently on my shoulder as she sat down across from me once again at the small driftwood table. She didn't bother to get anything this time. Our meeting was not about chitchatting over coffee. She had a large beige canvas bag slung over her shoulder that appeared to be filled with something heavier than rocks. Wincing in pain, she hoisted it off her shoulder and struggled to place it gently on the floor at our feet. She shed her red puffy coat and slung it over the chair behind her. "I shocked you. I just jumped right into my story without giving you any time to process everything, and I'm so sorry for that. I just, well, I'm not getting any younger, and I feel like time is running out. I couldn't take this to my grave. You know, Pete, my husband, and I moved here after he retired, sight unseen. We didn't know a soul, just heard about the nice people, the gentle climate, how good the hospitals were, and we just thought this would be a great place to live out our final days."

Why was this woman always talking about dying? I could feel my resolve melting away with each word she said. I wanted so badly to hate her for what she had done—keeping evidence from police in a murder case, finally telling me the truth decades after the crime, allowing my dad to spend his entire life behind bars. But there was something in the way she looked at me, like a small bunny, with wide, sincere eyes and short sprigs of fine white hair standing up in all directions on top of her head, that made me feel sorry for her. The way she spoke to me, her words catching in her throat, made me believe that she was truly sorry for what she had done that it had haunted her, maybe even *ruined* her life.

"I honestly had no idea you were Patty's daughter when I first saw you on the news. I had no reason to make the connection. But then I started doing some digging. I was determined to find Patty's little girl. I'm pretty good at family tree research, you know, genealogy; that's always been a hobby of mine. And when I figured it out, that *you* were right here in the same town where I lived, I felt like it must be a God thing. That God had put us here together in this place so that I could share the truth with you. I never meant to hurt you or your family. I was only trying to protect my son. I was a mother, after all. You know what that's like. You'll do anything to protect your children."

Quickly, anger flared up inside my chest, not just regular anger but fury. Yes, I wanted to protect Blake and Miranda at all costs. I wanted to protect them from the pain of losing their father to brain cancer at such a young age. I wanted to protect them from bullies and illness and from heartache, but I would not lie for them. I would not knowingly cover up a crime they had committed. *That* I would not do.

"I probably should have been clearer. Clifton didn't remember anything about how he got the rings. He told me he was drunk and high on drugs and that he had thrown up and peed on himself. He said he woke up in a pool of vomit in our basement, on the floor, lying face down in the green shag carpet in our rec room. That's where he was living at the time. His heart practically stopped as his hand brushed across something metal on the floor next to him. He opened one eye and turned his head to see what it was. Turns out it was a small pistol. He didn't *own* a gun. He knew it wasn't his, but it was right there next to his hand. He knew that something bad must have happened. He had a felony drug record. He wasn't supposed to have a gun. None of it made sense."

"Go on," I said, struggling to control my rage.

"He told me he panicked, the kind of panic that makes your heart race and your palms sweat and your vision get fuzzy. He honestly didn't know what to do. He didn't know what had happened, if he had done something *horrible.* He said he got up, grabbed the gun and ran out of the house. Somehow, in that inebriated state, he realized he had to get rid of it, which he did. Then, he ran back to our house, took a shower and went to bed. It wasn't until he saw the story on the news a few days later that he realized your mother was murdered just down the road from us, in your grandparents' house. He ran to the laundry room and found his dirty clothes. He was going to burn them, but first he turned the pockets of his pants inside out, and that's when he found the rings. That's when he knew he did it, *that he killed her.*"

I wanted so badly to interrupt her, to tell her this was all too much for me to bear, but I also wanted to know the rest of the story. So, I sat stoically while I was screaming on the inside. I was doing what I did best, compartmentalizing the various intense situations in my life so that I could function.

"As you can imagine, he was in a total tailspin. He didn't feel like he could confide in anyone, that he would surely end up in prison.

He had been there before, and he was determined *not* to go back. So, he sold the rings and told no one until I confronted him about where he got the money."

I tried to process this detail: My beautiful dead mother's rings were sold at a pawn shop. Those rings should have been mine, a reminder that she had given me life. But who knows where they were now? They could have passed through many hands by this time. They could have been melted down for the value of the metal and the stones. They were gone, just like Patty was gone.

"I told you about the car he bought, and then soon after that I noticed him with these big bills in his pocket, hundreds, fifties. I noticed them when he pulled out money to pay for groceries one night. He told me the groceries were his treat, that he had been sponging off us long enough. As soon as our eyes met, he knew I knew something was up. I knew he didn't have a job. *I knew about the rings.*

"We sat in the car in the grocery store parking lot, the ice cream melting in the back seat, as he told me about that night, about how disoriented he was, about how he could not remember anything concrete. He just had images, glimpses, flashes of moments in the house. He didn't know if they were real moments, or came from pictures of the house he had seen in the news coverage on TV. He begged me not to tell anyone. He promised me that he would live a clean life from here on out if I would protect him. I struggled with it; I really did. But I told no one. Not even my husband. The secret, it was like always carrying around a bag of explosives that might detonate at any moment if I said or did the wrong thing. The burden was so heavy, sometimes I just had to stop and sit and cry. My husband, Pete, didn't understand. He just thought I was unhappy with the hand that life had dealt me. I always felt bad about that, about making him feel like he couldn't make me happy. The secret put a wedge between us that only got bigger the longer I kept it. I never did tell him."

Esther's voice, not just because of *what* she was saying, but *how* she was saying it, so calmly with a soothing tone, mesmerized me. It was like listening to the rhythmic ticking of a metronome that subliminally lulled me into a trance. Still, it was hard for me to look directly at her. Her face was kind, but her words had torpedoed my life, and not just *my* life, but the lives of Roger and my mother.

"I even visited your grandparents, Rachel and Glen, right after the murder. Of course, I didn't know anything about Clifton's involvement at that time. But I was neighbors with your grandparents, Patty's parents, for many years. We weren't close; I mean we were a country mile through the field, but we still looked out for each other's properties and stopped to speak if we should see each other. Dilltown was, and still is, a small tight-knit community. I'll never forget their faces when I stopped by after she died—it was like someone had sucked the life out of them, like they had aged ten years overnight. They were sitting on the porch in their rockers, their faces long, drawn, eyes empty. I remember it was so quiet, I could hear those rockers scraping the hardwoods of the porch, and nothing else. Finally, I spoke, told them how sorry I was. I left a basket of food right there on the porch and went home. I don't even think they said thank you, or goodbye. They never recovered, as you probably know. They were quite unwell after that, both of them. I mean who could blame them? You're not supposed to bury your child."

"The gun, what happened to the gun?"

"I don't know."

"What do you mean you don't know?" I said, embarrassed by my own tone, knowing that if anyone saw me berating this frail, older woman, they would think I was an awful person.

"I don't know because I didn't ask. *I didn't want to know.* He had told me enough."

"You didn't want to know? Well, I want to know *everything.* For starters, why? Why did he do it? What did Clifton have against my mother?"

"Nothing, that's just it. He blacked out. He didn't remember much of anything. He had been involved in a lot of petty crimes before this, nothing violent. Just minor stuff, stuff to get money for drugs. He had never hurt anyone before. He didn't even own a gun. That's why when he woke up with that gun next to him, he was *terrified.*

He had no idea what had happened. Like I said, he panicked."

"I want to talk to him," I said boldly, with a resolve that came from somewhere deep inside of me. I needed to speak to the man who killed my mother. It was the least this woman could offer me after her years of deceit and the ripple effect it had exerted on my entire family. I *deserved* this, to spend a few moments with him to understand why he did what he did. Even if he didn't remember the details, I needed to see him in person.

"I'm afraid that's not possible," Esther said shaking her head and looking down at her hands clasped tightly together on her lap. I noticed that her knuckles were bone-white and blue veins protruded from just beneath her skin. I realized how keeping this secret had not only profoundly impacted my family's life, but also her life and her family's life. I felt momentarily sorry for her, but then I forced the thought out of my head. *Get a grip.* She was not my problem. I couldn't afford to be derailed by sympathy for her in this moment when I desperately needed more information.

"Why not?" I demanded, unable to keep my emotions in check. People at nearby tables were starting to turn to look at me, *the mean lady attacking the older woman.* They probably thought we were mother and daughter, based on the passion and vitriol in my voice. I tried to ignore them and focus on Esther.

"You can't speak to Clifton because he didn't make good on his promise. He did not go on to live a clean life. What he did, it *haunted* him. He spiraled out of control, got deeper and deeper into drugs, heavy drugs—cocaine, heroin, meth. Finally, one night he broke into our house in Dilltown to steal stuff he could sell to buy more drugs. We had kicked him out by then. Our car was in the shop, so he didn't realize we were home. We were sleeping. My husband heard a noise and grabbed his gun. All he saw was the silhouette of a large man in the doorway to our bedroom. He shot him in the chest. He died immediately. It was Clifton. It was my son. *My husband killed my son.* That was another reason we left Pennsylvania. We couldn't bear to live in that house anymore."

My head was spinning, trying to take in everything Esther was saying. He was dead. Clifton, the man who may have killed my mother, was dead. I stared at Esther, speechless. Clearly, she had also suffered a great tragedy in her life—the loss of a child at the hands of his own father. What could be worse? I still had one more question rolling around in my head, but I didn't dare ask it in this moment. Despite my intense desire to know, it felt insensitive. So, I kept it to myself. *Why did you continue to protect your dead son for all these years?*

12

SECRETS

I LEFT THE MEETING WITH ESTHER barely able to put one in foot in front of the other. The sun seemed brighter than it was when I entered the cafe. I ambled slowly to my car. Even with sunglasses on, I felt like the sun was burning holes in my eyes. I had Esther's heavy canvas bag slung over my right shoulder. It felt *exactly* like what I imagined a bag of rocks would feel like, heavy like the real burden she had carried around for so many years. Esther and Pete were among those who suffered at the hands of Clifton. It was a tragedy no matter how you examined it. In many ways, we were all his victims.

When Esther left me sitting alone in the restaurant, she had handed me the canvas bag and told me it contained important files, proof of everything that she was telling me. She said it was up to me now—that I could decide what I wanted to do with it—if I wanted to take it to the police, or to Roger, or to simply do nothing. Basically, she was now handing me her burden to carry or discard.

"What about you? If I go to the police, and they find out you knew about this, you could be charged as an accessory after the fact to murder," I said, wanting her to make sure she understood the risk she was taking, especially at her age in what appeared to be a fragile state of health.

"Don't worry about me. I've been through so much pain, there's nothing more anyone can do to me. I've spent my entire life walking across hot coals. Let them come for me." With that, she waved her hand in the air, gesturing curiously to the heavens, and then turned and walked away from me without looking back.

In that moment, I understood her. After so many years of living in fear, she was casting away the dark cloak in favor of being free. Her mind was made up that it was now *my* choice, my decision, my burden to bear or my burden to share. She had finally let go of her bag of rocks, and for her, it was over. I had no idea what I was going to do with what she had told me. Part of me wanted to light the bag on fire, or throw it off a cliff, but I knew myself better than that. Eventually, I would feel compelled to look inside, or at the very least let *someone else,* someone I trusted look inside.

I shoved the bag deep into the trunk of my car because I didn't want it near me while I was driving. I felt contaminated just holding it—this bag of secrets that threatened to tear open a whole new path in my life, in Roger's life.

I was on my way to Tilly's funeral. Nothing I did in the next two hours, two days or two weeks would bring my mother back, not even taking Esther's files to the police. I needed time to come up with a plan. I knew Kojak would no doubt help me with this if I chose to enlist him. But first, I needed to seek the truth about Tilly's death. I didn't want another family to live a life based on lies.

⌐

I slid into the back pew of the church. Technically, I wasn't there as a reporter. I wasn't covering the service for work. We only covered funerals of high-profile people in high-profile cases. Dex would never allocate resources to cover a funeral just because I had a gut feeling about a case.

But I wasn't there as a friend either. I didn't know this woman. I wasn't completely sure why I was there; it was just something I felt compelled to do, and I wanted to keep a low profile. I wasn't sure what I would learn by attending the funeral, but I wanted to see Tilly's people, the people in her inner circle, and maybe this would give me a sense of what really happened to her.

A soloist was singing "Amazing Grace" as mourners shuffled quietly to their seats. The people filing into the church were solemn and all dressed in black. It was not like the funeral of an older person who died after a life well-lived. Those services tended to be celebrations of life—this was something different. This gathering was cloaked in the shame that went hand-in-hand with suicide. People often have a hard time accepting that suicide victims could be suffering so deeply that this feels like their only way out. It is the result of a mental and emotional breakdown, of depression, not moral bankruptcy.

I started to pretend to focus on the program when I noticed two little girls out of the corner of my eye. They were sitting together at the end of the pew I was in, giggling as they looked at the screen of a cell phone held very low in between them obviously hiding it from the surrounding adults. They appeared to be somewhere between ten and eleven years old. I put them in fifth or sixth grade. I really couldn't blame them for wanting to look at something funny on their phone rather than paying attention to the very serious ceremony that was about to take place, but I did wonder where their parents were, and why they weren't reprimanding them.

When the soloist finished, everyone stood as Tilly's family came down the aisle. I wasn't sure who was who, but I did recognize her husband, Hubert, from Facebook and from his corny television ads. He looked just like he did in his commercials—big and burly, the buttons of his suit jacket straining to control his burgeoning belly, his jet-black hair slicked back with gel. He walked slowly at the front of the group, arm-in-arm with an older woman, maybe his sister. She wore a loose-fitting black dress that came down almost to her ankles. Her gray hair was wrapped in a tight bun at the base of her neck, and she stood stiffly and uncomfortably at Hubert's side, as if she would rather be anywhere else but next to him. She clutched a handkerchief with her free hand.

I studied Hubert as he passed me. I'm not sure what I was looking for, maybe some sign of insincerity, maybe a thin veil of truth that might crumble beneath the scrutiny of my intense gaze. But I saw nothing out of the ordinary. Hubert looked like a man who was genuinely grieving. His round, weathered face was appropriately sullen, and the corners of his eyes were tearing. But I then I remembered the Hubert from his cheesy television commercials— *Hubert the actor.* Surely, if you had killed your wife the funeral would be your biggest stage calling for a command performance by the widower.

On the other side of Hubert was a young, very attractive woman with long, black hair and pale skin. Unlike the older woman, she was literally clutching Hubert's other arm like she might fall down if not supported by his massive frame. She was also wearing a long black dress, but hers was form-fitted, and I noticed she had on stylish black high-heeled boots. This woman had to be Delilah, Hubert and Tilly's twenty-year-old daughter. She, too, looked like she was genuinely grieving, but there was something else about her demeanor that bothered me. She was *shaking* ever so slightly, like she was nervous. Maybe she didn't like all the eyes in the church on her.

"Excuse me," one of the little girls leaned over and whispered in my direction. "Do you have any tissues?" Suddenly, the girl I assumed was a bit immature because of her giggly behavior during the service seemed polite beyond her years. Maybe I had misjudged them.

I reached into my oversized bag and quietly rummaged for the package of tissues I knew lived somewhere beneath my wallet and hairbrush. The congregation was singing along to the hymn "How Great Thou Art."

"Here you go," I said just a little louder than a whisper in order to be heard above the singing as I handed the entire pack of tissues to the thin, tiny brunette girl with big brown eyes in the black taffeta dress. She looked like she was going to a prom instead of a funeral. She thanked me, took the package and gingerly opened it to remove a single tissue. She wasn't smiling, but she certainly didn't seem very sad. I wondered if she just wanted some excuse to interact with me.

"We will never know why a child of God is taken from us too soon, when her work on earth has yet to be finished. It's hard, if not impossible, to understand," the pastor who looked like a 1980s televangelist said with a booming voice as a low organ melody rumbled beneath his words. He was illuminated at the pulpit by a single spotlight that made him glow against the dark wood paneling behind him. "But it's not up to us to understand; only God has these answers. All we can do is try and live our lives to the fullest, and to remember our sister Tilly for the joy and kindness she brought to the lives of every single person she touched."

Several people took turns stepping up to the altar to speak tearfully about how Tilly would visit Hubert's Roadhouse on a regular basis and greet customers. They talked about how she knew all the employees by name and would often pop into the kitchen to survey the food line and take a taste of something that one of the cooks was preparing. While Kojak had told me her main job was to handle the accounting for the restaurant, it sounded like she was also very involved with the employees and was good at boosting morale.

"This is delicious! What spices are you using in this dish? Is it a new recipe?" She would say according to one of the speakers.

The kitchen staff who spoke at the funeral all said they got a kick out of Tilly's enthusiasm. It was just country cooking, after all. But she didn't treat it that way. Tilly treated them like they were world-class chefs making food for celebrities in a five-star restaurant. She treated them like they *mattered*. And that's how she would be remembered, for how she made them feel.

I glanced over at the girls and noticed they were using the tissues to spit out their gum and wrap it up. They then shoved the tissue balls into the little shelf on the back on the pew in front of them and giggled wildly. They must have felt my gaze on them, because they stopped suddenly and looked back at me with *pretend* solemnity. I nodded and smiled. Having twins of my own just a year or two older than these girls gave me a less critical lens through which to view their behavior. They were just being kids, after all, in a very adult setting.

The girl who had asked me for the tissues in the black taffeta dress slid down the wooden pew in my direction again, her dress crunching as it caught along rough spots in the aging wood.

"Who are you?" She said in a loud whisper, leaning into my ear with one hand cupped around the right side of her small face. "You look like someone I know. Do I know you?" The choir was now singing a soul-stirring rendition of "Hallelujah."

"Maddie," I said, as I continued to stare straight ahead and pretended to be listening intently to the music. I couldn't imagine that this child would know me from the television news. Who let their kids watch the news?

"Nice to meet you, Maddie," the girl said too loudly, reaching her hand out to shake mine. I quietly slipped my hand into hers and nodded, still looking straight ahead, pretending to be listening.

"I'm Penny. Tilly was my Great Aunt."

13

PRISON DOGS

"It's such a perfect fit for you," Janie practically shouted over the phone. I pictured her twisting her blonde curls around her index finger while she talked to me. She always did this when she got excited.

"So, if someone dies—like in a car wreck, or of cancer, or maybe they get hit over the head with a shovel,"

"Janie," I chastised.

"No, I mean for any reason—disease, murder. Then the local animal control takes the dogs to this program where they get fostered by prison inmates until a home can be found for them. So, imagine this. A guy in prison for murder could be fostering the dog of a murder victim. How bizarre is that?"

With that mind bender she got my attention. I had to admit, I was intrigued. It was a lot more interesting than most of the stories I covered on the animal beat.

"Okay, what's the plan then?"

"Meet Buster in the parking lot at the entrance of Creighton Correctional at eleven o'clock. The warden will meet you there and take you inside for an interview with an inmate. They're going to do it in the recreation yard so you can get video of him working with the dog."

"Awesome. Good work Janie. Sounds like a really good story."

"Really?" Janie said sounding appreciative of my rare complement. It made me think I should praise her more often. It just wasn't very common in our business to give anyone a pat on the back, which was a shame considering how most people sacrificed so much of their personal lives for the job. I made a mental note to take more stock in Janie's efforts and to point them out when it felt appropriate and not too effusive.

"Absolutely. By the way, did Dex ever get back to you about my request to spend a little more time on that suicide case from last week? There's just something funny about that one; I'm not sold on the official conclusion that it was a suicide."

"Yes, he did. You're not going to like it. He said, and I quote: *Not going to happen.* He then went into a whole long list of items that we don't have the time or budget for and said this request wouldn't even come close to making the list. And then he reminded me that you're not on the crime beat anymore and said, and I quote: *She should spend her time looking for runaway llamas that dart across the highway in rush-hour traffic or bears that break into people's houses, eat their food, and fall asleep on their couch. Now those are stories I would watch!*

"So, that's that."

"That's that," Janie echoed.

I had a little time before meeting Buster at the prison, so I called Kojak and asked him to meet me for a few minutes at the park. I wanted to fill him in on my conversation with Esther and ask him for his help. I was confident he would know what to do with this information.

I still had not looked at the files in the canvas bag. I had pulled the bag of rocks out of my trunk and set it on my desk in my home office. There it sat for several days. You would think it would have been a temptation, that the bag was burning a hole in my desk every time I passed it, begging me to open it. But every time I looked at it and considered opening it, I knew that it would be like opening Pandora's box. I would not be able to unknow what I learned from its contents. However, if I shared it with someone in law enforcement, it would be up to them to unravel the mess and figure out what should be done. So, I put it back in my car and carried it with me to the park.

I sat on the scratched wooden bench at Benton Road Park next to the small lake where people rented paddleboats on nice days. It was a rare, serene spot in the center of the busy city. In the distance, I could hear snippets of a conversation from two people on a paddleboat on the far side of the lake, their voices floating across the water as clearly as if they were sitting right next to me.

"No way. She didn't really say that?" A young woman's voice wafted over the glass surface of the lake. And then there were two female voices laughing, their guttural sounds hitting the water and bouncing in my direction like a rubber ball launched across a wooden floor. I couldn't help but smile at their infectious squealing.

Absentmindedly, I picked at the peeling green paint on the bench next to me as I tried to ignore the canvas bag at my feet. It suddenly struck me as ironic that Esther had passed the bag to me, and now I was going to pass it along to Kojak. Who knew where it would land after that?

"Fancy meeting you here," Kojak said as he approached me from behind, giving me a friendly pat on the shoulder. "What's with the Deep Throat meeting in the park?"

"No reason. I just have to go to the prison for an interview in a little while, so I thought this was a convenient spot."

Kojak was a formidable man—tall, bald, bespectacled, sporting a hipster goatee which was in direct opposition to his old-school, tough cop personality.

"What's up?" He sat down next to me and unwrapped a lollipop and popped it in his mouth.

"This is going to sound really strange, but I have to tell someone. And I figured you would know what I should do about it," I looked at him hopefully, and he nodded for me to continue. "A lady named Esther came up to me in the grocery store the other day and said that her son, not Roger, killed my mother. Apparently, he was young, messed up on drugs, and he broke into my grandparents' house and killed her. Or at least that's what she *thinks* happened. She says he woke up drunk and confused with a gun next to him, and he freaked out. He didn't realize what he had done until he saw the story on the news. His mom, that's Esther, the one who told me the story, found out about everything because he pawned my mother's rings, her wedding and engagement rings, and Esther noticed that he suddenly came into some money. She confronted him about the money, and he told her the truth. She also went to the pawn shop and saw the rings for herself."

"So where is the bastard now?"

"That's the problem, he's dead. Sometime after my mother was killed, the kid broke into his parents' house while high on drugs, looking for things to steal and sell, and his father thought he was an intruder and killed him by mistake."

"He *was* an intruder. That's rough for that dad. What a frigging mess. So, this broad, this woman Esther, why the hell did she keep this secret all these years?"

"I don't know. I can't figure her out. Maybe some sort of misguided loyalty to Clifton's memory. Clifton, that's her son. I mean, I think it really had a negative impact on her life, keeping the secret. She didn't look well."

"Are you sure she's for real? You do have a strong tendency to attract crackpots."

"I am sure. Well, at least, I think I'm sure. I don't know. I'm really confused. On one hand, I really want to believe her. If it's true, then Roger is not the monster I have imagined him to be my entire life. On the other hand, I don't want to believe her. If she's right, an innocent man may have sat in prison for almost four decades. I'm not sure what my ethical obligation is here. That's why I'm coming to you, to see if maybe you could touch base with the police in Pennsylvania and help me figure this thing out."

Kojak stared straight ahead at the little two-seater boat carrying the young girls that was now making its way back to the shore. It was quiet except for the squeaky grinding of the pedals and the whoosh of the water as they cut swiftly across the surface of the lake.

"Kid, are you sure you really want to open up this can of worms? I mean you're just barely getting back on your feet again after Adam's death. And then that last wacko case you got yourself all caught up in with the dead doctor and his stalker wife. *Take a break from the crazy.* You're going to stir up some shit with this one, one way or the another."

"I know. But I can't just sit here and do nothing. That's not right either." I reached down for my bag of rocks and struggled to lift it up. I handed it to Kojak.

"What's this?"

"Esther said all the information that proves her son's guilt is contained in these files."

"Have you looked at them?"

"No, but I thought maybe *you* could? I will look at it when I am ready. I thought you could make a copy and give it back to me. I don't want to let go of the original documents. But you could send a copy to the investigators in Pennsylvania and see what they think about it. See if there's really anything to this."

He shook his head and smiled, biting into the hard candy in his mouth with a loud crunch. He leaned down and picked up the bag effortlessly. It made me think about how weak I must be given that I had struggled to carry it.

"I'll do it, but don't kill the messenger when I find out something you don't want to know."

"I won't. I promise," I said crossing my fingers on both hands in front of him for good measure.

⌒

Buster met me at the guardhouse in front of the prison where they checked our identification, examined our equipment, and patted us down after we walked through the metal detector. Ironically, we could bring a big television camera into the prison, but we had to leave our phones in the car. This stemmed from an ongoing problem with inmates getting a hold of cell phones smuggled into the prison. They were considered contraband, and they were a hot commodity for obvious reasons. Even lawyers had to abide by the no cell phone rule.

Every time I entered Creighton Correctional, my stomach always did a nervous little flip when one door locked before we could enter the next door, trapping us momentarily between the two locked doors. We had to pass through multiple sets of these containment areas to get into the heart of the prison. It gave you a small sense of what it must feel like to be incarcerated with so many layers of security between you and the outside world.

"Today, you're going to meet Randall. He's a lifer, and he's been working with Sammy, a lab mix, real sweetheart. Sammy's owner, Cecile, died of cancer and the rest of the family has allergies, so no one could take him. The shelter called us and asked if he might be a good fit for the prison fostering program," said Warden Lane Bobbitt who walked in front of us rapping on locked doors that eventually opened like magic with the unseen touch of a button by a guard watching us on a security camera in a command center somewhere deep in the bowels of the facility.

Buster followed with the camera slung over one shoulder and the tripod in his free hand. We couldn't help but look at the prisoners in the dormitory areas behind the thick glass, dressed in their shapeless orange jumpsuits, as we walked down the long corridors. Some of them pressed their faces to the glass as we passed. Others sat at round metal tables playing board games or talking, paying us no mind.

It was a scene I had viewed many times before, but it always gave me a little shiver to think this was probably the kind of place where Roger was living in Pennsylvania. He had been moved several times over the years but served most of his sentence at the Penn State Grove Correctional Institution. I hadn't visited him since I was an adolescent with my grandmother, Belle.

When I was twelve, I stopped seeing Roger. The judge told me it was my decision. I'm still not sure why I let him go so easily. I think I knew he had something to do with my mother's death even though no one had come out and directly told me yet. Maybe I was also a little embarrassed about having a father in prison. Or maybe, prison was just a very scary place for a child, and I simply didn't want to go there anymore. But despite my unwillingness to see him, Roger continued to write me weekly letters from prison—letters I kept, but never read.

"Randall, this is Miss Arnette," the warden said as Randall extended his free hand to shake mine. Sammy was sitting obediently at Randall's feet attached to a leash in his left hand.

"Pleased to meet you. I'm kind of nervous. Never been on television before."

"No worries. It's easy. Just look at me, ignore the camera, and it's all on tape, so if you don't like the way you said something, you can say it again."

"Good deal. I will try my best."

"Why don't we do the interview walking together with Sammy around the yard, and then we'll get some separate shots of you exercising with him. How does that sound?"

"Perfect, you're the professional. I'll do what you tell me to do!"

Randall was a slight man with a wild mop of brown hair and complicated tattoos covering every inch of his exposed arms. As we walked, he got more comfortable speaking to me and almost seemed to forget the camera was there. Buster walked slowly backwards to capture our conversation as we ambled along the edge of the tall chain-link fence adorned with several rows of barbed wire. Sammy obediently stayed right by Randall's side.

"I was in a real low place after I was convicted. I was angry. Fought the system. Got into loads of trouble on the inside. Finally, after a few years, I accepted my fate, and settled down. But I knew I needed something to do, something that mattered. Always loved animals, and when the warden asked me to be part of this program, I knew this was *my destiny.*"

"What were you convicted of if you don't mind me asking?"

"Nope. Not at all. It was stupid. Broke into a few houses stealing crap—wallets, phones, laptops, jewelry. Nothing that had any great value on the street. I was high most of the time. Anyway, this one time the guy who owned the house was home and I didn't know it. He surprised me as I was going through his wife's jewelry box.

I heard the tiniest creek on the floorboard behind me, and I just turned around and he was there, up in my face. I panicked. Shot him in the head. It was a mistake, an accident, one that I have to live with for the rest of my life. He had a dog. The dog came running into the room and lay down next to the guy's dead body and started whimpering. I'll never forget that sound. It turned from a whine into a low moan, you know, straight from the dog's gut."

We were both quiet for a minute as we walked. The only sounds were of our feet crunching on the grass in the recreation yard and Sammy's panting as he walked close to Randall, often looking up at him, waiting for a command. I was trying to process what Randall had just told me, picturing this gentle, mild-mannered man shooting someone in the head and a dog grieving next to his owner's lifeless body. I couldn't imagine living with that burden.

"So, what's it like working with Sammy?" I asked, trying to lighten the mood, mine and his.

"Some people think we are saving these dogs, but *Sammy saved me*. I don't know what I will do when it's time for him to go. He's my best friend. Prison is a lonely place and life is long when you're locked up."

I suddenly thought about Roger being locked up for life and possibly being innocent. The thought of it made me feel physically ill. Randall had admitted to what he did. He was guilty of taking a life. But an innocent man living like this, like a caged animal behind layer after layer of locked doors and fences topped with barbed wire, it was almost too much for me to bear. If Roger was innocent, someone had to save him. The big question was, was *I* that someone?

14

A "PENNY" FOR YOUR THOUGHTS

I KNEW I HAD SEEN THAT LADY SOMEWHERE BEFORE. Her name is Maddie Arnette. She's on the television news. I don't really watch the news, but my mom does. Sometimes, it is on in the background when she's cooking dinner. If they start talking about bad stuff, like murders or tornadoes, Mom makes me leave the room. She tells me to scoot and go do homework until she calls me. But then I sometimes just watch the livestream of the news on my computer just because I can. It's like a silent protest to my mother's ridiculous need to shelter me from reality.

When I saw that lady at the church, I knew she looked familiar. But a lot of people look familiar in a small place like Oak City. When I finally figured it out, I looked her up on Instagram and started following her. Mom said I couldn't have an Instagram account until I was thirteen, but everyone at my school does. Plus, Mom doesn't do social media, so it's not like she's going to catch me.

I scrolled through Maddie's posts and found one from the night Aunt Tilly died. It was a picture of Maddie holding a microphone and standing in front of Aunt Tilly's house. There were police cars, big, bright lights, and yellow crime-scene tape behind her. I watch a lot of crime shows online about real cases that actually happened somewhere, and the yellow tape is always there when they find a dead body. It keeps people from walking around and contaminating the crime scene. The caption on Maddie's picture from that night reads: "Coming up at eleven o'clock, the latest on a death investigation at Conover Place."

I realized she must be investigating the case. That's why she came to Aunt Tilly's funeral, looking for clues like reporters did on Netflix. I love figuring out mysteries. I've gotten pretty good at it. When I watch the crime shows online I usually figure out who did it in the first seven minutes or so. So, I thought maybe I could help with Aunt Tilly's case. I decided I would start by sending that lady from the news a private message on Instagram and telling her what a creep Uncle Hubert is.

15

THE BREAKING POINT

WHILE I DIDN'T SEEM TO BE GETTING ANY CLOSER to solving the mystery of my mother's death, I decided I would take another run at Tilly's case. It would be a good distraction. I knew timing in her case was critical. I needed to find new evidence that would cause the investigators to reopen the case. They did not have the resources or time to be dealing with mere speculation that a suicide might in fact be a murder.

I had been to Hubert's Roadhouse a few times with Buster when we traveled out of town to other parts of eastern North Carolina for work. There was nothing he liked better than a country cooking belly-buster at a restaurant with peanut shells on the floor and bottomless baskets of hush puppies on the table. But, ironically, I had never been to the flagship restaurant in Oak City. Despite its size, Oak City had a surprisingly wide array of very good restaurants to choose from, and Hubert's Roadhouse didn't top many lists, unless you were Buster.

When I walked into the restaurant, the first thing I noticed was that it was very dark inside for such a sunny day. The wood paneled walls were covered in vintage signs for things like "Pepsi," "Esso Gas," and "Route 66." The floor was covered in sawdust and the requisite peanut shells; each table was adorned with a red and white checkered tablecloth topped off by a metal bucket full of dried ears of corn. It felt like I was stepping back in time. There were plenty of authentic home cooking roadside restaurants in North Carolina, but this was an over-the-top parody of one. It was as if someone traveled the country looking for the stereotypical things you might find in a rural, mom-and-pop eatery and then put them all together in this one place. The result was an explosion of stuff covering every inch of the restaurant.

"Just one today?" Asked the bubbly young hostess with two long blonde braids who was dressed in overalls and a red T-shirt—the restaurant employees' uniform.

"Yes, please."

She ushered me to a booth in the corner of the largest dining room in the restaurant. From my vantage point I could see just about everything, including the bar and the saloon doors that were continually swinging open to expose a frantic kitchen staff with steam rising from the hot grills all around them. Most of the tables and booths around me were full. They had a wide variety of clientele ranging from construction workers still in their yellow vests, to businessmen and women in their suits. I realized the food had to be good to draw such a large and diverse crowd.

"Tammy will be right with you. She'll bring you some cornbread and hush puppies to tide you over." The hostess handed me a brightly colored laminated menu with the specials paperclipped to the top on a small, pink piece of paper. I thought about how the hush puppies and cornbread wouldn't just "tide me over," they would be my entire lunch if I ate too many.

I couldn't reconcile the photographs I had seen of Tilly on Facebook where she looked so refined and sophisticated with the down-and-dirty feel of this restaurant. It seemed so incongruous that she would waltz in here with her demure look, sashay through the kitchen and praise the staff for their beer-battered chicken wings and loaded potato skins. *But it had happened*—at least that's what people had shared about her at the funeral. I was reminded, as I often am when I cover murder cases, that people have many facets. Tilly obviously did. Her looks made her appear like she was above a place like Hubert's Roadhouse, but her actions showed that she was not. She cared about the people who worked here, and she expressed that on a regular basis.

"What can I get you to drink, sugar?" The waitress who was clearly younger than me asked in a syrupy tone. I always got a kick out of this—younger women, probably wise beyond their years, who addressed me like I was a little girl. But I had gotten used to it. It was one of the niceties of the South that you either embraced or despised. I chose to embrace it.

"Just water, thanks."

Tammy's name tag was haphazardly dangling from the right strap of her overalls as if she might have put it on in a rush. She brought me a mason jar full of ice water with a straw and then set down a yellow plastic basket lined with white paper that was full of cornbread squares and hush puppies. I resisted the temptation to immediately grab something out of the basket despite the heavenly smell. She pulled out a pen from behind her ear and a pad from her rear pocket.

"Know what you want, baby?"

"I'll have the special, thanks," I said pointing to the homemade chili, baked potato, and side salad combination.

"Dressing?"

"Blue cheese."

"Ranch?"

"Perfect," I replied, quietly chastising myself for asking for blue cheese. For some reason when it came out of my mouth it sounded like I was asking for escargot at a fast-food restaurant.

"Coming up, sweetie," Tammy said replacing the pen behind her ear and turning to go.

"Can I ask you a question?" I tried not to hesitate, knowing she was busy, and I might only have a few seconds to get her attention.

"Sure, baby, shoot."

"Did you know Tilly? Tilly Dawson?"

"Sure did, hon. We all knew Tilly. Sweet lady. Always nice to me, nice to everybody here. Not like her husband. Plenty of people would tell you, *he's a real sonofabitch*. A real shame what happened to her. Hate that anyone gets that low. I've been praying for her soul and for her daughter, Delilah. She works here, too. You didn't hear this from me, but she didn't always do right by her mama. But I even pray for the sinners; they need prayers more than anybody. Who knew Miss Tilly was at that point?"

"What point?"

"You know, the breaking point. You know that low place people go where they can't see a way out. That's when I call on God. I don't know if Miss Tilly had God in her life or not, but I know she could have used some God. She was obviously hurting. That husband was meaner than the day is long and that daughter of hers gave her nothing but grief, grief and *trouble* with a capital T."

"What do you mean by *trouble*?"

"The kind of stuff that will push a mother over the edge if you know what I mean."

"Not really. What kind of stuff?"

Tammy then leaned down close to my ear, her hands grasping the edge of the table.

"Love triangle stuff," she whispered and then put a finger to her pursed lips in a "shush" gesture.

After Tammy walked away, I sat alone with my racing thoughts. Love triangle? Who was in the triangle? Was Hubert cheating? Was Tilly cheating? Did Hubert kill Tilly because she was cheating? Did Hubert kill Tilly because he was cheating and wanted his wife out of the way? Did Tilly kill herself because of the stress one of these potential scenarios had caused her? And why was Delilah so much *trouble*? What role did she have in all this? It was like Tammy had dropped a bomb in the middle of my basket of hush puppies and then walked away while they clung to the ceiling in the aftermath of the carnage. I didn't know what to think.

I took a break from my monkey brain and started scrolling through my social media accounts. I needed to see a few cats in sweaters and videos of babies with their faces covered in pureed carrots laughing hysterically. Within seconds, I was deep diving into my followers' weekend activities on Instagram. Shane went paddle boarding, Cameron went biking, and Leslie attended a surprise birthday party. Because this was my work Instagram account, I didn't really know Shane, Cameron, or Leslie, but their posts still made me smile and relaxed my runaway brain.

Louise, my best friend, who was a stay-at-home mom who became a successful event planner, had hosted a wedding at a local farmhouse turned party space. It was a beautiful country-chic soiree with tiny sprigs of baby's breath in little round glass vases on a long table dressed in a stark white tablecloth. Twinkle lights garnished tall potted trees around the room. I made a mental note to call Louise and check in. We were both so busy but had recently made more of an effort to stay in touch. My effort had waned since Adam's death in 2016, but for the past year, I had been trying to reconnect with my closest friends who stood by me through all the pain.

I rarely checked messages on Instagram because they were almost always unimportant and often bizarre. For some reason, strangers seemed to like to connect with me in private messages on this platform when there were hundreds of other more efficient ways to reach me—email, texting and phone calls being three of them. I noticed I had three unread messages.

One was from a man named Richard who said: "Hello there. Do you want to have coffee with me?" *Delete*. The second one was from a woman named Rhonda: "Something is happening on Walter Springs road. Lots of cops." It was dated a week ago. Too late. *Delete*. But the third one was curious. It was from a little girl named Penny. Her picture looked familiar. When I clicked on her account it was private, so I couldn't see her posts. I clicked on the message and it read:

> Hi, it's Penny from the funeral. I know ur investigating what happened 2 Aunt Tilly. I read lots of mysteries, and watch tons of crime shows on Netflix, so I have a pretty good handle on solving cases. U should look at my Great Uncle Hubert. He's a mean man. Hope u read this. Thanks!

I looked up from my phone to see a young girl with long auburn hair in overalls and a red shirt bringing me my meal. She had fairy hair—several strands of sparkling twine artificially attached to her long locks. Her name tag read "Brenda." Tammy was nowhere in sight.

"Thanks," I said, trying to sound casual. "Where did Tammy go?"

"She's on break," Brenda replied quickly, with more than just a hint of annoyance in her voice.

"Oh, okay. Well, can you ask her to call me?"

I slid my business card across the table and Brenda exchanged it for a ticket that she peeled off her pad and slapped on the table using the salt shaker to hold it in place as a ceiling fan whirred above us creating a mini-hurricane breeze.

"Have a good one," she said already turning away with her empty tray in the direction of the kitchen.

The saloon doors to the kitchen swung open again with a whoosh sound, and for just a second I could see Tammy talking to someone across the food line, hands on her hips, with a serious look on her face.

16

CHASING CHICKENS

"CHICKENS ARE RUNNING EVERYWHERE!" Janie said with an exuberance in her voice that I hadn't heard in a long while. It used to be that *I* was selling stories to my managers. Now, *they* were trying to sell stories to me. "The highway is shut down. The firemen are chasing them. We have great aerials from the helicopter. I need you and Buster to go on the ground."

I got Brenda's attention as soon as she finished taking an order at the next booth and asked her to pack up my lunch to go. I spent much more time eating in a car than I ever did eating at a table. I was pretty sure this wasn't the healthiest way to consume a meal, but many days this was the difference between making it on the air or not. As I paid the bill at the register, I noticed the framed awards and the newspaper articles that had been written about Hubert's Roadhouse on the back wall of the restaurant. Brenda came up behind me and tapped me on the shoulder to give me the to-go container in a white plastic bag. She leaned in behind me and whispered in my ear.

"I gave Tammy your card. She said to tell you to be careful, that you're playing with fire."

Brenda then turned and walked away again after making this cryptic statement without looking back. I wanted to run after her, to ask her to explain herself. I wanted her to get Tammy out of the kitchen and make her come talk to me. Obviously, Tammy regretted saying anything to me. She must have realized after she talked to me who I was. She would probably not have knowingly said those words to a news reporter—*love triangle.*

I hustled to the car with the fairy-hair waitress's words still gliding through my head—*playing with fire.* What in the world was she talking about? Was Hubert the fire? Was Delilah the fire? If not, who was the fire?

And then Tammy's words—*love triangle.* As a reporter, this wasn't something I heard about on a regular basis. Movies made it seem like love triangles were common and were the foundation for almost all domestic homicides. In reality, the reasons why a man killed his wife were usually pretty mundane. Men killed their wives so they wouldn't have to pay alimony and child support. They killed their wives to prevent the inevitability of a messy divorce and public shame. Jealously was way down on the list of reasons to kill someone. And Tammy made it clear that Delilah and her *trouble* had something to do with what happened to Tilly. But what?

But now wasn't the time for me to ponder these cryptic words from the women at Hubert's Roadhouse. I had a chicken story to chase. As I pulled in behind Buster's car on the side of the highway, I could see people running in every direction, their arms extended, hands splayed, hunched over trying to grab the elusive chickens that were literally streaming out of the overturned tractor trailer making the scene look like a fire hydrant unplugged. The truck lay on its side blocking two lanes of the I-80 highway, the main thoroughfare in and around the city.

"Good stuff," I said as I patted Buster on the back. His camera was on his shoulder and his eye was in the viewfinder as he swept the lens from one side of the chaos to the other.

"Damn straight. Can't make it up. Firefighters trying to grab them and they're running for the hills. Does sour me a little on wanting Chick-fil-A for lunch, though," Buster said with a chuckle pulling his face away from the camera momentarily. Buster always knew how to turn anything into a joke.

Buster was married to Hugh, a high-powered salesman for a top technology company. He traveled all over the country and made a very good living. They had a nine-year-old son named Noah who was adopted from an agency in Idaho that specialized in pairing same-sex couples with newborns. Because Hugh traveled so much for work, Buster was essentially a single parent, albeit in a fancy urban townhouse with a rooftop deck that had killer views. Buster had a lot on his plate, so I tried to give him a break, even when he refused to give me one.

"We need to get some sound," I said with as much cheer as I could muster given the high-pitched chicken carnage going on all around us.

"Here's the mic." Buster said, handing me the microphone with the big "Channel 8" logo on the square.

I made my way through the crowd to a firefighter who was sitting on the metal stairs of one of the trucks. His jacket was off, and he was pouring water over one of his hands. It looked like he had been injured, which didn't surprise me based on how frantic the chickens were—pecking and kicking at the people who were trying to grab them.

"Hey there. Maddie Arnette from Channel 8."

"I know who you are," the firefighter said still staring down at his hand. It looked like he had gotten a good gash from one of the chickens on his palm. It was about an inch long and blood mixed with the water was running down his arm. "She got me good. I mean I guess it was a *she*, I don't know. Happened so fast. Hurts like a bitch. Sorry."

"No worries. We're just trying to talk to people about what happened."

"Well, I can't talk. My supervisor is over there. Captain Wentworth. Tall guy with the moustache leaning against the other truck in the white fire hat."

The firefighter gestured with the elbow of the hand that was hurt. He looked up and met my eyes with a weary look. I assumed this wasn't exactly the kind of call firefighters expected or were trained for.

"Thanks. I hope you feel better. You might need a stitch or two. You should get that looked at."

"You're probably right. Thanks." He went back to tending to his wound and I sidestepped around the chickens on the run that threatened to trip me, winding my way over to the captain. Thankfully, I had worn closed-toe shoes instead of my standard springtime sandals.

"Captain Wentworth, Maddie Arnette, Channel 8. Can we get a quick interview?"

"Sure," the captain said as he straightened his helmet and told the other firefighter to "handle everything" for a moment with an emphasis on the word *handle.*

"So, this is a pretty crazy situation. Not something you train much for I would guess?" I said, trying unsuccessfully to keep the winnowing sarcasm out of my voice.

"Well, actually, a handful of my guys did a fair bit of chicken wrangling down east when they were growing up on farms. But no, for the most part, most of these guys are city boys who have never seen a chicken on a highway, or for that matter, anywhere else, before. In fact, about the only place they've seen a chicken is on a bun or a plate," he said, smiling devilishly at his own joke. It was hard not to see a little humor in the situation.

"So, it's harder than it looks, to wrangle chickens that is?"

"Yes, it is. It can be a bloody mess. They like to fight. Best thing is to grab 'em in your arms, two or three at a time. Same way they catch 'em on the farm to take them to the slaughterhouse. It's not easy. But we'll get them, one way or another. They can't outrun us forever."

This time I saw a twinkle in the captain's eyes, as if this might be about the best thing that had happened to him all week, maybe all month. Given the fact that firefighters often dealt with tragedy and loss, this was probably a much better assignment for his crew, even with the pecking injuries.

"I know it's a big inconvenience for people. You can see how long the line of traffic is from the air. When do you think the road will be open again?"

"When the chickens get gone, young lady, and not a minute before then. If you'll excuse me, I should probably be helping my guys. Y'all have a great day now."

The captain turned and became absorbed back into the crowd as the cacophony of the birds squawking and the firefighters shouting at them reached a fever pitch. Just then, my phone rang. I backed up about ten feet. It was hard to hear over the escalating noise, but I could just barely make out Kojak's voice.

"Hey, Kid, there's a lady you know at the hospice house right now. You know, Marion volunteers there. It's all confidential, but she put two and two together. I told her about the broad you had been talking to whose son was killed by his father. Well, she told Marion that story. It's her. It's that same lady. *It's Esther.*"

"Esther? I just saw her last week. What in the world?"

"Apparently, she has stage four colon cancer. Ugly stuff. Been fighting it for a long time. Went downhill real fast, just a few days ago. Has a DNR, do not resuscitate. Husband, Pete, I think his name is, couldn't deal with it at home. Not talking, in a coma. So, whatever she knows, unless it's in those files she gave you, it's going with her to the grave. Pete is with her. Kind of a broken guy, Marion says. You can understand that. Killed his own kid, now he's losing his wife. Sad story if there ever was one."

"Okay, as soon as I put this chicken story to bed, I'm going to go visit her. I just feel terrible, like I could have been so much nicer to her."

"Not your fault. You had no way of knowing. By the way. I copied the stuff in the bag. Gave the originals to Marion. She'll give it back to you when you see her. I'm not telling you what to do with it. But it's yours. You need to hold onto to it and decide when you're ready to look at it. Or *burn it* if you want to."

His mention of the bag put a lump in my throat. My last meeting with Esther came back to me in a rush, how I had bristled when she told me her story, how I had blamed her for keeping the secret all these years and putting Roger and my family through hell. I hated her in that moment; and I feared that I had made this very clear. And now, I was regretting how I acted. I had no idea what she was dealing with at the time. I didn't stop to think that maybe her need to unburden herself was part of a dying wish to cleanse her soul of this awful truth. After a long silence on the phone, Kojak finally spoke again, trying to calm me during what he could tell was an intense internal struggle.

"Again, not your fault, Kid; you were stun-gunned by what she told you. You didn't know she was getting ready to check out. You can't beat yourself up about it now. But it might make you feel better if you paid her a visit. I know how you are. You'll chew on this forever if you don't at least make the effort to see her."

As usual, Kojak knew me almost as well as Adam did. His ability to see me when others couldn't always amazed and quietly comforted me. It made me feel like I knew a little bit about what it would be like to have a real father. I wondered if anyone would ever know me again like Adam did. It made me sad to think that the answer was *no*.

17

GRACEFUL EXIT

THE OAK CITY HOSPICE HOUSE was the definition of serenity. I could understand why people chose this place as their final stop before as they left the earthly world. The waiting area felt like a friend's cozy living room with overstuffed couches, fuzzy throw pillows and light streaming in through large picture windows. There were a few subtle pieces of art hung on the light gray walls, all abstract pictures with muted but pleasant, soothing colors. Everything here seemed to say, *it's going to be okay, relax, be calm, be present.*

After watching Adam die at home with the aid of hospice nurses who came over on a daily basis to help me navigate everything from morphine doses to turning him in the bed, I had gained a tremendous amount of respect for the men and women who helped people exit the world with as much grace as possible. I knew nothing about death before Adam got sick. I thought I knew everything considering I was a crime reporter who covered death almost every single day. But watching someone you love die is different than covering it for the news. The hospice nurses taught me how to balance my intense emotions with caregiving duties. They also showed me the calmness a caregiver needs to master to truly help someone in the last moments of life.

Marion came out to speak with me when I arrived to see Esther and told me that they had a rule about the number of people that could be in a room at one time. At that moment, Esther had a group from her church visiting. Marion told me she would come and get me as soon as they left. I was glad that Esther had friends who came to see her before she died. So many people came to see Adam, and I chalked this up to the way he lived—open, receptive, engaging. I decided that people really did die the way they had lived. If they surrounded themselves with love in life, that's how they would die, surrounded by love. I was happy that despite Esther's lonely secret, she had obviously not isolated herself from others.

Without a word, Marion placed the canvas bag with Esther's files at my feet. I stared at it like it was radioactive. I decided I needed to get it out of my sight for now. This moment was about paying my respects to Esther, not chastising her for the mistakes she had made. The bag was a tangible reminder of those mistakes. So, I quickly took it to the car and put it in my trunk, shoving it to the back recesses of the dark cavern and then returned to the lobby.

I leaned into one of the large, gray fuzzy pillows fearing I might fall asleep. The chicken story had been chaotic, and the early March day was much warmer than usual. Thinking about what Tammy and the fairy-hair waitress, Brenda, had said at Hubert's Roadhouse was still eating away at my emotional bandwidth. My energy was *zapped*.

To stay awake, I scrolled through the comments beneath my story about Tilly's death on the station's Facebook page. I knew better than to take them seriously, but I also couldn't help myself. I wanted to know what people were saying. Sometimes, the comments revealed new leads or even new evidence in a case. More often, they just made me mad as people often wrote cruel and insensitive things that I couldn't imagine saying publicly about a stranger.

"Something here is fishy. This doesn't sound like suicide to me," Princess Deb wrote.

"Has anyone looked at the husband? I mean come on, isn't that always the first place the cops look?" Graham from Graham wrote.

Most of the comments were vague, speculative, even reckless, and they came from people who had no personal connection to the case. But as I scrolled through them, half paying attention, willing the cozy couch not to pull me down into a black hole of sleep from which there was no recovery, one comment caught my eye.

"Everyone knows that Hubert Dawson has a bad temper. If you've ever worked for him, you know what I'm talking about. And he treated his family—his wife and daughter—just as badly as he did his wait staff. Come on Oak City Police, when are you going to shine a light on this case and tell us what really happened????????????" It was signed "Chef Andy."

Chef Andy? It had to be someone from the restaurant. Maybe a disgruntled ex-employee? I didn't have time to ponder this question. But I was intrigued. Marion was at my side again, her gentle hand on my shoulder. Her calm, kind demeanor fit so well with this place. It wasn't hard for me to see why Kojak treated her like she walked on water. I was convinced in this moment that *she did*.

"You can come back now Maddie. She is sleeping, but I believe she can still hear you. Her husband, Pete, is with her."

I was nervous to meet Pete. I wondered if Esther had told him anything about me. I wondered if he knew that I knew he had killed his son. It was all too much to parse in the short walk to Esther's room. I decided I would deal with whatever he threw at me, and just hoped none of it would matter given the circumstances.

I followed Marion down the long corridor with its muted pastel green walls and the drifting sound of piano music from a room at the end of the hall. She was an attractive older woman dressed in an understated beige sweater set and black pants. Her curly, brunette hair was pulled back in a low ponytail and she wore no makeup and little jewelry with the exception of her wedding ring and a long gold pendant with a small angel dangling from it. I imagined this might have been a gift from a grateful family.

"Here we are," Marion gestured with one hand toward a room with a door ajar. Her angel pendant swung across her chest as she turned to go back down the hall looking like it might be about to take flight. "Just let me know if you need anything, okay?"

She gave my arm a little squeeze before she turned and left. Kojak must have told Marion something about my connection to Esther, but whatever he told her, it really didn't matter. She was the kind of person who didn't pry. As I watched Marion walk away, panic welled up in my chest. *I hardly knew Esther.* What right did I have to be here? How would I introduce myself to Pete not knowing what, if anything, Esther had told him?

As I peeked inside the room, not fully committing to entering yet, I saw an older, frail looking man with white hair in a green golf shirt that hung loosely from his thin frame. In his hand was a comb, and he was gently running it through the sprigs of white hair on Esther's head as they fanned out across her blue pillowcase. It was one of the most moving moments of true love that I had ever seen. I knew instantly that I would not tell Pete the truth about who I was to Esther as I suspected she had not told him anything. Like Kojak had said, she was taking everything that wasn't inside the tote bag with her to her grave.

"Hello, may I come in?" I said gently rapping on the door gently with my knuckles as I eased the door open. Pete kept combing and looking at Esther as he spoke to me.

"You may. I'm just tidying up her hair. She's real particular about her hair. You know how ladies are," his voice trailed off into what sounded like a tiny whimper. I could feel my chest constricting. I just wanted to throw my arms around this man and tell him how sorry I was, not just because he was losing his wife, but because of the way I had treated her the last time we met, and because I knew his tragic story, that he had killed his son. But I stopped myself.

"I'm Maddie, a friend of Esther's," I said extending my hand, and then thinking better of it when I realized his hand was occupied, I pulled it back before he looked up.

"You're the television lady," he said matter-of-factly, meeting my eyes with a weary gaze.

"I am, that's right. But we were in a book club together, a long time ago. I heard she was sick, and I—" I couldn't stop my stammering. I knew I sounded ridiculous.

"You don't say," Pete said, again, without judgment. He gestured for me to sit in the chair to the right side of her bed.

I eased into the brown recliner and sat upright on the edge of it so that I could lean in and speak to Esther. I felt sure she couldn't hear me, but when Adam was dying the hospice nurses told me you would be surprised by how much the dying can hear even if they don't react. Esther's small hand lay lifeless on the blanket near me. Her breath rattled as she struggled to inhale, but her face looked peaceful. The tension I had seen when we met in the coffee shop had melted away and was now replaced by a serenity that I'm sure had a lot to do with morphine. I remembered how the morphine had calmed Adam when he was dying—it also took him away from us—but the hospice nurses assured me that in the final stages of life it was the only way to allow him to slip peacefully from this world into the next.

"I'm going to step out for a moment and get some coffee down the hall. Do you want anything?" Pete asked in the tone of a well-raised southern gentleman.

I shook my head, and watched the sad man slink out of the room carrying the incredible weight of his grief with him. I knew I only had a few minutes before he returned. I leaned in and spoke softly to Esther. My words tumbled out quickly for fear that Pete might come back at any moment and hear me, and I would lose my chance and my nerve.

"Esther, I have turned the information over to investigators in Pennsylvania. I promise we will get to the truth, and the right thing will be done. You can let go of this burden now. I forgive you. I want you to know that. It's so important to me that you know that. Go in peace and know that you have given me the gift of your truth, a truth I will handle with care. I understand the responsibility that goes along with it. Rest peacefully my friend."

On impulse, I reached over and squeezed her little hand. It felt warm and tiny in mine, like a child's hand. I may have imagined it. I probably did. But just as I finished squeezing, I felt the faintest pressure of her tiny hand squeezing back. I had accomplished what I came to do. I turned around to see Pete in the doorway giving me a sad, but unknowing smile.

18

PICKING TAMMY'S BRAIN

As I DROVE HOME FROM THE HOSPICE HOUSE, I kept wondering if I had said the right words to Esther, and then I wondered again if she could hear me. Pete had been more than kind when I left, giving me an awkward sideways hug, and looking at me with his sad eyes and the best half-smile he could muster. There was no suspicion in his gaze. I was sure Esther had not told him about me. Who I was to his wife was a mystery to him and he didn't seem to need to know the answer. My kindness to her in this moment was enough for him.

Everything was swirling around in my brain—Esther was dying, someone may have killed Tilly, Clifton may have killed my mother. With everything happening, I had almost forgotten about Penny's message to me on Instagram. Clearly, she had some insight into this situation, but I could hardly reach out to a child and begin communicating with her online. Not only was it unethical, but I had no guarantee that what she was telling me was the truth. Although, her assessment of Hubert did jive with that of "Chef Andy" from Facebook.

I decided I needed to find Andy first and see if he might speak with me. Tammy, the waitress from Hubert's restaurant, seemed like my best possible connection to employees there. But after the way she had acted at the restaurant, hiding out in the kitchen, and giving the table to the fairy-hair waitress, I wasn't sure if she would help me.

I found her Facebook page easily because when I was leaving the restaurant, I glanced at a framed article from the newspaper hanging on the wall near the cashier. It was from a few years back and featured some of the Roadhouse staff after the restaurant was named number one in the area for customer service. "Tammy Rankin" was front and center in the caption beneath the picture that accompanied the article. Luckily, I had a photographic memory. I only had to see something once to remember it forever.

Tammy Rankin's profile picture on Facebook was her standing on a beach in front of a magnificent sunset with a large tropical flower in her hair sipping a pink drink through a straw. When I looked closer at the picture, I realized the beach and the sunset were part of a backdrop, and she was obviously at some party where you could take your picture with props in front of the dazzling beach scene.

I knew that not everyone checked Facebook Messenger, but I decided to give it a try and send Tammy a message to see if she might be willing to help me. I knew it was a longshot, but if the alternative was using an eleven-year-old girl as my source for the story, I decided it was a longshot that made sense.

"Tammy—this is Maddie Arnette. You waited on me today in the restaurant at lunch. Was just trying to figure some things out about the situation with Tilly. Do you know a Chef Andy? Do you know how I might get in touch with him?"

I tried to sound as casual as possible, like I hadn't seen her standing there in the kitchen when she was supposed to be waiting on my table, like she hadn't sent another waitress to do her job because she was suddenly uncomfortable about what she had told me.

I stared at my phone, willing her to respond. It was early evening, surely, she was off work by now if she worked the lunch shift. Just when I was about to give up, I heard the "ping" telling me I had a new message.

"Yes, of course I remember you. I realize who you are now. I'm embarrassed that I didn't recognize you earlier," Tammy wrote.

Maybe that was it. Maybe I was reading too much into the whole thing. Maybe she just felt weird about talking to me about the case and not realizing I was reporter. I wanted so badly to ask her about the "love triangle" she mentioned at lunch, but I decided that, for now, I would stay focused on my mission to find Chef Andy.

"No worries!" I replied trying to keep the casual tone going.

"Chef Andy used to work at the restaurant. He was the head chef here for many years, oversaw menus for all the restaurants in the chain. Hubert fired him for coming on to his daughter, Delilah. Frankly, I don't think she minded it too much. But I don't want to say anything that might get me in trouble. I need this job."

I paused for a moment to think about my next move. Tammy was letting me in, little by little. I didn't want to spook her. Clearly, she wasn't very fond of Delilah. Could Delilah have had something to do with Tilly's death? Maybe I was reading too much into what Tammy was saying or *wasn't saying.*

"Thanks Tammy. I won't out you. You have my word. But I would like to speak with Andy. Do you know where I can find him?" I waited for a few seconds, staring at the screen willing her to write back. After about a minute had passed, I assumed I had lost her. Then, suddenly, a new message popped up.

"Divorced. Shares custody of his little girl Emmy with his ex-wife, Liz. She got the house. He moved out of Oak City to his grandmother's farm in Ogburne. Lives in a cabin on her property. Verdine Parnell is her name."

"Thanks so much!"

I was eager to start searching for Verdine Parnell's farm in property records. I assumed Tammy and I were done, although I heard another ping and looked down at my phone again. Three words appeared in all capital letters.

"WATCH YOUR BACK," Tammy's note read.

Clearly, Tammy knew more than she was telling me about the situation. And I had a feeling I was about to find out what her warning was all about.

19

CHEF ANDY

I DIDN'T USUALLY WORK ON SATURDAYS, but lately, there simply weren't enough hours in the week to do everything I needed to do. Candace, my babysitter, had graciously agreed to ferry the twins around to their activities and two birthday parties so that I could take a road trip to Ogburne to see Chef Andy.

Candace had been with me since she was in college. I don't know what I would have done without her when Adam was dying. During that time, I didn't always know exactly where the twins were, I just knew Candace had whisked them out of the house on some new adventure and they were safe. I was thrilled when she decided to get a graduate degree in biology from the local state university. It bought me two more years of the unbelievable safety net she had always provided my family.

Saturday mornings were usually my long-run days with my running group at Benton Road Park, but I had missed the meetups so many times lately due to conflicts with the kids' schedules that no one questioned my absence. Now that the kids were old enough to stay home alone, I often went on predawn runs by myself to clear my head before work. Sometimes, my neighbor Melissa tagged along. Running equaled sanity to me. When I didn't do it, I felt anxious all day long. Today was going to be one of those days.

I had learned with a little digging that the "Chef Andy" on Facebook was Andy Parnell. I knew there was a good chance I would drive all the way to Ogburne and that Andy would refuse to speak with me. This happened a lot as a reporter—people refusing to speak with us despite our valiant effort to show up in person at their door. The way I looked at it was that if I called first and he said no, I couldn't in good conscience knock on his door. But if I went straight to the door-knock, there was a chance I could wedge my foot in the door, both literally and figuratively, and get him to speak with me. In my experience, face-to-face encounters trumped phone calls and digital connections every single time. You can't trust me if you don't see my face. And if you don't trust me, there's no way you're going to speak with me.

The GPS told me the farm was an hour and forty-eight minutes from Oak City. I had invited my good friend, Louise Chance, to come along for the ride so that we could catch up. Being a former reporter, she loved a good mystery. We had met as interns at a Washington, D.C., television station right out of college in 2000 and had randomly both ended up in North Carolina. Louise left television because the schedule and the stress didn't bode well for her family life. But a few years later she opened Elegant Event Planning in the spare bedroom of their house, and due to her tenacity, it immediately took off. The next thing she knew, she was helping plan everything from weddings to birthday parties to family reunions on a grand scale that even she had not expected. Now, she had four employees and a fancy office in the back of a fabulous downtown event space that was once a meatpacking company.

When Adam was alive, we socialized a lot with Louise and Scott. Their three boys—Aaron, Alex, and Avery—grew up with Miranda and Blake. They spent every Halloween together trick-or-treating, every Fourth of July together watching fireworks, and every New Year's Eve together staying up until midnight and toasting with sparkling cider in champagne glasses.

Because Scott was a local defense attorney, I sometimes interviewed him about criminal law topics. Every once in a while, Scott represented someone in a case that I was covering. Even when he could not do an interview due to privacy issues involving his client, he would always talk to me off the record and give me the background that I needed to get a running start on a story. In short, my friendship with Louise translated into a mutual professional respect between Scott and me.

Besides being a great friend, Louise was good company. She was a tiny, blonde, perky woman, a spitfire full of frenetic energy. But she was no wallflower. If you crossed her, she went from miniature poodle to pit bull in seconds. She was beautiful, funny, fiercely loyal, and had remained my friend even when I distanced myself from everyone after Adam's death. While Adam was dying, she was at my door every single day bringing ice cream, flowers, or just some corny joke. Her best quality was that she never made you feel like she didn't have time for you, even when she really didn't. When you were talking to Louise, you were the most important person in the room. She was always there for me, and I vowed to always be there for her.

I told Louise the basics of the case and said I was working on it behind the scenes because Dex didn't want to give me time to do it on the clock. I knew her reporter instincts would kick in, even though she hadn't used them in years, and she would start asking pointed questions and pulling apart my theories, which was exactly the kind of feedback I needed from her.

"Okay, so one more time. Let me get this straight. He worked for this guy, Hubert. Hubert's wife is dead, allegedly from a self-inflicted gunshot wound. This guy, Chef Andy, goes on Facebook and talks junk about Hubert, implying that the guy killed his wife. And a waitress named Tammy told you that Andy was fired by Hubert for coming on to his daughter, Delilah. *And* she implied that Delilah welcomed Andy's attention. But at this point, we don't really know what, *if anything*, transpired between Andy and Delilah and whether or not Andy is posting crap on Facebook because he is a disgruntled ex-employee, or because *it's true.* "

"Wow, you got it!" I said giving her a quick high-five. Louise was good at puzzles. She liked to talk things through which, in turn, helped me get my thoughts in order. She had been the education reporter at Channel 8 for a few years until she decided to stay home with Aaron and Alex. Once her business took off and she had Avery, she was even busier than she had been as a reporter. All three boys played sports, so there were travel league games on the weekends that Scott mostly handled so that she could be at the events she planned. I was lucky she didn't have a wedding to organize on this particular Saturday.

"Okay—so this Chef Andy character, what do we know about him? We know he's most likely angry because Hubert fired him. And we think he was fired because he came on to Hubert's twenty-year-old daughter, Delilah, which makes sense for sure because he's what, like thirtysomething? Late thirties? Too old for her, plus it's not very ethical to go after the boss's daughter. I can understand why Hubert fired him. We also know that he's divorced, shares custody of his little girl with the ex, and his finances and career pretty much tanked after he was fired—that's why he's living in the middle of nowhere in his grandmother's cabin. So, I think we can pretty much agree that he's a disgruntled ex-employee. Makes sense that he would spread gossip online about the person he thinks screwed up his life. But the real question is: Is he just talking junk, or *is he for real?*"

"We don't know if he is or isn't credible, but he could be an important piece of this whole puzzle. If he's bold enough to attack a powerful businessman like Hubert, his former boss, he might actually *know* something. That's a hell of a lot of liability to take on if he's wrong."

The country road curved around withering cornfields and old barns with caved-in roofs and weeds growing through their walls. Modest, brick ranch homes popped up in clusters every few miles around a bend. Their lawns were manicured, and every porch had a rocking chair and a swing. Some of the driveways were adorned with regal columns, gates and gilded lions that dwarfed the entrances. Some of the yards had small fountains and gazebos surrounded by colorful gardens lined with shiny reflective lawn ornaments.

As we snaked down Verdine Parnell's long driveway lined by a fence made of whitewashed rails, I swiveled my head in both directions looking for a "No Trespassing" sign. If a property was posted, we couldn't risk going to the door. If there was no sign, we could go to the door, but if we were asked to leave, we had to do so immediately, or face being charged with trespassing. Most television crews knew the law and followed it.

I spied the cabin behind the main house. It literally looked like someone had scooped up a genuine log cabin from the mountains on a flatbed truck and then dropped it in the backyard of Verdine Parnell's homestead in the sprawling farmlands of eastern North Carolina. Verdine's home was a large, white turn-of-the-century clapboard farmhouse that had seen better days. The closer I came to it the more it revealed its age with its peeling paint, loose shutters hanging on by a few rusty nails, and sagging eaves laden with pine needles.

I noticed right away that there was a big red pickup truck parked in front of the cabin and took this as a good sign that Andy Parnell might be home. I had seen his truck proudly displayed in the profile picture on his Facebook page.

Propped against the house was a small purple bike with streamers coming from the handlebars. It had a white plastic basket adorned with pink flowers. Hanging on the handlebars was a multicolored child's helmet with a Disney Princess theme adorning it. This had to be Emmy's bike, I thought, the daughter Tammy had told me about.

Strewn around the front yard were various children's toys and dog toys. There was a jump rope, a pink soccer ball, a rawhide bone, a couple of well-worn tennis balls, and a skateboard missing two wheels.

The cabin was charming, like something out of a fairy tale, nestled among the pine trees and azalea bushes. It had a wide front porch with a bench swing and white rocking chairs, and wind chimes that were silent on this breezeless day.

"What's the plan?" Louise chimed in.

"Well, normally I have a camera, and I have to decide whether or not to bring it with me and ambush the person, but since that's not the case, I think I'll just knock on his door, tell him who I am, and see if he will just talk with me off the record. You should probably just stay here. If he's as volatile as he appears to be in his Facebook comments, I don't want to expose you to that."

"No worries; I have plenty of Words With Friends to catch up on, and I'm super behind in my Netflix bingeing."

I knew Louise probably had tons of work to do, emails and phone calls to return, but she didn't want to make it seem like I was pulling her away from something more important. That's how Louise always was; she was a true friend. She smiled, waved me off, and put in her AirPods, preparing to descend into her own little world on her phone.

I quietly closed my door and bounded up the steps of the sturdy cabin. Suddenly, the silent wind chime hanging from the eaves made out of tiny spoons played a little melody in an errant breeze as if it were signaling my arrival. A stack of firewood was piled high next to the door. The mat in front of the door read: "Y'all Come Back Now." Not seeing a doorbell, I rapped on the glass storm door with my knuckles, as the main wooden door to the house appeared to be slightly ajar. After the second knock, I waited a full minute. I could hear a dog barking somewhere inside, and figured if someone were home, they surely knew I was at the door based on the dog's alert. Then I felt a firm hand on my shoulder. For a moment, I thought about picking up a piece of the firewood from the nearby stack as a weapon to defend myself. I imagined that I could turn and swing it at the person, knocking him or her down the steps and buying me enough time to get away.

"Can I help you?" A handsome man with a head full of rumpled dark hair, big brown eyes and a slight smile on his chiseled face was standing about a foot behind me. He had taken his hand off my shoulder, and now had both hands on his hips. He wore a tight black T-shirt and baggy, worn jeans. Muscles rippled through the thin material on his shirt when he moved. There was no doubt in my mind that he knew exactly how good-looking he was. His face revealed the air of confidence of a man who liked what he saw in the mirror every morning.

"Yes, are you Andy Parnell?"

"Who's asking?" He replied with a slight snicker, like we were playing some kind of game that only he knew the rules to.

I jutted out my right hand, hoping the polite gesture would disarm his sarcasm and kick-start his Southern manners.

"Maddie, Maddie Arnette. I work for Channel 8 News. I read some of your comments online about Hubert Dawson beneath our coverage of Tilly Dawson's death, and I felt like I had to talk to you. Just chat, I don't have a camera with me or anything."

I knew I was talking too quickly, but I wanted to get out as many words out as possible before he shut me down.

Andy stood there studying me for a moment. He looked me up and down. He looked back at the car where Louise was trapped in some kind of an iPhone rabbit hole, oblivious to what was going on outside the car. It occurred to me that she wouldn't be great backup at this point if things started to go south. He did not remove his hand from his hip to shake my hand. His grin turned cold, like I had just dumped a bucket of ice water on his head when I mentioned Hubert.

"Why would I talk to you, or anyone else for that matter about that asshole?"

"Well, you seemed to have something important to say or you wouldn't have made those public comments on Facebook. So, I figured I would just try to talk to you in person."

"You figured? Let me tell you something, miss television reporter: You are missing the real story here. This is no suicide. It's obvious. You don't need me and my comments on Facebook to tell you that. If you and the police would just do your damn jobs, you would figure it out."

"What's obvious?"

"Oh, come on, for Christ's sake. Give me a break. Do I have to spell it out for you?"

"Yes, I'm afraid you do," I said standing my ground. I could see over his shoulder that Louise had rolled the windows down in the car and was now listening to us. She must have heard him raise his voice. I could also hear a dog whimpering at the storm door and scratching the glass to be let out behind me. But I didn't dare turn around. I wanted to maintain eye contact as part of my bid to wear this man down and make him talk to me.

"That man killed his wife. Anyone with half a brain could figure that out. But cops don't care because he's a big-time businessman. It's all about the money. They turn their heads and call it a suicide, *case closed.*"

In his voice, there was a crack, like merely the act of talking about Tilly's death was breaking him. This was not about business. This was *personal.* I suddenly realized that Andy Parnell wasn't just some angry crackpot casting aspersions on the man who had fired him, but he was *grieving.* He was grieving for Tilly. I backed off then and gave him some space.

Chef Andy breezed past me, opened the storm door, and let the dog out.

"Chestnut, come on boy, let's go."

I watched as Andy and the auburn-haired goldendoodle hopped in the front seat of the red pickup truck. He slammed the heavy door with a loud thud, and the engine roared to life. The dog made his way to what looked like a familiar spot in the back seat, while Andy made an abrupt U-turn. The tires spun gravel and dirt in their wake as the truck headed away from the house down the long driveway in the direction of the main road. I stood there for a few seconds staring at it, wondering what his connection was to Tilly Dawson.

"Maybe we should hang out until he gets back?" I said to Louise, pretty sure she was going to reject my idea.

"Are you crazy, girl? He's a pissed-off redneck. He could be going to get a gun and come back out and shoot us. We need to get the hell out of here!"

"You're reading him totally wrong. He's not pissed off at *us.* He's in pain. I think there may be a lot more to this situation than we know."

Louise had slid over to the driver's seat and waved at me to get in the car. Out of instinct, I pulled a business card out of my pocket and stuck it in the storm door with the improbable thought that Andy might have a change of heart and contact me. As we rumbled down the long dirt driveway, kicking up our own dust storm from my big silver SUV, I wondered what Andy Parnell really knew.

20

PENNY'S WORLD

I'M SO MAD THAT THE TELEVISION LADY isn't getting back to me. I know she read my Instagram message. You can tell in your account when someone has opened your message. So why is she ignoring me? Doesn't she know that when you're solving a mystery, timing is everything? I think maybe she isn't taking me seriously because I'm just eleven. I think I know what I need to do.

Adults act like they understand things like the Internet and social media, but they really don't. Kids know a lot more than they do. I'm going to create a "Finsta," a fake Instagram account. I'll use a picture of an adult and then message her, pretending to be someone who has information about the case. I'll find a nice picture, someone who looks like a credible person. The TV lady won't ignore a grown woman. She can't. It's a murder case, and I'm pretty sure I know who did it.

Like I already said, I watch a lot of crime shows online, and I know you have to have real evidence to arrest someone. But I also know there's something called "circumstantial evidence." That's when you don't have physical evidence like blood or the murder weapon, but you have a bunch of facts that all point to one person. I'm pretty sure there are a lot of things that point to Uncle Hubert, if that television lady would just pay attention. It's funny how adults are always accusing kids of not paying attention, when they are the worst about that. My mom never hears anything I say. I have to say it like ten times. She's very distracted by her phone, which is ironic because she's always telling me to get off mine.

I overheard my mother and my grandmother talking about Uncle Hubert the other day. They were trying to whisper, but they weren't doing a very good job. They were in the kitchen in my grandmother's house, and I stood just around the corner in the den, backed up against the wall in case one of them decided to suddenly come around the corner.

"It just doesn't make sense. The way she did it. Where she did it. I've known Tilly to be a lot of things, but never depressed, never suicidal," my grandmother said in her most confident tone, the same way she told me when I was little that grandmothers always know if you're lying because they've lived a long time and know a lot more than we do.

"I know, Mom," my mother said in her best attempt at whispering which was no attempt at all, "But you can't just accuse someone of murder because you don't like him, or because he has a temper. The police know what to look for. They investigated. They said it was a suicide. We need to accept that and move on."

"I know my brother. If he found out she was messing around, well, I can imagine him doing almost anything. He's a jealous man. A territorial man."

I had heard all I needed to hear. Someone had to investigate Uncle Hubert before it was too late. If the police wouldn't do it, the television lady needed to do it.

So, my new name on Instagram is Fiona Lively. Fiona is my favorite character from a book I just read, and Lively is the last name of my fourth-grade teacher who I really liked. Her name was Janice Lively, but that would be too obvious. Plus, you can't create a fake account using a real person's name. That would be illegal, I'm pretty sure.

I found a picture of a woman on the Internet who looks honest. She is on a website that teaches kids how to cook. She's wearing a flowered apron and is mixing something with a long wooden spoon in a huge metal bowl. She has a nice big smile. I'm pretty sure Maddie Arnette won't ignore Fiona Lively.

21

RESOLUTION

KOJAK HAD GRACIOUSLY AGREED to meet me for brunch on Sunday at the Oak City Bistro. Despite their healthy, sometimes tasteless fare, they served a pretty delicious weekend breakfast. I couldn't ask Candace to work more hours on her days off; I had already inconvenienced her on Saturday when I went to confront Andy. So, I brought the twins with me to brunch. They sat at another table in the corner. I watched as Miranda drowned her large stack of pancakes in sugar-free syrup and cut them into big chunks that didn't look like they could possibly fit into her little mouth. Blake, meanwhile, was so engaged in a game on his phone, that his waffle topped with homemade whipped cream and strawberries sat untouched and getting cold on the plate in front of him. I wanted to yell across the restaurant for him to put the phone down and eat, but I resisted the temptation.

"They're getting big," Kojak said proudly, gesturing to the kids, as if they were his grandchildren. "Pretty soon they'll be heading to college."

"Not so fast. Don't rush it. We've got a few more years. Although Miranda was telling me the other day she might want to go to boarding school."

"Where in the world did she get a fancy idea like that?" Kojak said, putting down his coffee cup and wiping the foam from his latte off his lips with his napkin. The irony of a hardscrabble cop drinking a latte and then calling my daughter "fancy" was clearly lost on him.

"I don't know. I think she watched some show online where the kids go to boarding school and they have a fabulous time away from home out from under the burden of their parents' watchful eyes. According to her, they eat junk food in their rooms, get to stay up late watching Netflix with their friends, and attend dances with cute boys. I'm sure it's some vague romantic notion that will soon pass. Although, I'm not doing the best job of being both mother *and* father."

"You've got to stop beating yourself up. Grief isn't something you outgrow; you just learn to live with it. It takes a lot of time. You're doing the best you can." He reached out and patted my hand.

"Am I? I'm working too many hours again. I'm getting too wrapped up in this case that I'm not even supposed to be covering, and the entire narrative of my life may soon be undermined depending on what the investigators in Pennsylvania find in Esther's secret files."

"Listen, I told you not to worry about that. Take that off the table for now. I gave them everything, and they promised me they would take a good look at it. I got a guy up there, Zack Brumson, with the Pennsylvania State Police. He's a little younger than me, but we went to the academy together here. He started right after college, and you know I was coming off my first career as a washed-up race car driver, if you can believe that. Anyway, he didn't stay here long. He moved up north because his wife got a job as a professor at some snooty, high-dollar college. That didn't work out. Got divorced. Tough luck. But his career took off. Anyway, he's a good guy. He's not going to let you down. And he will let us know when and if there's something to know. Got it?"

I nodded my head, but I really didn't believe it. I didn't believe some stranger in Pennsylvania with no connection to the case or to me would all of a sudden reopen it and possibly blow apart the work that his predecessors had done. But I had to trust Kojak. And I definitely didn't have the emotional energy, or time, to investigate it myself. I had taken the bag with Esther's original files that Marion returned to me and shoved it in the back of the closet with Roger's unread letters. I wasn't ready to climb that mountain yet.

"So, back to Tilly Dawson's case, it's official. They're closing it. *It's suicide*. We told the family yesterday. Hubert and Delilah. They took it hard. But they seem reluctantly resigned to our decision. Especially the girl, she thanked us profusely for looking into it, and she ultimately agreed with our conclusion. Although, they both seemed pretty stunned that she would take her own life."

"What do *you* think?"

"I think something ain't right. The husband, apparently, he was the OCD one in the family. You know the type—no shoes in the house, everything has to be perfectly straightened, nothing on the kitchen countertops, bedspread so tight you could bounce a quarter off it. She was the messy one. Her closet looked like a bomb exploded in it—lopsided clothes dangling from hangers, piles of inside-out laundry, dirty, worn makeup brushes laying around, single earrings, empty disposable contact cases, stuff everywhere."

"Your point?"

"My point is that he was the one who cared about the damn driveway. Why would she put a towel down to keep the blood from staining her husband's precious concrete if she was checking out? Why would she care? Clearly, she was upset with him if she did take her own life. It's just that crazy detail that keeps bothering me, kicking me in the gut every time I think about it. But police work isn't a dictatorship. I've got to let my team do their work and come to a conclusion they all think is reasonable. And they all agree on this one. I'm outvoted."

"But you're in charge of the Major Crimes unit. Can't you demand the case stays open, gets looked at again?"

"It doesn't work that way, kid. Like I said, we've got people killing each other every other day on street corners. We don't have time to go deep on this one unless there's some strong evidence to the contrary. Sometimes things look like one thing, and they're really another. She may have offed herself, and you and I, we're just hung up on a few details that may not mean anything—the towel, the weird note. I think part of it is we don't want to think of anyone's life being that bad. *It's tragic.* I get it."

"I'm actually hung up on the daughter being so quick to accept this resolution. I mean, why is she okay with the fact that you ruled it a suicide? Wouldn't she be fighting for you guys to get to the truth, especially if there's any possibility that her father did it?"

"Excellent point; I hadn't thought of it that way. But look at it like this: maybe she *knows* her dad is involved, and she's protecting him?"

"True, but the other day at the restaurant I spoke to this waitress named Tammy and she gave me a funny feeling about Delilah, implied things weren't great between her and Tilly. But she didn't elaborate. I hate to think the worst about a young woman who just lost her mother—but women *are* capable of violence. I know that firsthand from experience."

"Kid, you got to stop beating yourself up about that case—look at it as a one-off. She had a lot of people snowed, not realizing she was so low. But you're not wrong, broads can be dangerous, and devious, that's for sure. The girl could be trouble."

Suddenly, I felt a little tug at the sleeve of my jean jacket. I looked up and saw Miranda, her mouth shrouded in a thick glaze of syrup remnants. He hair was piled in a messy bun on top of her head, and she wore an oversized sweatshirt with her school logo on it and baggy, stretched-out sweatpants. This was her idea of what was appropriate to wear to a restaurant for breakfast. I didn't dare say anything lest I wake the angry sleeping dragon that I knew was inside her. It was Sunday, and I didn't have the energy for her drama.

"We're done. We want to go, Mom. Can we please go?"

Even though she was not quite there yet, I already knew that Miranda was going to be a hell of a teenager. She was a professional brooder who rarely thought I did anything right. While other kids spent their time and energy trying to please their mothers, I spent my time and energy trying to please her.

"Here's my credit card. Give it to the waiter, and then we'll go after we pay the bill."

She snatched the card from me and stomped away back toward the table where her brother was still deeply ensconced in a game, but his waffle was almost gone. I took comfort in the fact that he had at least paused long enough to eat.

"Kids," Kojak said, smiling knowingly. His were long grown, married with kids of their own. I knew he wished he had been more present when they were growing up. But it had been hard to do as a young race car driver trying to make it big, and then as a beat cop working crazy hours.

"I know. What am I going to do with them? Apparently, I have to keep them until they are at least eighteen, and word has it I also have to pay for four years of college after that. Can you believe that? Someone sold me a raw deal." I said with a smile on my face, my words dripping with sarcasm. I knew our conversation about Tilly would have to be put on hold for now. Children didn't wait around for you to do business. When they were ready to go, they were ready to go.

"I don't know, but that one is going to be a handful in a few years," Kojak said pointing directly at Miranda who looked like she was tallying up the tip on her phone as she signed the bill.

"You don't have to tell me! By the way, real quick, before I go. I went to see that Chef Andy guy, Andy Parnell, you know the one I told you about? The one Hubert fired who then wrote some pretty damning stuff about him on Facebook?"

"And?"

"Well, he was very defensive. Angry guy. Basically, walked away from me and got into his truck and sped off. We didn't talk for long. But he was extremely clear on what he thinks about Hubert. There's something else. I'm not exactly sure what his relationship was to Tilly, but I could tell that he is grieving."

"Interesting. So, do you think there was something going on there? What did he say?"

"He didn't have to say anything about her. It was just so obvious that he was in pain over her death. And then he said that he thinks Hubert killed Tilly and the cops either missed it, or simply ignored it. He implied that because Hubert has some money, he has the power to make the investigation go away."

"Well, I don't think that's fair. I don't think anyone on my team would willingly ignore evidence in a potential murder case," he said with an uncharacteristic level of defensiveness. "There just isn't any evidence to the contrary. That's the deal. *No evidence, no murder case.* Done. It's that simple. People can gossip and say whatever they like, but it's not like it is in the movies or those one-hour crime dramas on Netflix. We don't have some magic blue light that shows us all the evidence and a smoking gun to connect the murderer to the crime in the last five minutes of the show."

"Okay, so what if I bring you some?"

"Some what?"

"Some evidence to the contrary."

"Then I would look at it. But you're not a cop. You're a reporter. You start stirring this pot and you piss off the wrong people, it could be dangerous. I don't like it. I don't like it at all. I don't think this is one that you want to be messing around with." Kojak sat up straight to make his point, but this only made me more determined to change his mind.

"Just the fact that you're telling me to watch my back means there's more to this. Now, I can't walk away. I won't walk away. That waitress, Tammy, she said something else, something pretty provocative. She said there was a "love triangle." She made it seem like this was the reason that Tilly's life had turned out this way, that this "love triangle" had something to do with it."

Kojak rolled his eyes like what I was saying was the most ridiculous thing he had ever heard, and then immediately broke into a fake smile as the twins came over and circled me, each taking an arm and lifting me up to my feet amid cries that they had to go home because they had lots of homework to catch up on. I threw a few dollars on the table, which Kojak promptly handed back to me. He saluted me as I was dragged out of the restaurant by two children who couldn't afford to lose me.

22

COOKIE CHOMPSTER

"COOKIE CHOMPSTER. You can't make this up," Janie said gleefully. She knew my penchant for covering weird stories. The weirder, the better.

"True that," I responded, picturing an alligator in a drug dealer's house guarding his stash. What I couldn't wrap my head around was how the drug dealer prevented the alligator *from attacking him.* As far as I knew, they weren't the kind of reptiles that could be domesticated.

"Anyway, there's a press conference at the zoo at eleven o'clock with the reptile specialist. They're going to talk about how they got the alligator out of the house and what will happen to it now. They're sending it to like some kind of a nature preserve in Florida. I'm pretty sure they have video of the crew taking it out of the house. So cool. Can't wait to see that. We could just play that on a loop for the entire newscast and people would watch it. In fact, I think they might prefer it to the doom and gloom we're so fond of sharing with them."

"How did they know it was in the house?"

"Amazon."

"What?"

"Amazon guy was delivering a package and saw the alligator

through the glass in the door. He took a picture of it and posted it on Twitter. North Carolina Wildlife people saw it there and contacted him for the address. Don't think he meant to start anything. He just saw it and thought it was wild. So, he posted it. It was shared like a couple hundred thousand times. Went *viral.*"

"Do we have any contact information for the Amazon driver?"

"Not yet, but I'll work on that. I'll message him on Twitter and see what happens."

"Okay, in the meantime, we'll hit the neighborhood first, see if anyone knew about the alligator and then head to the zoo."

"Sounds good!"

When I hung up, I paused for a minute to think about the bizarre nature of my job. No one would believe the things we did. A few seconds later I received my "assignment email" from the newsroom. It was titled: "Alligator in Drug Dealer House." Every single day the stories I covered had simple, but dramatic titles with just a few words to describe the story to the producers so that they could decide how to plan their shows. The viewing public would be horrified by these titles: "Dead Guy in a Ditch," "Swim Coach Child Molester," "Drunk Mom Crashes Car." It was the most efficient way to tag them so they could be easily and quickly explained. But they were not exactly the titles you would want to share with *everyone.*

Because my job was so strange at times, it was hard to explain the disconnect between news life and normal life. Without Adam as my firewall with the kids, I didn't have a choice but to chuck my armor aside every night, put on a smile and assume my place at the table as their run-of-the-mill, carpool-driving, suburban mom.

⌐

"We need to knock on a few doors and see if anyone knew about the alligator."

"They're not going to talk to you," Buster said without waiting for me to finish my sentence. "If they knew there was an alligator there, they knew *drugs* were being sold. No one is going to rat out a drug dealer in their own neighborhood. *That's not smart.*"

Buster always had a long list of reasons why something couldn't be done. In my head, I always said, *Okay, so what's your brilliant suggestion?* But I held my tongue and, instead, brokered a deal.

"Why don't we just take the little camera instead of the big one. I'm sure if anyone is willing to talk, it will be an ambush situation at the door anyway. We'll just do the three houses that are the closest to the alligator house. Think about it, all we really need is one person. And then we're done. We can head to the zoo and call it a day."

Buster sighed and reached into the back seat of the news car to get his little Sony camera. It shot video that was about the same quality as that of the television camera. The beauty of it was that it was not nearly as intimidating as a large camera. People were more likely to say yes to our request for an interview when we just had the little camera. The downside was that it did not have an external microphone which meant we had to get very close to someone's face to get useable audio. This understandably made people even more nervous than the big camera. But I had cajoled him into following me from door to door, and that was a small victory at the moment.

The neighborhood was populated with modest 1950s ranch-style houses, some brick, some wooden with vinyl siding, and some with sunrooms that had been haphazardly added later making them look like puzzle pieces that didn't quite fit. The drug dealer's house was in a state of disrepair, with a blue tarp on the roof, years of peeling green paint, and a porch elevated by cinder blocks. It stood out among the other homes which, by contrast, had clearly been cared for by the people who lived in them.

"Let's go to this one," I said, pointing to a little white house to the right of the alligator house. The front door was open, and a television was blaring from inside. I rapped softly at first, and then a little bit harder on the storm door. Buster stood one brick step below me holding the little Sony camera at his side trying to be subtle.

"Come in," yelled a disembodied voice from inside.

"Hesitantly, I pushed the storm door open to see a large shirtless man sitting on a couch with a laptop and a beer in front of him on a low coffee table. The laptop was partially blocking him, but it looked to me like he had no pants on, like we had caught him in the middle of *something*. I was horrified and stood frozen in the doorway, comforted to hear Buster's breathing just a few paces behind me. I was hoping he was seeing the same thing I was seeing.

"Bet you're here about that damn alligator," the man said without prompting, as if he had been expecting us. "Crazy stuff went on over there. Lots of people coming and going. Illegal stuff, I'm sure. But don't quote me on that. I was on the porch when they brought him out. Goddamn thing must have been eight feet long. They had its mouth tied shut with some kind of rope, and four guys, I think it was four, were holding the body like it was radioactive. Crazy, I mean *crazy*. You couldn't pay me to touch a damn alligator."

What was "crazy" to me was that man without pants on was casually talking to me in his living room like nothing was wrong, like we were chatting in line at the grocery store. I kept looking back at Buster wide-eyed, wondering what he must be thinking. He too looked a little stunned, but I would later discover it was for a very different reason.

I thanked the man for the information and backed out of the doorway after he politely told me he would not go on camera. I was relieved because I didn't want to have to step any closer to him. I practically ran down the steps toward the car. Buster and I didn't speak until we were safely inside the car with the windows up and the radio blaring so no one could her us. We were both shaking a little.

"That was insane!" I said at the top of my lungs so he could hear me over the radio.

"It sure was," Buster replied with an unusual amount of concern.

"Why would someone with no pants on casually invite you to come inside his house?"

"No pants?" Buster said, whipping his head in my direction.

"Yes, no pants. You didn't notice that?"

"Nope. I was too busy looking at the gun on the table next to the beer. The barrel was pointing right at us."

"Gun?"

Once again, it never ceased to amaze me how Buster and I could be in the same exact moment and observe completely different things. I wasn't sure if it was a man/woman thing, or a Buster/Maddie thing.

"Well, they're both equally bad in their own way—no pants, gun on the table pointing at us. Let's get out of here," I said, still a little shaky from the experience.

"Agreed."

It was the first thing we had agreed on all day.

⌒

As we waited for the press conference to begin at the zoo, I started scrolling through my social media feed. Most of the time I did so out of habit and boredom, but it was truly a part of my job. Television companies tracked how well their on-air talent was doing online—how many interactions we had compared to other on-air people in the station and in the market. This information was part of how we were evaluated during our performance reviews.

I tried to "like" comments my followers made under my posts as long as they were appropriate. I stayed away from liking anything controversial or editorial for obvious reasons. But, if the comments were universally benign—*so sad, praying for the family, hope they get a resolution*—then I saw no harm in acknowledging their posts. I rarely responded to questions in the comments because there were, frankly, too many to handle. But I tried to respond to all direct private messages.

I clicked on Instagram and saw a message in the file from the people I did not follow. I rarely checked this folder, and often the messages were weeks, even months old. But in this case, the message from a woman named Fiona Lively was less than twenty-four hours old. It read:

> You need to look closely at Hubert Dawson in connection with the death of his wife. He is not a good guy. I don't know why the police aren't paying more attention to him. If you want to meet, I can fill you in.

I clicked on Fiona's profile and could see that she appeared to be a chef. Most of her page was set to "private," but there was a pleasant photo of her in an apron happily stirring something in a large metal bowl with a long wooden spoon. I wondered if she might be a former employee of Hubert's, a cook from one of his restaurants. Without hesitation, I replied: "I'd like to know more."

I waited for a full minute, watching my phone like I was watching bread brown in my toaster oven—with painful patience. Nothing. So, I tried to refocus my attention on the press conference. A tall, thin woman in a white lab coat had just come up to the podium; she was holding up a photograph of the alligator discovered in the drug dealer's house. Because I was so distracted, I only caught snippets of what she was saying—*wild animal, not meant to be a pet, cruel, dangerous, needs a permanent home.* I was banking on the fact that Buster would capture the whole event and give me the video on a USB so that I could watch it again later and pay more attention to it as I figured out exactly what sound bites I needed to use for my story.

Just when I was about to give up on Fiona messaging me back, my phone vibrated. I immediately clicked on the message: "Will meet you at Benton Road Park at 2:00. Will drop a pin with the exact location."

Could kill you very quickly, I heard the woman at the podium say. *Especially dangerous if you stumbled upon him.*

These words made me think of Tilly Dawson and wonder if she had stumbled upon someone dangerous who decided to take her life.

23

CATFISH

As I sat on the park bench observing every woman that walked by, I imagined what Fiona Lively might look like in person. Would she be wearing jeans? Maybe workout clothes? Maybe a chef's uniform? She could be coming straight from work. And why the park? What an odd place to meet a stranger. I had met Kojak here plenty of times, but he wasn't a stranger. This seemed like the plot of a bad movie, meeting your source on a bench in the park. Fiona had dropped me a pin to tell me exactly where to meet her. I was here, right where the pin landed on the map.

And what did this woman really think she knew anyway? Through the years, many people had contacted me to say they knew something about a case and could help solve it. Often, what they thought they had was really just circumstantial evidence that was already known to investigators. But I always listened, and if I thought what they were saying had real merit, I would encourage them to contact the police directly. I always explained to them that we couldn't try the case in the media, and the responsible thing to do with new evidence was for them to give it to the investigators and let them decide if it was important or not. While people always berate the media for not supporting truth and justice, I begged to differ. Justice was always more important to me than getting a scoop.

For some reason, the interaction online with this person, this *stranger* named Fiona Lively, felt different. It felt personal. I sensed that Fiona may have a real connection to Hubert Dawson that transcended mere speculation and circumstantial evidence. I had nothing to base this on but a gut feeling. So, I waited patiently on the park bench watching the world go by, trying not to get too absorbed in the nonsense on my phone. I watched the dog walkers amble by me, moms with strollers, joggers, the occasional cyclist or roller blader who must have made a wrong turn at the 1980s. Most of them were smiling, enjoying another typical blue-sky Carolina day, something that was easy to take for granted when you lived here.

Finally, I spotted the woman I thought must be Fiona walking in my direction. She had on black leggings, pink sneakers, and a zip-up green hooded workout jacket. Her hair was in a high ponytail and she wore a baseball hat that bore the logo of Duke University, which was located in the next town over. She was walking very fast and was wearing AirPods that seemed to be absorbing her focus. She was deeply ensconced in whatever she was listening to—her music, book, or podcast. And while she didn't make eye contact with me directly, she was walking straight for the bench. I tried to catch her eye, but she didn't avert her gaze from where she was looking, straight ahead on the path. Just as she neared my personal space, she made an abrupt turn in the direction of the water fountain to the right of the bench.

"Hi," a high-pitched childish voice rang out from the left side of the bench. I turned to see a young girl slide in next to me. It took me a minute to realize where I recognized her from. "Hi, I'm Penny. We met at my great aunt's funeral."

I sat there staring at the girl for what seemed like minutes, but it was probably just ten seconds or so. I was trying to wrap my head around what I was seeing and figure out how an adolescent girl had catfished me online, pretending to be a grown woman with information about a potential murder case. But I was here now, so I decided to play it cool and see what she would say.

"Penny, nice to see you again. I'm actually waiting for someone."

I kept up the ruse to see how she would react. Maybe I was wrong. Maybe this was just a weird coincidence. I sincerely hoped that it was and that Fiona Lively would come around the corner any minute and tap me on the shoulder.

"Actually, I'm the person you're meeting. I'm really sorry I pretended to be someone else online. I just knew you wouldn't come if you found out you were meeting me."

I stared at her again—this girl was dressed like a girl and looked like a girl but was acting like an adult. She wore purple leggings, an oversized T-shirt emblazoned with a cartoon character that I didn't recognize, and white sneakers with silver stars on the sides. Her thin brown hair fell limply around her face, just skimming the tops of her shoulders. But those big brown eyes, that's what I remembered about her from the funeral. In her hand was a cell phone with a sparkly pink case covered in tiny gold stars.

"You're right, Penny. I would not have agreed to meet a child. Does your mother know you're here?"

"Nope, of course not. She's at work. But this is really important. I read a lot and watch a lot of those true crime shows on Netflix. I know how important it is to get it right early in the investigation. The police will never listen to me, but I thought a reporter might. You seemed nice when I met you at the church. My mom always told me to look for the adults you can trust, the ones who make you feel safe. Look for the helpers. So, that's why I'm here."

I sat with her last statement for a moment, readjusting my position on the bench to turn in her direction, closing the space between us so that no one else could hear what we were talking about. She was stroking my ego, and it worked. She had gotten under my skin and flipped the switch with the phrase "look for the helpers," a line from one of my favorite children's television hosts, Mister Rogers. Somehow, she knew I wouldn't be able to walk away now. But I had to stand my ground. I had to do what was right.

"Penny, while I appreciate what you're saying, your mother would not want you speaking to an adult about your private family issues; it's not ethical of me to speak with you without her permission."

"I get it. I figured you would say that, so I'll just leave you this note. You can pick it up, open it, read it, *or not.* You can just leave it here and walk away. Your choice. It will be like we never talked. I didn't even sign it, so there won't be a trail," the girl flashed me a pirate's smile and laid the small, sealed envelope on the scratched wooden bench between us. "Have a great day!"

And then she was gone. She skipped off into the parade of dog walkers, joggers, and strollers, her tiny frame almost disappearing in the distance as she was swallowed by the movement of the people around her.

I held the envelope in my hands tentatively, like it might contain anthrax. What could a child possibly know that would solve the case of a dead woman? What could she know that the police didn't already know? Nothing. So, what was the harm in opening the envelope?

I opened it up and slid out a single sheet of white paper with a typed note in bold black letters.

It read:

> I overheard my mother and my grandmother talking about Uncle Hubert. They were in the kitchen. They didn't know I was there. I was just around the corner in the den. They said he was a mean man with a bad temper and that he was jealous, jealous of a man Aunt Tilly had "eyes for." They think he had something to do with her death. So do I. Please investigate this. Please find the truth.

I tried to picture one of my kids writing this note. I couldn't. This child's voice was such a throwback, almost as if she came from another century. I read the note again, and then again, trying to figure out what I was supposed to do with it. The police would find it laughable—it was the circumstantial theory of a little girl who overheard her family speculating. It *wasn't* evidence.

To Penny's credit, she had come to the right adult. She was looking for the helpers and she found one, albeit a reluctant one. Despite the source, it was information I couldn't ignore. In my mind, there was a growing list of reasons why Hubert Dawson might be a suspect in his wife's death. But I knew, from what Kojak had told me, the police would not reopen the case based on hunches or speculation—there had to be something more than that. I had to offer them solid evidence. It was time for me to find out who the mystery man was that might have cost Tilly her life. I knew exactly who might have access to that piece of the puzzle: Tilly's daughter, Delilah.

24

LIGHT OF MY LIFE

It wasn't hard to figure out Delilah Dawson's routine. She posted *everything* about her life on Instagram. Whether she was at work at the restaurant, working out at the gym, or socializing with friends, there was almost always a photo of her with a pithy caption documenting her every move.

She was a beautiful, photogenic girl who looked like a much younger version of her mother. She had long dark hair, very fair skin, large dark eyes, and wore red lipstick when she was out on the town with her girlfriends. She had clearly mastered the art of shooting herself at just the right angle, with perfect lighting and then editing the photo to achieve that final bit of magic. It was an art that had escaped me. My selfies were mostly poorly lit, out of focus, and unflattering, something my daughter Miranda reminded me of on a daily basis. For teenagers, and twentysomethings, selfie taking was in their DNA. For anyone over thirty-five, it was a learned art. I had chosen *not* to learn it.

I kept seeing photos on Delilah's timeline from Yardley Yoga, a new downtown studio opened by local yoga guru, Yardley Samuels. Samuels had been written up by several online magazines and newspapers and had recently been featured on Channel 8's "People to Watch in Oak City."

While some people would wonder why Delilah was still posting on social media and going to yoga so soon after her mother's death, I actually felt like it was pretty normal behavior for a twentysomething who had lost a parent under tragic and confusing circumstances. Social media was her generation's way of reaching out and getting love and support in return. Yoga was a great way to decompress and put her pain aside for an hour.

Yet, I was still not completely sure that Delilah was actually grieving over her mother's death. Tammy's strange comment about Delilah causing her mother "trouble," and then implying that she was flattered by Andy's interest in her, kept coming back to me, not to mention her eagerness to let police close the case, according to Kojak.

I tried to put my swirling thoughts aside. I had always wanted to try a class at Yardley, so I decided to kill two birds with one stone. I would sign up for a starter pack—four classes—and see if I could casually run into Delilah. I figured that she was the one most likely to know if her mother had an affair, not that she would tell me, but I might at least be able to start a conversation with her if I met her in person. She was also the one responsible for getting Andy fired, according to Tammy. Basically, Delilah seemed like the key to answering a lot of my questions.

It was an evening class, and the room was almost pitch dark as we gathered on our respective mats next to the wall for restorative yoga—a practice dedicated to deep stretching and meditation. In the dim light, I could barely make out Delilah setup on her mat on the opposite wall. Even in the almost-darkness, I recognized her long dark hair and pale skin immediately from her photos on Instagram. She was already lying flat on her back with her legs straight up against the wall when I came in. Her arms were crossed on her chest, and her eyes appeared to be closed.

I got into a child's pose and tried to put Delilah out of my mind. Dwelling on her throughout the entire class was going to be counterproductive to achieving something at least mildly restorative from the practice. But my mind was racing. I couldn't help myself. I tried to concentrate on my tight hip flexors, to get them to release the tension they held from years of running, but all I could think about was the twenty-year-old young woman ten feet from me who lost her mother. Here I was, twice her age, and I was still grappling with the loss of my mother decades ago.

On one hand, it made my heart ache for her. I wanted her to have the truth, the closure that had been so elusive for me. But on the other hand, I wasn't convinced that she was totally innocent. Was it possible that she was covering up for someone? Did she know what really happened to her mother? Was she protecting that person? And then, an even darker thought crept into my brain as I lay there, my back flat on my mat, my hips turned to the side, feeling a much-needed stretch down the length of my spine. *Is it possible that she could have had something to do with her mother's death?*

When the class finally ended and the teacher turned up the lights just enough for us to gather our things, I angled my way in Delilah's direction. I was feeling a bit drunk from having almost fallen asleep during the Savasana part at the end of the class where you lie still on your mat with your eyes closed. I was also drunk from the toxic thoughts about this young woman bouncing around in my head. I had to pull myself together if I wanted to make the encounter with Delilah look casual and coincidental.

"Delilah? Delilah Dawson?"

"Yes," she turned and looked at me hesitantly. Her hair was piled in a messy bun on top of her head with individual hairs sprouting in every direction. She hugged her coiled purple yoga mat tightly to her chest as if I might try to take it.

"I'm Maddie, Maddie Arnette. I was at your mother's funeral. I am so sorry."

She eyed me up and down carefully, clearly trying to assess who I was and why I was approaching her, and even more importantly *why* I was at her mother's funeral. Despite the dimly lit room, I could see the spark of recognition the moment it came across her face. She went from hesitation directly to a cross somewhere between fear and anger.

"You're *that reporter*. I know who you are. I'm sorry, but I can't talk to you."

With that, she turned to leave the room, but there was a bottleneck at the door with the rest of the class pausing to speak in soft tones with the teacher and exchange hugs as they left. Delilah couldn't escape me. She turned her back to me to signal our conversation was done, but I was right behind her. The woman behind me had no boundaries and had pushed me so close Delilah that I'm sure she could feel my breath on the back of her neck.

"I'm not trying to bother you," I said, leaning in close to her ear from my awkward space in the line, speaking in an almost whisper. "I was just trying to figure some things out and thought you might be open to having coffee."

This time when she turned around to look at me, she held the yoga mat aggressively, stiffly away from her body, like a grenade that she might be getting ready to launch at me.

"Let me tell you what I'm trying to figure out. I'm trying to figure out why my beautiful, amazing, kind mother would take her own life. She was the light of my life, and I was the light of hers. And none of this is anybody's business but mine," she spit the words in a loud whisper through gritted teeth. The whispering seemed like a strange homage to the yoga setting. But it was so loud compared to the quiet murmurs of the other students thanking the teacher, that everyone stopped talking at once and turned to look at us.

"I understand," I said calmly, trying to regain some sense of control over a situation I had clearly not thought through. "There are just some people who think she didn't take her own life. Some people who believe her death needs to be thoroughly investigated. I thought you might be one of those people."

At this moment, I felt like she was launching daggers at me from her eyes as they darted up and down. The line was starting to move, and I knew I was about to lose her. I had decided to go for it, and put all my cards on the table, but in hindsight, it felt like the wrong move.

"If you're implying that my dad had something to do with this, you're dead wrong, lady. Those are just Internet rumors started by jealous people. My dad is not perfect, but he is not a killer. How dare you follow me here to say all this. My mother killed herself. It's a tragedy. Please get away from me, now!"

"I'm so sorry I bothered you. I just noticed you and thought—never mind. This was a very bad idea. I see that now. Just call me if you want to talk," I blabbered, pressing my card into her left hand. She reluctantly took it, probably just to get rid of me and barreled through the door, not bothering to stop and speak with the teacher.

"Don't count on it," I heard her say, her voice drifting away from me as I finally stood at the front of the line staring at the diminutive yoga teacher, wondering what to do next.

25

TEACH YOUR PARENTS WELL

As soon as I heard Candace shut the front door, I climbed the stairs and peered into Blake's room. He was sound asleep, his tufts of brown hair peeking over the edge of the blue comforter covered in rocket ships that he had wrapped around his body like a mummy. I gently stroked the top of his head. He murmured quietly, and I tiptoed backward out of the room trying not to hit the creaky board three steps from his bedroom door or snag my sock on the protruding nail in the door jamb. These were things you knew about in a well-loved, well-lived-in house, things Adam always intended to fix, but never got around to. Now, I didn't have the heart to fix them because they were *our* imperfections, the things that made this old house our home.

Next, I poked my head into Miranda's room. She was sitting up in bed, throw pillows all around her propping her up as she read her book with one of the headlamps I used for running in the dark.

"What are you doing, honey?" I asked, trying to brush a long lock of hair out of her eyes unsuccessfully as it was stuck inside the elastic band that fit snugly around her forehead. "Why don't you turn a light on?"

"I'm practicing for summer camp. We're not allowed to have electronics. So we have to bring *real* books—isn't that ridiculous?

And lights-out is at ten, which is also stupid. But you're allowed to read if you have a personal light that doesn't bother others."

I looked at the blinding beam that cut a path clear across her dark bedroom illuminating her gray shag rug and pink bean bag at the foot of the bed. I made a mental note to get her a proper reading lamp that wouldn't make her bunkmates feel like they were staring into the high beams of a car.

"That makes perfect sense. But camp is still a few months away."

"I know, but I've got to get used to this. Everything I read is on the computer or the iPad. This is old-school, Mom. The way you grew up," she said without a hint of sarcasm, never taking her eyes off the page, as she moved her index finger across the line she was reading.

"Okay, well don't stay up too late." I kissed the top of her head and then left her room, quietly shutting the door behind me as not to wake Blake next door.

I didn't normally drink on weeknights, but I decided I needed a glass of red wine to calm my nerves. For some reason, seeing Delilah and the look of horror in her eyes when I mentioned her father brought back so many memories of Roger. Of course, I was only a little girl when Roger was first accused of murdering my mother, and Delilah was a grown woman, but I could still identify with her disbelief. It wasn't hard to imagine that she could be in such denial, that in her heart she may know her father had something to do with her mother's death, but she didn't want to face it.

It took me so many years to come to terms with what Roger had done; in fact, I ignored all the signs. I ignored the fact that he was in prison. I ignored the gossipy girls at school who whispered about my family in the locker room when they thought I wasn't listening. I ignored the curious stares I got from strangers in the grocery store. I knew that *something* had happened, but I never asked what that something was.

I had discovered a file in Belle's attic which contained newspaper articles about the investigation and the trial. It told me everything I needed to know about Roger's guilt. But even then, I wasn't convinced. I thought maybe the journalists had it all wrong. I'd heard people say before that the media lied and made things up. *Maybe that's what happened to Roger? Of course, now I know that people said things like that about the media when they simply didn't like what was being reported. People only like the media when the reporting reflects their opinions. When it doesn't, they become critical of us. I learned a long time ago that people's opinions of us was very rarely based on truth or facts.*

Finally, when I was sixteen, Belle sat me down and told me the truth, that Roger had been convicted of killing my mother. But even then, Belle's misguided loyalty to her son caused her to lie to herself and me. She said he was railroaded by a broken criminal justice system, that there was no physical evidence connecting him to the crime, and that he had an alibi, that he had been home in New Jersey at the house I grew up in when my mother was killed in my maternal grandparents' house in Pennsylvania, 120 miles away. But I so clearly remembered my dad being there, holding me in his arms soon after I discovered my mother dead. Belle told me that, obviously, I was mistaken. She said he jumped in the car and came right away when he heard, when the police called him. She said I was in shock, so I must be remembering it wrong.

Belle's arguments to the contrary didn't sway me. Once she told me the truth, all my former doubts about the situation melted away. Somehow, I made peace with the fact that Roger was the person who took my mother's life, and Belle's refusal to see the truth drove an impossible wedge between us that couldn't be overcome, not even by her immeasurable love for me.

So, here I was, thirty-nine years after my mother's murder thinking about how Delilah might also be experiencing the same complicated feelings I had experienced in my late teens, just a few years younger than she was now. There was still a tiny part of me back then that wanted to believe Belle was right, that the jury got it wrong, that Roger really didn't kill my mother. And now, with this latest wrinkle, with Esther suddenly appearing in my life with her bizarre story about Clifton, that tiny shred of unwelcome doubt had crept back into my brain.

I could see the conflict in Delilah's eyes when she turned to stare me down in the dim light of the yoga studio. Her dark eyes dared me to challenge her belief that her father was not involved in Tilly's death. And the truth was, it was very possible she was right; it was just as possible that she was wrong.

But I also saw something else in her eyes—*fear.* Was it possible that Delilah had done something to her mother? That the "trouble" Tammy had told me about between them had escalated into some kind of violent altercation? I shook my head vigorously, trying to shake away the ugly thought. I couldn't go there. I couldn't blame the daughter of the victim. I had to keep reminding myself that Delilah was also a victim, whether her mother committed suicide or was murdered.

As much as I needed to get to the bottom of Tilly's unhappy ending, I also needed once and for all to understand what happened to my mother. Delilah's situation had revealed that much to me, that I was still a lost soul in limbo somewhere between clarity and confusion. It was time for me to pay Roger a visit in prison.

I lay in bed that night searching for flights to Philadelphia. It was the closest airport to the Penn State Grove Correctional Institution where Roger was an inmate, but I would still have to rent a car and drive at least an hour or so. I checked with Candace to make sure she would be able to stay with the twins for a couple of days. I also went on my work website and requested two vacation days that I felt certain Dex would approve. I would worry about a hotel later. My final act was to check the visitation hours and policies at the prison on their website. I discovered that I had to be on Roger's "approved list of visitors" to see him. I didn't want to waste time with snail mail, so I wrote a quick email to the warden explaining who I was and asking him if he would request that my father put me on his approved list. I had no idea how Roger would react to this. Frankly, I didn't care how it made him feel. It was about *me,* and what I needed for my own sense of closure.

Finally, I turned out the light. My head was spinning with visions of Roger, an old man sitting in a dark cell somewhere in central

Pennsylvania, biding his time until his death. What would he look like after all these years? Would I recognize him? Would I see part of myself in him?

Again, I thought about Delilah in the dark yoga studio trying to wrestle with the possibility that her mother may have been murdered. Based on the way she had responded, I was sure she had already heard rumors to this effect, but it was a different to hear this theory from a reporter than to read comments on Facebook. Who was she really protecting with her anger and her defensiveness? Was it her father or *herself*?

Just as I was dozing off to sleep, I heard the familiar vibration of a text message on my phone. Against my better judgement, I rolled over, picked it up, and squinted my eyes, trying to adjust to the bright screen in the pitch-dark room. There was one new text. It read: "We need to talk." It was signed "Andy." As in *Chef Andy*.

26

SQUIRREL WHISPERER

"IT'S RIGHT UP YOUR ALLEY. It's *weird*," Janie said, emphasizing the "d." On my new beat, I seemed to be increasing the tally of stories in the weird column. "It's also sweet. She scoops up dying squirrels in the middle of the road and nurses them back to health. Most people would call them roadkill, but she's totally into them. She calls her house a "squirrel sanctuary."

I smiled over the phone at Janie. She always knew how to sell me on an insane story. But it was getting harder to switch my brain from one topic to the next. One minute, I was still stewing about Delilah, trying to figure out what her deal was, and the next I was thinking about my trip to see Roger, and then, suddenly, without warning, one of the kids was pleading with me for help with something. All the gear switching was making me dizzy.

"Hold on, Janie. What is it, Miranda?"

"I told you I needed you to sign the permission slip for the field trip to the planetarium," she said stamping her foot for emphasis as she pushed her laptop into her already overstuffed purple book bag. My tough, anxious little girl. What was I going to do with her? Would she ever soften?

"Okay, bring it to me," I said reaching out my right hand as I held the cell phone in my left while Janie patiently waited on the other end of the line. I put her on speakerphone and laid the phone down on the kitchen island, muting my end. I could hear Janie raving to someone in the background about the Krispy Kreme donuts that were sent by a viewer to the newsroom with multicolored sprinkles on them.

"Mom," Miranda said stamping her other foot this time. "It's not an actual piece of paper. It's an electronic signature, online. Duh. You have to log in to the school website. How many times do I have to explain this to you?"

Whoever said parenting in the digital age was easy? *No one.* Between passwords and all the hoops we have to jump through to sign a simple form, I would much rather just do it the old-fashioned way, with a pen and a piece of paper. When did everything in life get so complicated? Technology was supposed to make our lives easier; instead, it just added more steps to everything that used to be so simple. I felt like I spent half my life filling out digital school forms.

Miranda rolled her eyes as I put a finger up to tell her to hold on a minute so that I could finish with Janie. I unmuted myself as Miranda found my laptop in the den and brought it to me.

"Mom!" she said with the exasperation as she shoved the laptop in my direction.

"I should let you go," Janie said in her singsong voice. "Sounds like there's trouble in paradise. Give your little gremlins a hug for me. Why don't you try bribing them? Krispy Kreme donuts might work. They always work for me!"

Janie hung up and I quickly opened my laptop, found the permission slip on the school website, and added my electronic signature. I slammed it shut and then hustled the kids in the direction of the front door. It was my day to drive carpool. I wasn't dressed for work yet, which meant I would have to take them first and then rush home to get ready.

Blake and Miranda hopped into the back seat, while the new neighbors, Carter and Cameron piled into the far back. We used to carpool with a brother-and-sister duo who were always quiet and well-behaved, but they moved away, and now we had the Poplar boys from down the street who sometimes wrestled in the far back of the SUV. They were also famous for leaving things behind— homework assignments, books, phones, laptops. It was not unusual to get a hysterical text from their mother, Billie, at all hours of the night asking me to look for something the boys had left behind. But the flip side of the arrangement was that Billie worked for a big payroll company from home, and she was very flexible, which meant she could usually fill in on short notice if I got tied up.

I was inside my head ticking off a list of everything I had to do today, but I kept getting interrupted by thoughts of Delilah, Roger, and the Squirrel Lady.

"Mom, don't forget I have piano after school," Blake chimed from the back seat.

"And I need a trifold board for my science project," Miranda added.

"And I need to clone myself to help me do all this!" I said with a laugh, looking at them in the rearview mirror. I could see Carter and Cameron arm wrestling in the far back row of the car. They were in their own little world, ignoring my gaze. But my kids were suddenly silent. My joke had not gone over well. To them, it sounded like I was saying I couldn't do what I needed to do for them on my own, that I needed Adam to help me. But Adam was gone, and I had no choice but to make this single parenting thing work. It pained me to think they had lost a father at a young age just like I had. The only difference was that my father was *technically* still alive even though he had been dead to me for decades.

"Got it, guys. I'm just kidding. I'm Superwoman, remember? What are my superpowers again?"

"Speed!" Blake cheered, raising a fist into the air, and lightly punching the roof of the car.

"Organization," Miranda snarled, crossing her arms across her chest.

It was a little game we played. Blake loved it; Miranda thought she was too old for it.

"All of the above!" I chanted, trying to get a rise out of Miranda who was already nose-down in her phone. How I wish I had made them wait longer to get phones, but after Adam died, I wanted them to know they could connect with me anytime they needed me, and I would be available to them. So, I gave in. Plus, most of their friends had them at this age, and given what they had already lost, I didn't want them to be left out when it came to having a social life that was almost exclusively defined by digital connections these days.

I pulled up slowly and Mrs. Millinsky greeted us with a little wave as I aligned my SUV with the edge of the curb and the kids piled out with their bags, jackets, and sports gear dangling clumsily from their shoulders. The Poplar boys mumbled a quick "Thank you" without making eye contact with me as they exited the car. Miranda gave me a brief "Bye" without turning around. But my sweet Blake turned and blew me a kiss, almost losing his balance as he stumbled out of the car onto the curb. As I pulled away, they were swallowed by the swarm of kids heading toward the front door of the school, and I was reminded that even in the face of tragedy and loss, life does go on.

The weirdest thing about the Squirrel Lady, Karin Bowman, was that she wasn't weird at all. She greeted me at her front door wearing a fitted, light-gray V-neck T-shirt, distressed blue jeans, and black flats. She was a petite Asian woman with long, silky, jet-black hair, a lovely round face, and a welcoming smile.

"Come in, come in. Your photographer is already here," she motioned down a long hallway where I could see Buster setting up his camera and tripod by a slender, distressed wooden table. "We thought the light would be best in the sunroom. It's in the back of the house."

She gestured for me to follow her. I expected her to bring me into a room full of squirrels. I imagined them in little doll beds with white bandages wrapped around their tiny, damaged limbs, maybe sipping water from teeny straws.

Instead, she took me to a bright, cheerful room at the back of the house with windows looking out on a forest that was just beginning to turn green with new spring growth. We climbed over a baby gate to get into the room. I could see that Buster had already made friends with four little brown furry squirrels that were sniffing around his feet. He was bent down, stroking two of them at the same time, one with each hand. It reminded me of the time he insisted on petting a wandering bull while we were on a medical mission shoot in Uganda. At the time, I didn't think that it was a good idea, but he did it anyway and nothing bad happened. But he did get bitten by a monkey on that trip when he got too close to it while trying to take her picture. I wasn't with him at the moment, and he ended up having to get rabies shots. Based on how he was cozying up to the squirrels, I was pretty sure he hadn't learned his lesson.

"So, as you can see, these little guys are doing really well. They're almost strong enough to go out there, back into the woods *where they belong.* It's always really hard to see them go, but it's awesome at the same time to know that you've saved a life and returned that life to the wilderness where it belongs."

Karin knelt down on the floor beside Buster with a big smile on her face. She reached out to stroke one of the squirrels that had been vying unsuccessfully for Buster's attention in the middle of the gaggle at his feet.

"For some reason, squirrels have this reputation of being mean, dirty, or dangerous. No one ever thinks of them as pets. They think of them like pigeons, like a nuisance. But they really are the sweetest animals, and they can be tamed. Still, they are wild animals, and they need to be outside on their own as soon as they are strong enough to go. I am in no way advocating that people *keep* squirrels as pets."

I thought about "taming" an animal, versus taming a person. Taming a person was a lot harder, because to tame someone, you had to be able to control his or her impulses. I thought back to Tilly's letter, the alleged suicide note. The person she was writing to in that letter had obviously gone rogue, done something horrible and unforgivable, proof to Tilly that she could never tame whatever evil existed inside this person. I was still trying to figure out exactly what she was saying in the letter, and more importantly, to *whom* she was saying it. It still didn't feel like a suicide note to me. It sounded more like a goodbye note after someone had behaved very badly. The person she was writing to did more than just disappoint Tilly; the individual devastated her.

"So, as you can see, they will eat right out of your hand," Karin said gleefully, jarring me back into the present moment. She had a small bottle and was cradling one of the squirrels like a baby in the palm of her hand and feeding it milk. The squirrel greedily sucked at the bottle, making loud slurping noises, and curling its paws around one of Karin's fingers in an adorable gesture that reminded me of a scene from a Disney movie.

"I think we've got enough," Buster said, turning the camera off, and then dropping to the floor to gently wrestle with the smallest squirrel who seemed thrilled to be getting his attention. I was sure Buster would sit here and play with these squirrels all day long if we didn't have more work to do.

With the two of them enthralled in their squirrel-play, I looked down at my phone and texted Andy back that I would be happy to meet with him. He responded right away that he would like to meet with me tomorrow if I was available. For some reason, I felt sure that he really did know something about what happened to Tilly, that it wasn't just angry whistleblower speculation about Hubert being involved. I wasn't exactly sure *what* he knew, but I had to find out.

27

REASONABLE DOUBT

"I AM NOT LETTING YOU MEET THAT BASTARD by yourself," Louise said to me over the phone, the word *bastard* rolling off her tongue like liquid poison. She didn't mince words. I silently thanked God for putting her in my life.

"It's okay, for real. He really wasn't that bad. I think he was just upset about Tilly's death. We will be in a public place in the middle of the day. It will be *fine*, I promise."

"He was just such a jerk when we went to his house the other day. I'd hate for you to subject yourself to his anger again."

"Again, I think you're overdramatizing it. It was no big deal. He was just pissed off at the situation, *not at me*. I got this. I promise!"

I appreciated Louise's concern. It had increased exponentially after Adam died—*Are you getting any sleep? Are you eating enough? Have you done anything kind for yourself today?* She reminded me over and over that my mental and emotional health were critical to my children's well-being, and that I had to do the things I needed to heal so that I could be the best parent to them. And while she knew I could handle myself in dicey situations, as I had many times in my job as a crime reporter, she always made it a point to let me know she worried about me. Having someone care about me like that in Adam's absence was a gift that kept me going, kept me sane, and kept me grounded.

Frankly, I *was* a little nervous about meeting with Andy again. But I wasn't about to tell Louise that. What could he possibly have to say to me? Why couldn't he just email me or talk to me over the phone? I knew based on his need to meet in person that it must be something very important and sensitive. My gut told me he had some details, or evidence that might solidify Hubert's involvement in Tilly's death. Or maybe even Delilah's involvement? But why tell me? Why not go to the police? Did he think they wouldn't believe him? That they would just see him as a disgruntled ex-employee?

Despite what I told Louise about meeting Andy in a public place, I agreed to meet him at a property his family owned and rented out about forty minutes from Oak City. It was in a rural community called Windle, the same place the creepy taxidermist, Frank, lived. Andy said his tenants had moved out and he was doing some work on the house. He told me it was best that I came there because he was extremely busy and intended to work from sunup to sundown. He apologized profusely for the inconvenience, but said he needed to speak with me urgently.

As I pulled down the street lined by small, clapboard, shotgun houses, I wondered out loud what kind of rental properties Andy and his family owned. The houses in the neighborhood were all in various states of disarray, but they appeared to be lived in based upon the fact that there were cars in the yards, pets lounging on sagging front porches, and the occasional person walking to a mailbox.

"My God, is he a slumlord or what?" I said to myself in the side mirror as I pictured just how far I would have to backtrack to get out of the neighborhood quickly. *One way in, one way out,* I noted.

I suddenly wished I had taken Louise up on her offer to come with me. I knew what she would say right now. *Girl, we need to get the heck out of this sketch neighborhood. He's bringing us out here to shoot us and bury our bodies in a soybean field where they'll never find us. You watch Netflix, you know what I'm talking about.*

The truth was, I didn't need to watch Netflix to know this type of scenario could be true. I had covered so many murder cases in my career full of strange details that little surprised me in terms of how people killed one another and how they acted in the aftermath of those murders. Cut her body up and put her in coolers to get her out of the house? Sure. Feed her dead body to wild boars or alligators? Why not? Bury her in your basement and then pour a new concrete floor? These were all real cases that I had covered as a television news reporter—a reporter who knew better than to meet a stranger on a dead-end country road alone. *But here I was.*

As the blue house at the end of the street came into view, I saw what looked like piles of personal belongings on the lawn in front of the home—clothing, furniture, lamps, children's toys. It all looked soaked. Andy was in the middle of the mess with a big green trash bag picking up the waterlogged items with his hands clad in what appeared to be thick gray work gloves. Even though he was a muscular man, he seemed small in comparison to the endless piles of wet junk that surrounded him. He was stuffing items into the garbage bag as fast as he could, but it didn't look like he was making the slightest dent in the waterlogged mountains that rose all around him.

He looked up when he heard my car approach and directed me with a raised gloved hand to park on the other side of the circular gravel driveway away from the piles. I got out slowly and walked hesitantly in his direction, even though he didn't look like much of a threat standing there in the middle of the heaps holding an overstuffed garbage bag.

"Sorry we had to meet here. As you can see, I'm in the middle of a huge mess."

"I see that. What in the world happened?"

"Flood. That big nor'easter we had in the fall sent about three feet of water into the house. There's a creek back there—we're in the hundred-year floodplain. Go figure. First time this has ever happened since we've owned it. Had it for about fifteen years. My tenants, they just up and left. Left this shit for me to clean up. I've been putting it off, but my parents want to sell it now, so I have to clean it up and do my best to get it on the market. Although, I can't imagine anyone wanting this piece-of-crap house. Can you?"

I looked at the old blue house with the shiny tin roof. The paint was peeling in large sheets, windows were broken, the front porch sagged under the weight of the roof. It looked like the posts holding supporting the front eaves were straining so hard to stay upright that the entire structure might collapse in on itself at any moment. Then I looked more closely at the roof. Spray-painted on the pitched tin front were the words "Screw the Stoms." There was a floating "r" above the "o" and the "m" with an insertion arrow pointing downward. It made me chuckle.

"I know," Andy said as he caught my laughter and lobbed it back. He nodded up at the roof. "At least if you're going to vandalize someone's property, spell it right!"

I looked back at Andy and decided he had morphed from the angry, defensive, grief-stricken man I met a few days earlier at his grandmother's cabin, to an affable, humble man standing here in the middle of this dump. He was upset the day I met him. I had caught him off-guard. Maybe I had misjudged him. I decided I would give him another chance.

"So, you're probably wondering why I asked you to come here, to come all the way out here?"

I nodded affirmatively, putting my hands in my jean pockets waiting for what he was about to say next. I didn't want to give him too much leeway in case I was wrong, and he was just tricking me into thinking he was going to be nice in order to get my defenses down.

"Well, first of all, I owe you an apology," he said dropping the garbage bag at his feet and peeling off the work gloves so that they were inside out. He shoved them into his back pocket and wiped sweat off his brow with the back of his right hand. His brown wavy hair was untamed, falling into his eyes. He exhaled with his bottom lip pointed upward to move the hair away from his eyes. "Clearly, I've been broken up about this situation. I lashed out on social media, and I lashed out at you. It wasn't right for me to do either and it definitely wasn't fair to you. You didn't deserve that, and I'm sorry."

"Thank you for that. I appreciate it. But you could have told me that over the phone."

I was used to people treating reporters badly. I tried not to take it personally. It was rare that anyone ever apologized for being ugly to us. I think they just saw us as characters in a movie, or in a television program, not as real people with feelings. With so many vitriolic exchanges on social media where everyone always had to be right, to one-up someone else, this pattern of people blaming journalists for everything had only gotten worse in recent years.

"I know. But I really was an *ass*. Please tell your friend I'm sorry, too."

Louise will love this story, I thought, especially the part about "Screw the Stoms." But she will also be mad at me for meeting a strange man in such a desolate spot by myself. Silently, I decided when I told her the story I would have back into it, leading up to the part about me being there alone with this man in the country as a footnote.

"I will tell her. Thanks again. I appreciate it. Most people don't apologize to reporters. Is that it?" I was confused. I felt certain there was more that he wanted to tell me.

"Can we sit for a moment?" Andy gestured to the sagging front stoop of the house where two white stairs were remarkably free of junk. They didn't appear to be very clean, but as I looked around, there didn't seem to be any other viable choices.

"Sure," I said with more hesitation than I had intended. I didn't want him to take my repulsion about sitting on a dirty step in black pants as a rejection of him. Now that he was being kind, and I could see him for more of who he was, I realized that he seemed like a very humble man, at least in this moment.

He was also handsome—something I had noted when I first met him. He was broad-shouldered with a small waist, muscular arms, warm brown eyes, and a mess of brown hair that he kept sweeping away from his forehead. He had a wide smile with white, straight teeth that meant either he was lucky or someone who had benefitted from good dental care growing up.

We made our way carefully through the maze of wet trash that was once someone's treasure—a baby's bassinet, a guitar with broken strings, a pile of soiled women's clothing, a toaster oven. We sat down at the maximum possible distance from one another on the small top step, an unsaid gesture of mutual respect. Andy looked down at the ground and wrung his hands.

"You see, the reason, the reason I'm so upset by all of this is that I know Hubert was out to get Tilly. He knew she'd had an affair, and he wanted to punish her. Not because he loved her, but because he thought of her as his property, and she had embarrassed him."

Andy looked up at me earnestly, as if to make sure what he was saying to me was sinking in. *It was sinking in.* I was listening so intently I forgot I was sitting on a dirty set of stairs out in the middle of nowhere with a man I barely knew.

"I told all this to the police, but they didn't think I was credible. They said I was a *disgruntled employee.* They said there was no evidence to support Hubert had anything to do with his wife's death, and that I should just leave it alone and go on about my life."

"Are you?"

"Am I what?"

"Disgruntled?"

"Sure, I mean, yes, of course. He fired me. Obviously, I don't like the guy. But that's not a good enough reason to accuse him of murder."

"Some people might think it is," I replied, not trying to push him too hard. But I wanted to push him hard enough so that he would really examine what he was telling me and how it all sounded. "I was told you were fired for coming on to Delilah."

"That's *crazy* talk. There's no truth to that at all. I never did anything to that girl. I don't know what she told her parents, but if she said I did anything to her, she's making it up. Believe me. I don't need to go after my boss's young daughter. If anything, she was the one flirting with me, not the other way around. But you'll have to ask her about that. The real reason I got fired is that Hubert had it out for me after I told him I wanted a share of the business. I wanted to be partners. It was *my* cooking, *my* recipes, that put us on the map. It was only fair. But that's not important. What is important is that I just wanted to do the right thing by telling investigators what I knew about Hubert. About his violent streak. He blew up all the time at his staff, at his wife, and at his daughter. I've seen it on multiple occasions.

After the police ignored me, I decided I had to tell someone who might listen, someone who might believe me. That's why I called you. He threw a pan at Delilah one time, barely missed her head. I saw him nearly dump boiling water on a sous chef's feet one day. I heard him call his wife a 'slut' and a 'bitch.' He's a creep. I know that doesn't prove he killed his wife, but it sure should at least make him *a suspect.*"

"Okay, I'm here, and I'm listening. But you've got to give me more. What about Delilah, what was her relationship with her mother like?"

"Delilah? Why do you care? I'm trying to tell you about Hubert."

He shifted his position on the step awkwardly, like he was trying to create more physical distance between us where none was possible.

"I just heard she and her mother may have had a troubled relationship."

He snorted and turned away from me, and then turned back abruptly.

"It was complicated. Like I said, Delilah had a thing for me."

"And Tilly was upset about that."

"You could say that."

"Why?"

"Because it was *me.* I was the one having the affair with Tilly."

28

SKELETONS UNEARTHED

"Kid, I agree that's some compelling stuff Andy told you, but it doesn't prove anything. Plenty of people have affairs every single day and their spouses don't kill them. Where's the proof tying the husband to her death?"

Kojak and I sat on a bench at Benton Road Park, the same one where I had met Penny. It was starting to become one of my favorite spots. We both stared straight ahead at the joggers, the skateboarders, and the mothers with strollers.

"I admit, it's not the smoking gun. But it's something. Right? He told me it was a very brief affair that ended several months ago. That it started after Tilly confided in him that Hubert had had many affairs of his own. They were alone one night, Delilah and Andy, closing up the restaurant. They had a few drinks, and that was the beginning. He said it was brief, but passionate. She ended it when tongues started wagging in the restaurant. He said she told him that she couldn't let her daughter see her in this light—*as a cheater*. That Delilah wouldn't understand what had led up to it, how unhappy she had been in her marriage for so long, how badly Hubert had treated her. She was afraid Delilah would feel sorry for her father, take his side, and she couldn't risk losing her. Even though she and Delilah had their differences, her daughter was her whole world, the main reason she had put up with Hubert for so many years. So, the affair ended abruptly, and Tilly went back into her self-protective shell, treating Andy like any other employee."

"So, where did the 'trouble' come in with her daughter? She must have found out about the affair and been pissed. And didn't you tell me that Tammy chick, the waitress, implied that Delilah had a thing for Andy? There's your *love triangle* right there. Mom, Andy, and the daughter. How's that for some crazy, incestuous shit? Maybe we should be looking at the girl instead of the run-of-mill jerk of a husband? Do we know for sure that Hubert found out about her affair with chef-boy? And if so, how?"

"Andy told me he thinks it was an email from a hotel chain where the two of them had met for a little afternoon delight. It was a survey asking Hubert how his stay was at the Oak City Inn on a particular Tuesday the previous month, asking him to rate it. When Tilly used her credit card it was attached to a joint hotel rewards program. The problem was *he* had *not stayed* at that hotel, not ever. Tilly saw the email on Hubert's computer screen one day in his office when she was working on the company's books. It was like he left it up there for her to see, to torment her, to destabilize her. Hubert never confronted her, but he made her life a living hell from that point on. And the really weird thing is he didn't fire Andy right away. He didn't do it for several months. That's why Andy doesn't think his firing was about the affair. Personally, I think it *was* about the affair, but he just took his time doing it because above all, Hubert is a businessman. Andy thinks Hubert kept him on until they solidified the opening of two more restaurant locations with the bank, and then he was done with him, had no more use for him, and definitely had no intention of financially partnering with him. Andy says that's what Hubert told him outright, that he was firing him because they were never going to see eye-to-eye on a partnership agreement, and he thought it was best to go their separate ways. He never mentioned the affair, or even *knowing* about the affair to Andy. But Andy assumed that Hubert knew because Tilly told him about seeing the email. I still think the affair was the underlying reason for firing Andy. Hubert is just too arrogant and proud to admit that was the reason. It was easier to pretend he didn't know, get what he needed from Andy from a business perspective, and then get rid of him."

"I agree, it's pretty strong circumstantial evidence, but it's still not enough. I'll take it to my guys and see what they make of it. We need some physical evidence to tie the creep to the crime; without it, the bad marriage just gives her more of a reason to kill herself. The story is pretty much a *motive* for suicide. And honestly, after what I've heard about this broad Delilah, the kid lusting after the man her mom was having a thing with, I'm not ruling her out as a suspect."

I thought about everything he was saying for a moment, how everything I had just told him could be a motive for murder, or a motive for Tilly to take her own life. She could have been so broken up about Hubert finding out, about the ramifications of Delilah finding out, that she simply couldn't take the pressure anymore. Or maybe Hubert killed her in a jealous rage when *he* couldn't take it anymore, the secret he knew for months eating him up inside, questioning every look that passed between his wife and Andy, every time she got a text and shielded her phone from him. But why kill Tilly at all? Why not kill Andy instead?

And then there were these lingering questions about Delilah. Could her *jealousy* have pushed her to do something over the top like hurt her mother? Maybe Andy didn't return her affections and she felt spurned and wanted to punish him by taking away Tilly.

There were so many questions and so few answers. And there was still another possibility that I had to consider: that someone else took Tilly's life, someone who was *not* on my radar.

⌒

"Kid, I need to switch gears here," Kojak said in a tone he reserved for his most serious moments. I felt my stomach tensing. "Been talking to my contact in Pennsylvania. My buddy, Zack Brumson, he's got something for us."

I sat very still for a moment taking in Kojak's words. A cyclist in a bright pink jacket and matching leggings whizzed by us. The "whoosh" she left in her wake seemed to hang in the air between us for more than just a second or two until Kojak finally broke the silence again.

"Do you want to know, or not?" He asked gently, not wanting to upset me even more, but wanting to offer me a door to the truth that I could choose to walk through or not.

"Yes."

"Yes, what?"

"Yes, *I want to know*. I want to know what he found out."

"Okay, so that Clifton dude, Esther's son, he was a drug dealer. And he knew your dad. He sold him a little cocaine and pot from time to time at a local bar called the Blue Moon, near your grandparents' house in Dilltown. Your dad would sneak away when they visited the in-laws for a little man-time at the bar, and that's where he met the loser. Apparently, they were seen together at the bar a day or two before your mother was killed."

"So, there was a connection?"

"There was."

"But what does it mean?"

"It means they knew each other. That's all. Beyond that, Zack doesn't know anything yet. He's still digging. Remember this happened nearly forty years ago. Not many people around who are still alive to talk about it."

"But could it also mean that Esther was telling the truth. That Clifton was high, wasted, that he broke in and killed my mother, and that Roger had nothing to do with it?"

"*Anything* is possible. You know that."

This time, another cyclist in full biking gear zoomed by us. His head was bent over the handlebars, his body hunched like an animal getting ready to launch at a prey, There was so much silence between me and Kojak that in that moment I felt like I could hear the feverish turning of every single spoke in the cyclist's wheels.

"But that doesn't answer my question. Do you think there's a possibility that Clifton did it or not?"

I knew it was unfair to put Kojak in this spot. He had no idea what the truth was. How could he? I turned to look directly at him, still searching his eyes for the answer. He looked at me helplessly, his glasses about to slide off the bridge of his nose as usual. He raised his palms in the air as a sign he was giving up; his symbolic white flag was flapping in the breeze.

"I can't answer that question, kid. At this point, I know of only one person who is still alive who can answer these questions for you, and that's Roger."

29

THE BOSSMAN

ONE TIME WHEN I WAS WORKING on a serial murder mystery podcast, a man that I interviewed kept putting me off. He refused to answer my questions either by email or over the phone. He kept telling me I had to talk to "The Bossman." I couldn't figure out who he was talking about. Finally, I realized he was talking about God. He told me that I could find the answers to all my questions by talking to *Him*.

So, in Tilly's case, short of talking to God, I decided I would try to speak with "The Bossman" of Hubert's Roadhouse. He was the source of everything. He was at the middle of the intricate web that was starting to define this case. About ten days had passed since Tilly's funeral, and I felt like it was now appropriate for me to reach out to Hubert. The worst that could happen would be that he would get upset with me and tell me to leave him alone, and probably in much less diplomatic terms. As a reporter, I had doors slammed in my face almost every single day. I had nothing to lose.

After much deliberation, I sent Penny a message on her fake Instagram account, or "finsta," asking if she could help me get Hubert's cell phone number. I figured calling his office or one of his restaurants would get me nowhere. I would simply be an unanswered message in a stack of unanswered messages on his desk in the wake of his wife's death.

As expected, Penny was more than happy to help me. She secretly went through her grandmother's phone, copied the contact information, and sent it to me. Then she erased the text as soon as I confirmed that I had it. While I was still more than a little uncomfortable about having a child informant, I convinced myself that a greater good was at stake and that I needed Penny's help. I figured if it came back to haunt me later, I would deal with it then.

After exchanging a few missed phone calls and texts, Hubert agreed quite cordially to meet me at his office in downtown Oak City. The office was in one of the older high rises in the young city that was still flexing its new might with a budding skyline that was dotted with massive construction cranes. But Hubert's building represented *old* Oak City, the one before progress came to town. It had a tiny elevator with dark wood paneling and gold buttons that squeaked when you pushed them. While Hubert had small offices at his various restaurants, this was the headquarters for the chain.

As the elevator came to a grinding halt on the seventh floor, it felt for a moment like the door was not going to open; I thought I was stuck in this tiny cage with no cell service. I quickly scanned the small box for an emergency button. Just as I spotted it, the doors creaked open to reveal an unmanned reception desk.

The office was small and tidy. On the shiny white counter was a gold bell with instructions to ring it if the receptionist was not at her desk, which she was obviously not. A nameplate that said "Barbara" sat next to the bell. A blue swivel chair with a bright green sweater draped over the back sat behind the counter at a neat desk. A 3-D orange-and-blue screen saver that said "Carpe Diem" wobbled in and out across the desktop computer. I waited a second and then rang the bell.

Around the corner darted a petite brunette with a pleasant smile. I assumed it was Barbara. Her curly hair was pulled back in a tight ponytail, but stray curls escaped around the edges of her thick, black-framed glasses, which made her look a bit frenzied. She wore a loose navy dress with wide cuffs at the sleeves and a long gold necklace with a white fringed pendant dangling near her waist. I couldn't tell if she was thirty or fifty. I put her somewhere in between.

"Hello, I'm here to see Mr. Dawson."

Barbara cocked her head to the side and observed me with a wry smile.

"Honey, everyone just calls him Hubert. He'll tell you he doesn't know any 'Mr. Dawsons' but his daddy." She waved me off with a smile to make sure I knew she was joking. "I know he's expecting you. I'll let him know you're here."

And with that, she disappeared around the corner again. I wasn't sure why she didn't just pick up the phone and call him. I tried to relax my anxious thoughts by scanning the photos that seemed somewhat haphazardly hung on the beige wall. There were pictures of every single one of Hubert's restaurants. In most of them, he was in the foreground either cutting a ribbon or pointing to the building behind him like a game show host. There were a few photos of his staff over the years assembled for group photos in the parking lots in front of his various establishments. I tried to spot Andy in some of them, but I couldn't find him. I wondered if Hubert had directed Barbara to get rid of anything with Andy pictured. There were a few stark white square spots on the wall surrounded by a darker, more weathered wall where pictures had obviously been removed.

There were also a few photos of Hubert, Tilly, and Delilah. In most of them, Delilah was a little girl, or an adolescent, wearing a Sunday dress with a big awkward bow in her hair. She looked like a squirmy little girl, like she was always just at the edge of the picture frame trying to wriggle out of Hubert's firm grip on her shoulder. In these photos, it was impossible to ignore the uncanny likeness between Tilly and Delilah—their flawless skin, dark lush hair, red, rosebud lips. Delilah looked like a mini version of her mother. As an adult, the resemblance was *even stronger*—although Delilah came across to me as more of a natural beauty who didn't spend a lot of time on her makeup or hair, while Tilly was definitely someone who used the traditional trappings of female smoke and mirrors to make the most of her beauty.

The other thing I noticed about the photos was that Hubert seemed to be holding Tilly's small waist very tightly. The look on her face in every picture was a strained smile. She held her right hand over his hand that was encircling her waist, as if to guide him not to squeeze her any tighter. It certainly gelled with what Andy had told me about Hubert's literal grasp on his wife and daughter, and how he viewed Tilly as a possession. My guess was that he felt the same way about his daughter, that she was something he *owned*.

"Miss Arnette, he will see you now," Barbara said, after sneaking around the corner, again and startling me. She caught me staring closely at a family photo of the Dawsons on the deck of what looked like a cruise ship. It was the requisite entry photo on the gangplank of the ship at the beginning of the cruise with a big white life preserver on the wall behind them that read "U.S.S. Getaway."

"Okay, thanks," I stammered, abruptly turning on one heel, looking away from the photograph to meet Barbara's eyes.

"I can't believe she's gone," said Barbara with something breaking in her voice. She took off her glasses and began to clean the lenses with a tissue from her desk. "It's just so unreal. She was a great lady. Really smart. Really kind. Really funny. I mean, she had a wicked sense of humor. You probably already know this, but *we all loved her*. People always say that when someone dies, but this time it's true." She laughed, maybe remembering something funny Tilly had once said in her presence and then glanced over at a photo where Delilah was a little girl and they were wearing matching blue dresses adorned with pictures of butterflies; they were sharing a huge chocolate shake with two straws on a stool at one of Hubert's restaurants.

Barbara's look turned serious. Her mouth turned into a frown. Her eyes became watery. I stood silently waiting to hear what she would say next. Like Tammy, it was clear this woman was moved by Tilly and her death.

"I just wish we had known she was in trouble, that she was hurting. I wish we knew and could have helped, that's all," Barbara said wiping a tear from her right eye, shaking her head, and finally replacing her glasses. I mean I knew her life wasn't perfect. Even with all this," she said gesturing to the wall of photos which I took to mean Hubert's assets, and the kind of life it had afforded the family. "She had her struggles with *him*, and with her daughter. But still..."

Suddenly, it was clear that Barbara, not unlike Tammy, felt like she had said too much. Her words trailed off and she bowed her head and turned away from me. I followed her silently down the hall to Hubert's office, just the sound of our heels picking at the Berber carpet as we walked solemnly in lockstep. At his door, she gestured for me to enter and then closed the door behind me without a word, just a small click of the latch.

Hubert was sitting in a big leather chair behind a massive, dark wooden desk that held only a phone, a small laptop, a jar of pens, and a photograph of his wife. The picture was a close-up of Tilly with natural light coming in from a window. She was holding a wine glass at her chin that was almost empty and looking off in the distance at something off-camera. It made me think about how photographs so powerfully capture someone's essence and suspend the person in one single moment for eternity.

Hubert's office was just about the cleanest workspace I had ever been in. There were no stacks of paperwork, no errant pens or paperclips, no envelopes torn open and discarded in a pile. This was a man who seemed to like order and control in every aspect of his life, including his work environment. This snapshot of him jibed perfectly with the story Kojak had told me about him always wanting his driveway at his home to be pristine. He had it painted every two years to hide the normal wear and tear from cars and people walking on it.

Hubert stood up to greet me when I walked in, his dark suit jacket straining against his belly as he reached across the desk to shake my hand and ushered me to sit in a green, velvet straight-backed chair across from him. The office was so orderly, I wondered if he had one office where he met people and one where he did his work. But as I looked around at the framed awards on the walls and photographs of him shaking hands with famous people at his restaurants—

NASCAR drivers, football players, country music singers—I realized this probably was his real office and that he was just a very neat, organized person. I also assumed he had a lot of help from Barbara in this department and then expected Tilly to follow suit at home. A lack of attention to his need for strict order in all aspects of his life may have been a major source of marital strife for the couple. While I didn't think *my* need for order was anywhere near Hubert's, the amount I did crave definitely challenged Adam and our marriage.

"First, I wanted to tell you, sir, Mr. Dawson, that I am so sorry for your loss," I said, trying to open the conversation with Hubert on a personal level. "I'm sorry to be here at a time like this; I really appreciate you agreeing to see me while you are still grieving."

"It's my pleasure, and please, no 'sirs' needed here. No 'Mr.' Despite this big, fancy office, I am just a good old country boy. Call me Hubert," he chuckled, obviously pleased with himself as he sat down in the leather chair and leaned back, resting his clasped hands on the edge of his desk. The chair groaned beneath his weight. "So, what brings you here? I'm fairly sure this isn't a standard condolence call."

"No, you're right, Sir. I mean, Hubert. I am here because I think there's something that's not right about the investigation into your wife's death."

As soon as the words came out of my mouth, I noticed him studying me. The look was a combination of amusement and curiosity. *Why does this woman care about how my wife died?* it said. He leaned back even further, the leather beneath him crunching and the chair itself straining with a metal grinding sound as if it might collapse under his weight. He crossed his arms across his belly and laced his fingers together.

"I agree one hundred percent."

"You do?" I said, sounding more stunned than I had intended to.

"Yes, none of it makes sense to me. My wife was a lot of things, but she was *not* suicidal. If anything, she was a fighter. The last thing she would have done is take her own life. She had no use for me sometimes, but she adored our daughter, Delilah. Delilah was everything to her. I mean they had their differences like most mothers and daughters do, but she would *never* have left her in that way. And she cared a great deal about the people who worked for us. She worked hard to make them feel like she noticed them, noticed how hard they worked. I was never very good at that kind of thing. I left that up to her. But most of all, I know she wouldn't take her own life because she was a godly woman, very dedicated to her spirituality and the church, to the Lord. It just wasn't in her to do this."

I couldn't believe what I was hearing that Hubert, the man Andy and Penny thought may have killed his wife, was agreeing with me that this was *not a suicide*. If he did kill her, this was a crazy mind game to be playing with a reporter. But something in his tone sounded sincere to me.

"Have you told the police this? That you don't think she committed suicide?"

"I have, but they just wanted an easy, open-and-shut case. They don't want to hear anything I have to say. They basically forced me to sign off on their conclusion, because what choice did I really have? That's why I hired my own PI to look into it."

"I'm glad to hear it. I mean, not the part about the police not listening to you, but the part about you getting a private investigator. Something just seemed wrong about this from the beginning. It's been bothering me."

Without trying, Hubert, for all his bravado and brashness, was beginning to win me over. I couldn't reconcile the Hubert that Andy had told me about, the Hubert who was abusive to his staff and his family, with this concerned version of Hubert who wanted solid answers in his wife's death investigation. *This Hubert*, the one I was talking to at this moment, seemed like a man sincerely wanting to get to the bottom of what really happened to his wife. My mind was racing with every possibility. I couldn't see hiring a private investigator to look into your wife's death if you killed her. What sense did that make? Unless it made perfect sense. Unless it was a cover-up for what he did. But in that case, why not just let it rest? Let the police call it a suicide and ride off into the sunset as a free man.

"You know, when a woman is killed, her husband is always a suspect. But I've got nothing to hide. I told Paul Peterman, that's my PI, I told him to leave no stone unturned. I said 'Paul, do what you have to do to get to the bottom of this. Do it for me, but more importantly, do it for Delilah.' I've known Paul for twenty years. He retired from the police department ten years ago after thirty years in. Salt of the earth kind of guy, old gumshoe. He will get to the bottom of it if there's something to find. If Paul doesn't find anything, I'll move on, *let it go*. But not until then."

Suddenly, Hubert sat up in the chair and slammed his right palm on the desk for emphasis. It startled me so much that I almost fell out of my chair. I looked around to see if he was reacting to someone suddenly bursting into the office. But we were still alone.

"Maybe I should put you two together? Two heads are better than one, my mama always said. Maybe you should talk to Peterman, tell him what your theory is? What is your theory, anyway?"

"I don't really have one," I said bashfully. "But there are just things that don't add up."

"Go on."

I started to feel uncomfortable, like I had just received one of those fake emails telling me there was a million dollars waiting for me in an account in Belize and I just needed to give them my social security number. This man was probing me for information in a murder case where he could be a suspect. Somehow, I had to back of this gracefully without sharing too much. I decided I would just turn what I knew into questions and see how he reacted.

"The towel on the driveway, what's that about?"

"Good catch. Maybe you should have been a detective instead of a news reporter. I know my daughter Delilah often did yoga on the driveway on a towel. It was the only perfectly flat place on our property. So, I assumed maybe she just left it there, or nearby. She and her mother shared what I call the 'messy gene.' You might have figured out that I'm somewhat of a neat freak."

I was impressed with how forthcoming he was. It kind of put me off-balance. I wasn't used to people answering my questions directly.

I decided I had to go for it and ask the *money* question.

"And what about those wild posts from one of your former employees on Facebook, accusing *you* of being involved in Tilly's death."

"You mean Chef Andy?" He said, his voice thick with disdain, shaking his large head.

"Yes, Chef Andy."

"He's tore out of the frame that I fired him. Thinks he was some bigwig chef on his way to his own reality cooking show, but he was really just flipping burgers and making fries. He was *nothing* to me. He's just trying to make me look bad. I should sue his ass for libel," Hubert exclaimed with growing agitation in his voice. I was starting to see the *angry Hubert*, the one Andy and Penny had warned me about. He then slapped the desk again, this time with his left palm, for emphasis. I realized I had touched a nerve and decided to keep probing.

"He says you fired him because he wanted to be a partner in the business, and you didn't want him to have a share of it."

"He said that? *That's* what he told you?"

"Yes."

"Lying sonofabitch." Hubert unbuttoned his jacket and sat up straighter, the chair beneath him groaned with every subtle movement.

"So, that's not true, that's not why you fired him?"

"No, I fired him because the no-good loser was sleeping with my twenty-year-old daughter. Taking advantage of her. I think that's a pretty damn good reason, don't you?"

This time, I was the one leaning back in my chair taking in this new revelation. *Things were definitely starting to get interesting.*

30

RESTORATION

"WHAT?" I BLURTED OUT.

That's all I could say when Hubert told me this mind-blowing information. Then, his phone rang, he picked it up, and he held up a finger that silently asked me to hold on for a minute.

I sat there in the green velvet chair ticking off what I'd already been told. Tammy said Andy came on to Delilah and was fired as a result. Andy told me he had an affair with Tilly, but had *no relationship* with Delilah, and that he was fired because he wanted to go into a partnership with Hubert, and Hubert was having none of it. Now, Hubert was telling me that Andy and Delilah *did* have a relationship. So, who was telling the truth and who was lying? Why would Andy admit to one thing that was egregious—the affair with his boss's wife, and then lie about coming on to Delilah? And if Hubert did know about the affair with Tilly, *as Andy said he did*, wouldn't that be a good enough reason to fire him? None of it was making any sense to me.

Then a crazy thought crossed my mind—could Andy have been sleeping with both women, *mother and daughter*? Was that the "love triangle" Tammy was referring to? Was the genesis of the alleged suicide note Tilly confronting Andy about his affair with her daughter?

AMANDA LAMB

As Hubert talked in hushed tones on the phone, his big leather swivel chair now turned to face the wall so he could talk in private, the door to the office made a tiny "click" sound and Barbara came in and put a hand on my shoulder.

"Sorry, he's going to be tied up for a while, Ms. Arnette. So, he asked that I walk you out."

I couldn't figure out how Barbara knew to come into the office and rescue him from me. Had he shot her a quick email or a text when I wasn't looking?

I stood reluctantly, wanting so much to ask Hubert all the questions swirling around in my brain, but I knew that this was not up for negotiation. I reluctantly followed Barbara out of the office looking back to see if he would acknowledge me leaving; he did not.

As I handed the gate agent my phone with my digital boarding pass to scan, I thought of how many years I had been preparing for this journey to Pennsylvania to see Roger again. At this moment in my life, it was less about confrontation, and more about restoration. I wanted the truth to restore the part of my soul that had been wrenched from me as small child by the murder of my mother and the subsequent conviction of my father. I had lost both parents as a little girl, and while my paternal grandmother, Belle, did a great job of raising me and of filling in the gaps that my parents left behind the best she could, it wasn't the same. And now, with Adam gone, I literally felt all alone; Blake and Miranda were my world, but they were too young to be my support system. It was my job to be theirs.

The trip to visit Roger was the only thing that could possibly take my mind off what was going on with Tilly's case. I had purposely decided to hit the pause button on that investigation until I was back in North Carolina. I had to focus on fixing my life and my family's life. I needed to understand where I came from to understand where I was going in a world without Adam. As Kojak said, Roger was the *only living person* who could give me that clarity.

Thankfully, Candace agreed to stay for a few days with the twins so that I could make the trip. Kojak told me it was foolhardy, that I

148

should just let the investigators in Pennsylvania handle it from here. He said Zack Brumson was a pro and would fill me in as soon as he completed his investigation.

There was a part of me that was finally ready to know, to confront the tragedy that had been haunting me my entire life. I had learned through the stories of my friends that dysfunctional families were the rule, not the exception. But the unique quality of my tragedy made it isolating because I didn't think anyone else could possibly understand what it was like to have your mother murdered and your father in prison for the crime. They didn't have support groups for this particular trauma.

Yet, with the help of Belle, Adam, Louise, and Kojak, I had managed to cobble together the semblance of a well-adjusted life. When you looked at me from the outside, I looked like I had it all together. I built a solid career and achieved a certain level of respect in my industry. Despite Adam's death, I had two beautiful children whom I adored. But on the inside, I was screaming. I was still that little girl who lost her parents. It wasn't that I wanted Roger back so much as I wanted to find the missing pieces of the story that had come to define my life.

As I sat in the window seat watching the plane ascend into the clouds, I couldn't help but wonder if things would look different to me after my visit with Roger. Would the sky be bluer? Would the clouds be whiter and fluffier? Or would the truth just bring me further down into the dark hole I had carefully crafted to hide my pain over the years? For the twins' sake, I was determined *that would not happen.*

I imagined what Roger would look like now. I pictured gray hair at first, then no hair. I could have looked his photo up on the Pennsylvania prison system's website, but I wanted to be surprised, not surprised in a good way, but part of me wanted to see *evidence* that prison life had been hard on him, that he was being properly punished. There was another part of me that was afraid to see what he looked like. If he looked soft and frail, would I pity him? Would this sway me in the direction of Esther's story, that Roger really was an innocent man decaying in prison for a crime he didn't commit?

I must have fallen asleep, because the next thing I remember the flight attendant was announcing that it was time to put up our seats and tray tables and turn off our electronics to prepare for landing. I had contacted the warden at Penn State Grove Correctional the previous week to see what I needed to do to get on Roger's visitation list. Roger had to approve me, which he did. I wondered what that conversation was like when a guard went to Roger's cell and asked him if he would like to see his prodigal daughter. It almost made me feel guilty because he must have been so hopeful, so excited to think I might want to have a relationship with him again.

My guilt about Roger's hopefulness to see me waned even more when I pictured the dog-eared, yellowing newspaper articles about my mother's murder I had stumbled upon in a file in Belle's attic when I was growing up. She and I never spoke about my find, but it was the moment I felt in my gut that Roger was truly guilty, even though at that point no one had told me directly. I had always suspected it. Kids talked about it at school. People in the community still whispered about it even though she was raising me in New Jersey, a full state away from where the murder happened at my maternal grandparents' house in Pennsylvania. Thankfully, the Internet wasn't much of a thing yet, so the news about the case wasn't as widespread as it would have been today.

After I found those articles, I told my guardian ad litem, Lucy, that I was done with Roger. She asked for the family court to rehear the custody and visitation order that was in place. The judge took me into his chambers, without Belle, and he asked me what I wanted to do. I told him that I no longer wanted to visit Roger. I was in middle school at the time and the judge said I was old enough to make the decision for myself. He asked me if it would be okay if Roger wrote me letters, and I said it was. Hence the decades of unopened mail from him that I kept in large plastic bins in the back of my walk-in closet. In the same way that I wasn't ready to read the files in Esther's bag of rocks, I wasn't ready to read Roger's letters.

"You sure you don't want to read *just one*, just to get a feel for what he's saying? I could open it and read it to you," Adam used to say when one of Roger's letters would come in the mail with its big, awkward block printing on the front and his inmate number in the return address portion of the envelope.

"No, I'm sure," I always said with too much confidence. But the truth is, *I was never sure*. I made a decision and stuck with it. There was a part of me that ached to read what Roger had written, to find some clue as to why my life had turned out this way. I suspected the answer was in the letters, yet, I didn't give myself permission to find out. In a way, I imagined the truth would be harder to accept than what I had made up all these years. And the last thing I wanted was to do was to *feel anything* for Roger, anything that might make me want to know him again.

Because there wasn't a good way to get from the Philadelphia airport to the prison in Inverness via public transportation, I decided to rent a car. I would get to the town in central Pennsylvania too late for visiting hours, so I had booked a hotel room online in what looked like the cleanest hotel chain that was close to the highway. I had never been a big fan of driving in unfamiliar places, but I tried to look at the drive as an opportunity to decompress and get my head in order before I saw Roger. Thirty years was a long time. A lot had happened in my life in three decades. It would be impossible for me to condense all that time into a single brief meeting.

As I wound through the narrow, winding roads of Pennsylvania, I was struck by how much farmland there was all around me. Cows grazed on rolling green hills in the early spring day—it was much colder here than it was in North Carolina. I had the heat blasting in the little blue rental car. Even so, I was shivering; my tolerance for cold weather had thinned from living in the south for so long.

Every mile or so an old red barn would pop up that looked like something straight out of an Andrew Wyeth painting. Bales of hay coiled into massive circular objects sat spaced evenly apart in fields that seemed to go on for miles.

I briefly recalled my time here with my grandparents—my mother's parents, Rachel and Glen Hartsell—both gone now. I remembered how they always seemed to be *of* this place, of this land. The Hartsells had lived here for generations, and when my mother, Patty, moved to New Jersey with Roger, they could never understand why she wanted to leave this country paradise. But I understood her reasons. This was a place of isolation, a place where you were far from your neighbors and miles from the closest town. The suburban town I grew up in New Jersey had the illusion of being in the country—trees all around us, winding creeks, and sweeping, green manicured lawns where you could hang a tire swing or run through a sprinkler. But it was just an illusion. The Acme grocery store and a Kmart were within two miles of where I lived, first with my parents, and then with Belle. It had a small-town feel with modern conveniences; New York City was just a forty-minute train ride away.

While I didn't ever really know my mother, I saw her in photographs as an ethereal being, her red hair catching the light and the wind, a whirling dervish of positive energy. I sensed that she was a woman who craved connection to the world around her, and especially to people. She was never meant to be trapped in a place like this so far from others. But I couldn't help thinking that maybe if she had stayed here instead of moving with Roger to New Jersey, she might still be alive, but then, of course, I would not exist.

I could barely eat the free continental breakfast at the hotel; my stomach was churning. I did, however, down a large cup of coffee; this turned out not to be the best choice because it made me even more jittery than I already was.

Warden Archie Porter had given me the heads-up in an email about what I could and could not bring into the prison. Basically, he told me no phone, no purse, and not to wear anything with that might set off the sensitive metal detectors like jewelry, an underwire bra, or shoes with steel in the heels. I specifically chose an exercise bra for this reason underneath a pullover workout jacket. He said I could bring my car keys, which they would hold for me at the front gate, and glasses, if I needed them. But that was it.

As a reporter, I had done many interviews in prisons throughout North Carolina. So I had been through the drill of leaving everything in the car and being searched after I went through the metal detector. But this felt different. Today, I was not a journalist; I was the family member of a convicted murderer. They didn't know what I did for a living, so I would be categorized like everyone else who came through the doors to visit a family member, as someone who was potentially dangerous and as someone who might have a reason to bring contraband into the facility.

Thankfully, I chose my outfit well, right down to my running shoes, which would not set off the metal detector. I sailed through security quickly, turned over my keys, and then followed an officer to the visitation area. We passed through several gates beneath tall chain-link fences outlined in barbwire. The gatehouse where visitors entered was a separate building from the prison. As we walked down a long sidewalk lined with recreation yards, I saw in the distance groups of inmates dressed in orange jumpsuits, playing basketball and sitting at picnic benches talking or playing cards.

I wondered silently if Roger interacted with the other prisoners or if he was a loner who sat in the corner of the yard reading a book or writing letters to me. Was he bullied? Did he get jumped and beaten up? Or had he been here so long that he was left alone like a lot of the lifers who just quietly did their time once they aged out of their bravado.

When we got to the front of the prison, we entered a series of containment areas—where one door opens and the other remains closed until the first one closes. I was used to this process—but again, this day felt different as I went deeper and deeper into the bowels of the prison realizing how many doors I would have to pass back through to exit. Just thinking about being locked up in a place like this made me cold.

When I interviewed inmates in prisons, the wardens usually let me sit in a conference room, face-to-face with the person. It was like any other interview I conducted on the outside, just with a line of correctional officers in the back of the room for protection. But I had not *personally* visited anyone in prison since I last saw Roger thirty years ago. I had no idea what it would be like. I imagined it might be like it was in the movies where Roger would sit in a cubicle on the other side of a scratched Lucite window and talk to me through an old-fashioned phone handset. I would be in a similar cubicle on the other side of the fake glass on my own phone handset. I pictured us both putting our hands up to the window at the same time, flattening them together to simulate us touching. But then I shook that image out of my head. This would never happen. I did not love my father and never would. Even if he didn't kill my mother, too much time had passed for us to form a relationship. He was a stranger to me. He would never be part of my life.

To my surprise, the visitation space was not at all like it appears in the movies. It was a big room with small round metal tables spaced evenly apart. There were several families gathered around the tables visiting. The cacophony of voices was broken only by the occasional sound of someone getting a drink or a snack from the vending machine—a thud as their purchase hit the metal drawer behind the flap. Officers ushered me to a corner table, which I was glad about because I didn't want these strangers hearing the critical conversation I was about to have with Roger. Even in the corner, I felt exposed, but I knew it was not my choice. He was in prison and this was all I had to work with.

About thirty seconds after I sat down, a guard holding an older, balding man by the elbow steered him to the metal seat across from me. I knew right away it was Roger. He looked the same as I remembered him, but much more fragile. It wasn't just age that had debilitated him; it was as if prison had sucked the life out of his body and left behind a hunched over, feeble man with sagging skin and patchy sprigs of white hair around his very round head. I knew his eyes; they were familiar to me. Despite how much he had changed, his hazel eyes remained bright, smiling at me with a long-forgotten fondness.

"Maddie, I can't tell you how much this means to me that you came to see me," Roger said in a deep baritone voice after a few seconds of silence. He held my gaze with his eyes in an almost hypnotic trance. The hopefulness in his voice was tangible and unapologetic.

"Honestly, I can't believe I'm really here," I gasped, instantly regretting the longing in my voice.

We sat for another few seconds in silence, him looking at me, me looking down at my hands. Then I got my courage back. I remembered why I was here. I looked up at him again.

"Did you get all my letters?" He asked gently, trying to break the frigidity of our silence.

"I did."

"Did you read them?" He asked too eagerly.

"I did not."

"I wish you had. I think this would be a lot easier if you had read them. They explain a lot."

"There is nothing easy about this," I responded, my words cutting the air between us like a sharp knife.

"Sorry, you're right. 'Easy' wasn't the proper word. I just meant that if you read them you would understand better, and it might be easier for us to talk."

"Roger, what is there to understand?"

Clearly, my use of his name instead of saying "Dad" jarred him. He didn't know me as an adult, and probably couldn't picture me as one even though I was sitting right there in front of him.

"Well, you would understand what happened. It's all there in the letters."

"I think I pretty much know what happened," I said, this time through gritted teeth, trying to keep my voice down as we were just two feet from the other inmates and their visitors who sat at tables on either side of us. Unlike me, they were probably regulars who tuned out other people's conversations because they didn't want to squander their valuable visitation time.

"But you don't, not really," he said, shaking his head and looking down at his lap. "You don't understand."

"You killed my mother. You were arrested, convicted by a jury of your peers, and sentenced to prison for the rest of your life."

"That's one way to look at it."

"I'm pretty sure that's the *only* way to look at it."

"But there's more."

"Okay, I'm here. Now is your opportunity to tell me what you want me to know."

"It's hard to talk about it here. There's no privacy. I wish you had just read my letters."

"Well, I didn't read them. So, you're going to have to start talking quickly unless you want me to get up and leave." My hands were gripping the edge of the chair beneath my thighs. I knew this feeling, the beginning of a panic attack. My modus operandi was always to run, to get away from the trigger that was causing the anxiety. At the moment, Roger was my trigger. I wanted to be anywhere other than on this cold metal chair in a prison visitation room. Suddenly, I was a twelve-year-old little girl again.

"I just wish you would give me a chance. It's been so long, *so long*, and I just want to get to know you again. I think about you every single day. Losing you is my biggest regret in life."

I was regaining my composure now. I pulled my hands from the seat and rested them on the edge of the table as I breathed deeply in and out, trying to calm myself. I remembered that *I* was in control. Roger was in prison. He had no power over me. I was the one with the power.

Roger then did the unthinkable, something he had no right to do. He reached across the small metal table with his right hand and touched my left wrist. I recoiled like a poisonous snake had just bitten me. My hands went immediately to my lap and my pulse quickened again, my breathing became uneven and ragged like I had just sprinted three flights of stairs.

"You gave up that chance when you took my mother from me," I practically spit the words at him, no longer caring about what others could hear. "But because of that, you do owe me. You owe me answers. It's the least you can do for ruining my life. That is why I came all the way here, to look you in the eyes and get answers, not to rekindle some imaginary past father-daughter love story."

Roger sat back, moving away from me as far as he could into the back of the bolted down metal chair. He crossed his arms and gazed at me again with too much affection.

"I do owe you. You're right. What exactly do you want to know?"

"I want to know about Clifton. Did you know him? Was he involved in my mother's murder in any way?"

"I did know him, and it's complicated. Like I said, I've explained everything to you in the letters. If you would just read— "

I was centered again, ready to dig into him. I was so sick of him constantly referring to "the letters." I was right here in front of him. Why couldn't he just answer my questions with straightforward, honest responses? Didn't I deserve that?

Suddenly, a large, muscular officer came up behind Roger and tapped him on the shoulder.

"Time's up, Roger," the guard said gruffly.

"But sir, it's only been a brief visit," I protested, getting up out of my seat to meet the officer's eyes.

"He only gets a short time, miss. Sorry, those are the rules."

Despite my pleas, the officer was already maneuvering Roger up and out of the chair in the direction of the door, one hand on his shoulder, and one hand on the small of his back.

"Come back tomorrow, Midge," Roger said, his voice trailing away as it blended with the din in the room and seemed to disappear as the door started to close behind him. I stood motionless, watching the scarred heavy steel door slam behind the guard as the name "Midge" echoed in my head. It was Roger's nickname for me as a little girl. It was the name of a character in my favorite book, *Mighty Midge,* about a little girl who had special powers that allowed her to fly from building to building and from tree to tree. From her vantage point high up in the sky, Midge could see things all over the world that others missed. Right now, I could use some of those superpowers. I felt anything but mighty.

31

SECOND THOUGHTS

I COULDN'T SLEEP IN THE HOTEL ROOM with the clanking sound of the heater in the corner, a thin shaft of blinding light coming in from the parking lot through a space in the blinds, and what seemed like the continual sound of the pinging elevator doors opening and closing just down the hall. All that aside, it was Roger who kept me awake.

It was the way he looked at me, with *real affection*, like I was his little girl who might jump into his lap and throw my arms around his neck at any moment. I couldn't get the sound of his voice out of my head, the way he said "Midge," the way it rolled off his tongue so naturally like he had been calling my name for the past three decades. I refused to allow myself to be seduced by his misguided love for me after all these years. I had moved on. I was a different person now. Clearly, he couldn't see that I was a grown woman; he didn't understand the proper boundaries of the situation. He had misjudged me if he thought I was going to forgive him. Even with the slim chance that Clifton might be involved, I was not ready to absolve Roger.

Did he think we would just pick up where we left off before he killed my mother? What kind of a person did he think I was that I could just let go of my tragic past and forgive him for what he did to her, for what he did to me? As my brain was circling this black hole of questions, my phone rang.

"Maddie? Maddie Arnette?" A woman's shaken voice said on the other end of the call.

I looked at the cheap digital clock on the bedside table. It was just past one in the morning. I sat up on my elbows to get my bearings.

"Yes, this is she. Who is this? Do you know what time it is?"

"Yes, I'm so sorry to call you this late. I just, I was afraid I would lose my nerve if I didn't go ahead and do it now."

The voice was familiar, but in my sleep fog I couldn't immediately place it.

"I know I wasn't very nice to you when we met at the yoga studio. Okay, I was really ugly. I'm sorry for that. I just had so much going on in my head. But I'm ready to get rid of it, all the bad stuff, and I think you're the right person to talk to. I've got a vibe about you. I know that sounds so corny, but even though I was being a real bitch to you, you didn't crumble, you didn't break, or turn on me. That says a lot to me about what kind of a person you are. I need someone I can trust, and for some crazy reason, I think you might be *that* person."

I was awake now, putting the details of what she was saying together. I was starting to get a sense of who it was. Truthfully, lots of people were mad at me almost every day. That was one of the perks of being a television reporter. They got mad at me for little things, big things, and things they perceived I did or didn't do. One woman I had never even met said I was sending her subliminal, passive-aggressive messages one night through the television screen. But this woman on the phone was definitely someone I had met. It was Delilah Dawson.

"You see, I got so mad at people gossiping in this town behind my back, accusing my father of this horrible thing, of killing my mother, and I kept having to defend him. It so was emotionally exhausting on top of my overwhelming grief. So, when you came at me, well, I broke. I couldn't take one more person accusing him of this. I know you didn't say that directly, but it was *implied,* and I was so drained by the whole thing. You triggered something in me, and that's why I reacted the way I did. I'm actually a very calm and kind person, but you wouldn't know that lately."

"Delilah," I said even though she had not yet identified herself yet. "I get it. You're grieving. I wouldn't expect you to react well to the way I approached you. I used poor judgment in ambushing you in a yoga class, of all places. And you're right, people do not have the right to accuse your father of *murder*. The police have ruled it a suicide and frankly, I met with your dad the other day, and he was very forthcoming. I know how you feel, and I should never have approached you in that way."

"You know how I feel?" she said. The familiar anger from our first meeting was starting to build in her voice. I knew I had just trapped myself in a corner. I *did* know how she felt, but I hadn't intended to tell a stranger my backstory over the phone. I guessed it was the fact that I had just seen Roger that made what happened to me feel so close to the surface.

"Yes, I do. I actually do."

"And how is that?" She quipped, the contrition in her voice having vanished.

"Because the same thing happened to me. Well, not *exactly* the same thing, but I lost my mother too."

"I'm very sorry to hear that. But while losing your mother is hard, having your mother die like this is a little bit more traumatic."

I decided in that moment I had to placate her and find out what she knew, or at least what she suspected. I took a deep breath and decided I needed to give a little to get something in return.

"My mother was killed too, murdered actually, when I was just three. She was shot in the head at my grandparents' house. My grandparents were not there. I was alone in the house with her body, sleeping. I don't remember anything about it, really. I just know what other people told me."

For a minute it sounded like no one was one the other end of the line. I wondered if the cell had dropped out or if Delilah had hung up. But then I heard it, it was almost imperceptible, a muffled cry, like someone crying into a cupped hand with the phone on her lap.

"I'm so sorry, I didn't know. I feel horrible for speaking to you the way I just did."

"There's no way you could have known. Hardly anybody knows about it. I don't talk about it. But there was something about hearing you, the desperation in your voice, I felt like it was the right thing to do, to tell you. I can't walk in your shoes, but I *can* understand the pain of losing a mother tragically."

From that moment on, Delilah opened up. We talked for an hour. She told me that one of her father's employees had been sexually harassing her. He was an older guy, and he was constantly flirting with her, saying inappropriate things about how she looked, how sexy she was, how short her skirts were, or how tight her blouses were. She was so uncomfortable, she even began dressing differently, more conservatively. She didn't want to tell her father because she knew he was a hothead. She had seen his temper before, toward her mother and his employees. He would yell and throw things. Delilah said Hubert was all bark and no bite, that he would never actually hurt someone, but that he did have a legendary anger-management problem. She said he had never laid a hand on her or her mother, but there had been moments she thought he would.

Delilah didn't name the person she was talking about, probably assuming the name would mean nothing to me. But the entire time she was talking I couldn't help but think—*Andy. Chef Andy: It's got to be him.* It made perfect sense. Tammy knew about the harassment. It was probably hard to hide amongst a small group of coworkers at a restaurant. But was it sexual harassment? Or was it an affair as Hubert told me? I decided it was better to let Delilah's story unfold and then ask questions.

She continued. She told the guy at work to stop harassing her. That he was making her feel uncomfortable. He apologized and said it would never happen again. She felt good about her decision to confront him and even better about the outcome. She believed him. Whether he agreed to stop because it was the right thing to do, or just because he was afraid of losing his job, she didn't care. She just wanted it to end.

But it wasn't over. Eventually, this guy started texting her. It was easy enough to get her number, she supposed, from the on-call list posted in the office on the wall in the back of the restaurant. Waitresses were always calling out with car trouble, or a sick kid, or some made-up reason, and they had to find replacements quickly.

At first, the texts from him were fairly benign: "You look nice today." "Did you get your hair cut? It looks great." She responded with a simple "thank you." But then they started to cross the line: "I can't stop looking at you." "You're trying to drive this old man crazy, aren't you?"

Delilah explained to me how she felt like she couldn't tell anyone because she had been complicit. She had done nothing when he harassed her for months, whispering his obscene comments when she passed him in the kitchen. And then when she told him to stop, he started harassing her in a different way. He started texting her these compliments that she *accepted* at first. She accepted them because she was afraid not to, afraid that he might revert to his earlier behavior. So, when he finally crossed a boundary into the inappropriate texts, she felt like it was too late to tell on him, that anyone who looked at the thread would think she had been asking for it.

But then she confided in her friend Brenda, another waitress at the restaurant. I recognized the name—it was the girl with the fairy-hair who had subbed for Tammy the day I ate lunch at Hubert's Roadhouse. It was all making sense now, coming together. Delilah told Brenda about the harassment, and Brenda told Tammy.

Besides working together, Brenda was one of Delilah's oldest childhood friends. She had no social or personal connection to anyone else at the restaurant besides Delilah. She worked and she went home to her three-year-old, Daniel. As a single mother, she had no time for dating or going to bars. When she got pregnant as a teenager and the dad, her high-school sweetheart, took off, Brenda had grown up fast.

Delilah told me that when they were about seven, Delilah fell off her bike having just mastered riding without training wheels. She skinned both knees, both elbows, and her chin. She remembered that when she stood up with Brenda's help, she saw the red blood mixing with tiny pieces of gray gravel from the path trickling down her legs. Brenda told her she was fine. She took her back to her house and made Delilah sit on the edge of the bathroom sink while she cleaned up her wounds with warm water, soap, and paper towels. Then Brenda climbed onto the sink and foraged through Tilly's cluttered medicine cabinet until she found medicated cream and a box of Band-Aids. Brenda, Delilah said, was *always* like that—a soldier in a crisis, calm and focused. So, she knew Brenda would know what to do about this situation.

Brenda listened to Delilah without interrupting over chai tea at the coffee shop just down the road from the restaurant. Delilah said when she was done, Brenda unfolded her arms, took a sip of her tea, and then looked directly at Delilah to deliver her answer.

"It's obvious," Brenda told her. "You have to tell your mother. That's exactly what you need to do. Tell Tilly. She will handle it quietly. He will disappear from the restaurant, and your life. He's a predator, and he deserves whatever he gets."

At first, Delilah told me, she resisted this advice. Her mom was a fixer. Throughout her childhood, her mother was always the person Delilah turned to, to make things better, to make things go away, to solve problems that she didn't want to deal with. But she was a grown woman now, and she was determined to fight her own battles. Plus, she and her mother had gone through a rough patch lately. Tilly wanted Delilah to go to college and get a degree. She couldn't understand why Delilah was still working in the restaurant, spinning her wheels instead of trying to better herself. After all, they had plenty of money to send her to the college of her choice. Her mother just didn't get that Delilah didn't want to go to college because she didn't know what she wanted to do with her life. College would be a waste of time until she figured out some direction. This had caused a lot of friction in their relationship, Delilah said.

Yet, in her heart she knew Brenda was probably right. She knew her mother would know exactly how to handle it without embarrassing her in front of her coworkers. So, she finally broke down and told her.

"And how did your mother react?"

"Well, honestly, she looked really stunned. She had known this guy for a long time. She knew them all. She had a way with people that my dad just didn't have. So, she dealt with a lot of the staff very personally, in a way my dad didn't want to, or just didn't know how to. Everyone loved *her*. So, I think she was a little hurt that someone she trusted, someone she depended on, and someone she respected would do this to her daughter, to her family, after all we had done for him."

"So, what happened next?"

"I'm not exactly sure. She asked to see the texts. I showed them to her, of course. Despite everything we had been through, I knew she had my back. She was *my mother*. I had nothing to hide. I knew she wouldn't judge me for responding politely at first. She was so quiet after she read them. And then she told me she would handle it, like she always did. And the next day *he was gone*."

"The next day? That was fast."

"It was. I'm not sure if she told my father. If she did, he never mentioned it to me. But she must have told him *something* to allow her to get rid of such a key person in his organization that quickly."

Finally, we were getting closer to the name, the name that I already knew, but I needed to hear Delilah say it.

"Key in what way?" I asked nonchalantly.

"Well, he was basically the head chef at our flagship restaurant, and he developed the recipes and the menu for the whole chain, for all ten restaurants. He was important to the business, to my dad. He was there from the beginning."

I felt a chill come over me, and I pulled the scratchy bedspread up around my neck. I suddenly wished I had worn socks to bed. This case was getting quite complicated.

"His name, the name of the guy you're talking about?" I said, trying to sound casual again.

"His name is Andrew Parnell. He was basically my dad's head chef. But everybody calls him Chef Andy."

I sat up in the bed adding a pillow behind me to prop me up. I felt like I needed to be sitting up straight to figure out what was really going on here. Would Delilah be telling me this detailed story about sexual harassment if she really were having an affair with Andy? Every time I spoke with another person involved in this case, the framework of what I thought I knew blew up. It was like I was starting from scratch again trying to put together a puzzle with a hundred missing pieces.

"So, anyway, Andy was really mad when he got fired," Delilah continued. "He thought he and my father were eventually going to be partners, and then this happened. I know he blamed my mother, because he assumed, and he was right, that I had told her and that she told my dad. Everyone at the restaurant knew how close I was to my mom, even though we fought sometimes, how I relied on her, how I pretty much told her everything. He blamed her. That's why I think he may have had something to do with her death. I know it sounds crazy. Even just saying it out loud to you sounds crazy. But I can't come up with anything else that makes sense. My mother didn't take her own life. Sure, her life with my father wasn't easy, but she was tough. She was a lot like Brenda, a soldier. She believed life was a gift. And she loved me too much to leave me. I know that for sure."

"But you signed off on the police department's conclusion that it was suicide. Why?"

"I was in such shock, so riddled with grief. My dad told me just to go along with it, and he would hire a private investigator to make it right."

How did you know Andy was mad at you and at your mom?"

"Because he sent me a long, ugly text, calling me a bitch and saying I would pay for ruining his career. And he also said the apple didn't fall far from the tree, that my mom was a bitch, too. I screenshotted it. I saved it. I still have it. For some reason I thought it might come in handy someday."

I thought back to my meeting with Andy. He was affable, calm, even disarmingly charming as he explained that he and Hubert had a falling out over becoming business partners and that his firing had nothing to do with Delilah, that it was just *a rumor*. He also admitted he'd had a brief affair with Tilly, something he was almost positive Hubert knew about. And if Hubert *did* know, it gave him a strong motive for murdering his wife. Was Delilah just in denial, a young woman covering up for her father? Did she know about Tilly's rumored affair with Andy, and even more importantly, did *she* have an affair with Andy?

A strong part of me felt like Delilah knew more than she was telling me. She was casting stones at Andy so blatantly, I couldn't help but think that she was either protecting her father, or very possibly, *herself*. I couldn't help but wonder if she had either made up or exaggerated the situation with Andy to make him look like a viable suspect.

In a small way, I had done the same thing. I believed Roger was innocent all those years between the murder and age twelve when I stopped visiting him. I had visited him in prison, taken his gifts, hugged his neck. I even told him that I loved him when I left each visit. I made up other possible scenarios for how my mother died. None of them involved Roger. Yet, somewhere deep down inside of me I must have known the truth. I must have known that he was in prison for killing her. Even when that truth was confirmed by those newspaper articles I found in Belle's attic I didn't really embrace it until Belle told me why he was in prison when I turned sixteen. So, I really couldn't blame Delilah for whatever story she told herself so that she could sleep at night, not thinking about the possibility that her father was culpable.

I knew I had to tell her what I had learned and ask her to reconcile what she was telling me with what Hubert and Andy had told me. I just couldn't figure out how to broach the topic of her having an affair with Andy and of her mother having an affair with Andy.

"Delilah, I know this is all very sensitive to you right now, but I need to tell you that your dad told me you and Andy did have a relationship."

"That's ridiculous, I'm sure my mother just exaggerated the situation to him to make sure my dad fired him. Sexual harassment is not something my dad would have totally understood. She probably felt like she had to tell him something more dramatic, something over the top that would guarantee he got rid of Andy."

"Okay, that does make sense. For the record, Andy also denied you had anything going on."

"That's big of him," Delilah snorted.

"But there is one more thing that Andy said. I'm not going to sugarcoat it. I'm just going to tell you straight-up. He says he had an affair *with your mother.*"

There's was silence on the other end of the line. I could still hear Delilah breathing, but that was the only sound coming from my phone. Suddenly, in the dark hotel room my ears clued back into the other sounds—the rumbling heater, the elevator pinging, someone opening a hotel room door and then slamming it shut. I waited, and then there was one more sound, the sound of Delilah hanging up on me.

32

SKIPPING OUT

I NEVER INTENDED TO GO BACK and visit Roger at the prison the next day. Sure, I had left the possibility open, telling myself I could decide in the morning. But I knew I wouldn't go. The previous day had been so painful, the little girl inside of me getting pulled back into wanting the imaginary love of a father who might be a monster. But when I sat there in front of him, there was no way for me to separate the two needs—the woman who wanted the truth, and the little girl who longed for her daddy. It wasn't healthy, and it wasn't going to be productive. I had to let it go for the moment for my own sanity.

My flight wasn't until late afternoon, so after breakfast I decided to head toward Philadelphia and maybe stop somewhere along the way. I was sleep-deprived after my long talk with Delilah. I honestly didn't know what to believe anymore. *Someone* was lying to me. I didn't know if it was Delilah, Hubert, or Andy.

In my mind, Delilah's story gave Hubert as much, if not *more*, motive to kill Tilly than Andy. It seemed crazy to me that Andy would kill Tilly over losing his job, but given Hubert's "anger-management issues" and his obvious jealousy and need for control when it came to his wife, it didn't seem out of the realm of possibilities that *he* could have done it.

It also didn't seem too far-fetched that Delilah might have been jealous of her mother's relationship with Andy—whether or not she herself was involved with Andy. In that case, was it possible that Delilah had done something awful to her mother in a fit of rage? I shook the thought out of my head and focused on the scenery around me.

As I drove through the rolling green hills, farmland on either side of the road, I suddenly realized I was in a familiar area. I passed a sign on the right that said: "Welcome to Dilltown, Original Home of the Minty Mattie." I briefly recalled reading on Wikipedia how the mint chocolate candy was first made here and then later sold to Hershey where it became a huge success.

Dilltown was where my mother had grown up. It was where my maternal grandparents, Rachel and Glen Hartsell, had lived until they died. It was where my mother was murdered. Without realizing it, I was driving in the direction of their home. If I stayed on this main road, I would be going right past it. I had only been there a few times after my mother was murdered, but I had looked it up on Google Earth several times in recent years, wondering if seeing the house from a satellite view would spark any clear memories for me. It did not.

Belle took me there to visit my grandparents a few times when I was a little girl after my mother died. They were older and not well enough to travel to us. Rachel had diabetes and my grandfather, Glen, had been battling cancer for years. Thinking back on it, it must have been horrible for them to stay in that house, yet they probably didn't have a choice financially. No one wanted to buy a house where a woman was murdered.

Even as a child, I remember them being kind to Belle. They didn't hold her responsible for what her son did, and I think they were forever grateful that she was able to raise me when they could not. A few years after my mother died, they ended up in a nearby nursing home, and they died within six months of one another. I overheard Belle say to a friend one time that diabetes and cancer may have taken their bodies, but they had really died from broken hearts.

I knew the house in its original state. I had studied the pictures in the yellowing newspaper articles I found in Belle's attic. Years later, when I looked up the exact location online, the old red farmhouse was still there, but the trees obscured much of my view.

There was only one main thoroughfare through Dilltown, and I was on it. The farmhouse was on this road, just outside the little downtown which wasn't much of a downtown at all. There was a row of boarded-up stores with "For Rent" signs in dusty, cracked windows. The younger generations had fled to the suburbs of Philadelphia with their neat, cookie-cutter, family-friendly communities, manicured lawns, and country clubs. But there were also some beginning signs of gentrification—a handful of small cafes and boutiques in the next block that left me with a sense that Dilltown was not dead.

As I crested the next hill, there it was, looming in the distance like a disheveled heap of red planks that someone had dumped next to the road after a storm and forgotten about. It was as if the house had been waiting for me all these years to come back and see it in this ruin. This was the place where my mother had taken her last breath, but it was also the place where my mother had grown up. It was hard to reconcile these two different pictures of the old red farmhouse and what they meant to me.

I imagined her running through the rolling hills in the distance, her red hair flowing in the wind like a sail behind her, wearing the little blue dress I had seen in old photographs, brushing by the cornstalks as she leaped with abandon, as sunshine beamed down, making her fair skin pink. And then, in the next moment, I pictured the single, fatal gunshot wound to the head that took her away from me in that same place where she had sprung to life. I had always prayed that she didn't suffer, that one minute she was alive, breathing, and happy, and the next she was gone, without warning, without pain.

I slowed down as I approached the house. I knew I was going to stop. The temptation was too great. There was a good chance I would never be this way again. This was my opportunity to face the ghosts that had followed me through life. At one time, I imagined, it was a beautiful house. I wondered if anyone had ever lived in it after the murder, or if it just fell into disrepair because no one wanted to buy it.

My mother had two brothers, uncles I never really knew. Belle told me they had "issues," which I later learned meant they were alcoholics. They both died young. I assumed my uncles would have inherited the property when my grandparents died, but they probably knew the place was cursed. I had no idea who owned it now. As far as I knew, my uncles never married and never had children, so maybe it reverted to the state when they died. I honestly didn't know and didn't care. Based on the condition of the property, I didn't think anyone would mind if I stopped for a minute and looked around.

I glanced down the road and saw an old blue colonial house in the distance with a tall stone chimney. I suspected this was where Esther had lived before she moved to North Carolina after Clifton died and Pete retired. There weren't many neighbors, just a few houses in this distance, too far to even be called real neighbors. But Esther had told me she saw my mother walking with me. Was it on this country road? I tried to imagine it as I carefully drove the rental car into the jungle of grass in front of the house and stopped.

I sat for a minute in the car staring up at the house, wondering why I had come here. The roof dipped like a frown under the weight of fallen branches and was covered in soft green moss. Weeds were growing in between the sideboards, protruding from the peeling red walls of the house. A flagstone path leading to the sagging front porch was mostly obscured by cattails. My eyes filled with tears. What was I expecting to find? This was an abandoned house in the middle of nowhere that no one cared about—no one but *me*. To my great surprise, as I got out of the car, I felt an immediate sense of calmness as I stood in the tall grass facing the house. I closed my eyes and allowed the tears to roll down my face—they were tears for my mother, for my grandparents, for myself, and even for Roger.

With my eyes closed, I could hear the birds singing a little bit louder and the gentle wind rustling the springtime leaves that had just sprouted on the trees. I wasn't afraid, or sad, just oddly content as I realized this was just an old house. It couldn't hurt me. There were no ghosts here, no evil spirits haunting the ground I stood on or lurking within the dilapidated walls of the farmhouse. It was hard to explain the feeling of peace that came over me in that moment. It was as if my mother was telling me to let go of my anger for Roger, to let go of the past that had been my life's burden. She was giving me permission to unchain myself from this tragic story and move on. Suddenly, I realized that my trip here wasn't really about seeing Roger or learning the truth; it was about making peace with my past and learning how to move beyond it.

As I got back into the car, I noticed a thin shaft of sunlight peeking through the trees above the house. It almost blinded me, hitting me dead in the eyes. I reached for my sunglasses to block the glare and then stopped. I closed my eyes again and felt the warmth of the sun bathe my face with light. It was like my mother was sending me off with love. I wasn't much of a prayer warrior, but I said a silent prayer thanking God for granting me this moment, the moment of knowing that everything was going to be okay, somehow.

As I pulled out of the driveway of the old house, I knew what my next stop would be. I was not heading back to the prison to see Roger. Our reunion had been too overwhelming and took an emotional toll on me. I didn't need to hear what he had to say. I wasn't interested in hearing his version of the truth and feeling manipulated by his misplaced paternal instincts after decades spent apart. The person I really wanted to speak with was Kojak's friend, investigator Zack Brumson. He would be objective and tell me the facts. Facts were what I needed, not denials and half-truths spun through the biased lens of a convicted murderer who happened to be my father.

I texted Kojak to find out where Detective Brumson's office was. He worked for the state police, but the regional office was in the county somewhere near Dilltown. Reluctantly, Kojak gave me the address and told me he would give the detective a heads-up that I was coming. Kojak had not been on board with my trip to Pennsylvania, fearing it would only open old wounds and not provide the closure that I was looking for. But what he didn't understand was that this trip was a long time coming. For years, I had kept myself so busy that I didn't have time to reflect on my painful history, but after surviving Adam's death, I realized that I was capable of a lot more than I gave myself credit for. It was time to face my past. It was the only way I knew how to move forward.

⌐⌐

Zack Brumson's office was only about eight miles from my grandparents' old house. The state police regional headquarters was in an old stone house called the "Zelda Ergon House" that was donated to the state by a wealthy spinster heiress. I immediately Googled the woman after he gave me the address because I was so curious. Wikipedia had a short history of Zelda's life and a photograph of an elegant woman in a long, blue chiffon dress sitting sideways on an ottoman with a martini in one hand and a cigarette in the other. Her blonde hair was wound tightly on top of her head in a beehive, and her lips were parted in a slight smile as she looked off camera at someone or something that was making her laugh. Apparently, according to the biography, even though she never married, she always had a great affinity for men in uniform.

When I drove into the fancy circular driveway and saw the grand white stone house sitting on a sloping bluff that overlooked a walking path and a public park, I couldn't believe this was a police station. Zelda must have really loved the boys in blue, and she was certainly paying them back for their service to her.

An older blonde woman in a green sweater with glasses dangling from her neck on a gold chain met me at the receptionist desk.

"Miss Arnette? Investigator Brumson is expecting you. If you'll have a seat, I will let him know you're here."

The furniture, like the building, was a throwback to another time. I sat in a large mahogany wing-backed chair covered in checked blue silk. I realized Zelda must have also donated the contents of the house. This was unlike any police station I had ever been in.

"He'll see you now," the blonde woman said after a minute, looking at me with more concern than friendliness. She motioned for me to follow her down a narrow hallway that was lined by a long thin oriental rug and gold framed photos of rolling Pennsylvania landscapes. I imagined Zelda roaming these very halls, waiting for a suitor to finish his shift at the local police department and join her for drinks in the parlor.

"Hello, Miss Arnette," Zack Brumson said as he stood from his leather chair behind a large polished mahogany desk that held one silver-framed picture of an attractive brunette and three blonde girls in matching dresses. I remembered Kojak telling me he was divorced and had no children, so I stared at the photograph longer than I intended to, wondering if it came with the frame. He caught me looking.

"That's my twin sister, Jenny, and my three nieces. No kids of my own, but I'm a pretty amazing uncle, if I do say so myself," he said with a disarming smile and a chuckle.

Zack looked more like a fancy, high-paid defense attorney than a police officer with his slicked-back black hair, perfect white teeth, and a tan that didn't jibe with the harsh Pennsylvania winters. He wore a starched white shirt, a red bow tie, and black suspenders holding up his black dress pants. A suit jacket hung casually over the back of his leather office chair. I silently wondered what his hair would look like if it wasn't slicked back, if it was loose and wild.

"Hi, thanks for seeing me on such short notice," I said, shaking his tan hand and sitting in the wooden cane-back chair he motioned to in front of his desk. For some reason he made me nervous, which was an unusual feeling for me.

"Absolutely. I have had a chance to look at these files that Kojak sent me, and I've done some digging," he said patting a stack of papers on his desk that must have come from Esther's bag. "And I also went back to the vault. The vault is where we keep old files."

He turned around and pulled out two dusty, brown boxes from behind his desk and pushed them around the side of the desk in my direction. I stared at them like they might contain dynamite. I wasn't sure I wanted to know what was inside, but I was impressed that he had taken the time to go to "the vault," wherever that was, to retrieve the old files. It was more than I had expected.

"Wow, I really appreciate all you've done. I mean I know it's a solved case. And it probably doesn't make a lot of sense for you to waste your time on it."

"Yes, and no," Zack said. The way he dressed made him look like he belonged in another era, but when I looked at his trim physique and the fact that he had no hint of gray, I realized we were probably close to the same age, although I put him a few years older than me. "They did a good investigation, a solid investigation. But remember it was a different time. We didn't have the scientific tools then that we have now. I saw some things when I read through the files that no one probably caught back then,"

"I guess my biggest question is, was Clifton involved? Or is that just some wild story that his mother made up?"

"Here's what I know. Kojak may have already told you some of this. Stop me if you've heard all this. Clifton was a small-time drug dealer. Your dad, Roger, dabbled in drugs. You know, recreationally. He partied. When your parents would come visit your grandparents, Roger would occasionally hook up with Clifton to buy a little pot. Apparently, they met at the local bar, the *only* bar at the time in Dilltown, The Blue Moon. It's long gone, but it was kind of legendary in the eighties. You know—cinder block place, neon lights, dark, smoky, lots of fights. I guess when your dad had enough of the in-laws, he would head over there for a beer and a joint."

Even though Kojak had clued me in on the basics, hearing them from Zack in more detail made the hairs on the back of my neck stand up.

"So, what in the world would be the motive for Clifton to kill my mother? It doesn't make any sense."

"I agree; he didn't know her at all. As far as I can tell, they never even met. So, that makes it even more curious. I'm not done yet. I've got a few more rocks to look under. As you probably know, Clifton is dead, so that makes it more complicated. And I also understand his mother, Esther, the lady Kojak said gave you the files, also recently passed away. By the way, I did find something in one of these boxes I thought you might want."

Zack opened the second box and gingerly lifted out a five-by-seven black-and-white photo of my mother sitting in the grass next to me. In the picture, she is wearing a striped wraparound dress and has her legs folded beneath her. Large hoops dangle from her ears, and her red long locks are cascading down her chest, but a few errant strands are blowing to the side in the wind. I am young, maybe eighteen months old, sitting beside her in denim overalls with flowers stitched into the bib. I have on white Keds and I'm holding a large stuffed rabbit. I look stunned, but she is smiling, touching my arm, her fingers lightly encircling my tiny wrist.

For a moment it was hard for me to breathe. It was such a raw display of my mother's love for me in a way that I had never seen it before. The photograph was foreign to me, as if the people were strangers, people I had no connection to. Zack cleared his throat and brought me back into the present.

"Sorry, that was probably insensitive of me to thrust that on you. I just thought it was a sweet photo, and I thought you might want it. I don't have daughters myself, but I adore my nieces, been around them since they were born. And I can't imagine them surviving without their mother, my sister, Jenny. She's an angel, and your mother looks like she was an angel, too."

He cleared his throat again, appearing embarrassed by having shared too much with a stranger. He pulled away from me, sitting back in his leather chair to create some distance between us.

"So, back to Clifton. He had no motive to kill your mother. If Esther is right, there is only one possible explanation I can think of—*murder for hire.*"

33

NANCY DREW

I READ MY GRANDMOTHER'S BOOKS about a girl detective named Nancy Drew. Even though the stories were super old-fashioned and pretty corny, I still liked the idea of a girl solving mysteries. I had been listening closely to the adults again, lurking around corners, trying to pick up bits of truth, things they didn't want the children to hear.

From what I was able to put together from the conversations that I overheard between my grandmother and my mom, they thought that Uncle Hubert killed Tilly because he found out she was cheating on him, that he was jealous and angry that she made him look bad. My grandmother, my mother, and my Aunt Debbie talked about this a lot in whispers to make sure me and my cousins didn't hear anything. But it was too tempting for me not to listen. I had as much right to know as anyone else what happened to my great aunt.

No one ever wanted to give kids credit for understanding more than adults thought they were capable of. I understood plenty. Not only did I read a lot, but I was always researching things on the Internet. I knew from watching lots of crime shows on my iPad that my mom didn't know about that it was almost always the husband or boyfriend when a woman was murdered. Stranger murders were very rare—like serial killers who jumped out of the bushes and grabbed random women or kids. I also knew that it wasn't good to jump to conclusions because you might miss something important if you have blinders on.

I had been patient, taking notes in my journal, looking at the case like a bunch of puzzle pieces that I needed to sort and arrange until the full picture came into focus. And finally, I had put it all together. I just needed to get it to that reporter. I could tell the reporter lady wasn't very thrilled with me after I pretended to be an adult online in order to meet with her. I now realized that was wrong, but I also knew the lady wouldn't have met with me in the first place if she thought I was a kid. For some reason, though, I trusted her and felt like she was the best person to get the information to the police because I knew for sure the police weren't going to listen to me.

It all came together when I was in the tub the other night. I did some of my best thinking in the tub. I was watching a documentary about an unsolved murder on my iPad that was propped on a stool next to the bathtub when I heard my mother on the phone with my grandmother. I always knew when my mother was talking to my grandmother because her voice got really Southern. For the most part, my mom didn't really have a Southern accent. She had gone to college up north, and she always sounded like a Yankee to everyone who knew her here after that. Or at least that's what she told me. But when she talked my grandmother, it was like all the Southern just jumped right back into her voice, almost like she was a different person, someone I didn't know. I didn't have a Southern accent either, which I assumed was because I grew up listening to my mom and her Yankee-college accent.

So, I listened real close to them on the phone. I muted the volume on the show and sat real still so I wouldn't splash the water and miss something important. This was something Nancy Drew had taught me. It was in the stillness that you heard the most. A good detective had to learn to be as still and quiet as possible in order to hear the clues.

"Yes, Mama, I agree. It makes total sense to me. But what are we going to do about it? Are you going to go to the police and say: 'Oh, just in case you were wondering, I think my brother may have killed his wife.' I don't think so. I don't think that's a very smart thing to do. You know Uncle Hubert is and always has been a sonofabitch, and he's a powerful man. He's got money and power. He can buy people off. He can make people turn their heads. He can make things that don't look good for him go away. He's not someone any of us should be messing with," my mother stopped and went silent. I assumed she was listening to my grandmother's response which I imagined would be as long and excited as my mother's. They've both talked the same way, with lots of exaggeration in their voices, like they were competing to be heard over the sound of an oncoming train.

"Yes, I agree the affair gives him motive. It's the oldest and most cliched motive in the world. But why not just divorce her? Why kill her and risk everything? That doesn't make any sense to me."

I was proud of my mother for trying to make logical arguments to my grandmother, and I would have told her so except then she would know I was eavesdropping. The water was getting cold. I really wanted to get out of the tub, but I didn't dare for fear that I might miss something, some important clue that would help me solve the case, complete the puzzle, end the mystery we had all been living with for days now.

"I hear you. Yes, he is an egomaniac. When you look at it like that it makes sense. I think the best way to get at this is to get the boyfriend to talk. If he tells the police what he knows, about the affair, about how Hubert learned about it, and we're of course just assuming he did learn about it, and then how Hubert reacted, well that gives them something concrete to go on. But us speculating is really nothing but gossip. They're not going to listen to us, and it will put us in a real bad way with Uncle Hubert. I don't think you want to risk that, do you?"

Now, they had my interest for sure. I had heard the word "boyfriend." I just needed a name to seal the deal. I would take that name right to the reporter and let her take it from there. She would get him to talk, get him to go to the police and tell them Hubert killed Aunt Tilly in a jealous rage. I knew even if I was responsible for solving the case, I would never get the credit. But it didn't matter.

I would know that I made a difference, just like Nancy Drew. For her, it was never about getting credit, it was about the satisfaction of knowing she had solved the mystery.

"Yes, I agree, that's what we should do. We should talk to Andy and encourage him to talk to the police and then let it go from there. We will wash our hands of it. Uncle Hubert will never know we had anything to do with it. Andy is the one who will be in the hot seat; after all, it's really his fault. I knew she was lonely in her marriage, but he is the one who tempted her, who pulled her away. He charmed her, I'm sure of it. Tilly wouldn't have strayed on her own without some pretty strong coaxing."

I jumped out of the bath and grabbed my towel from the rack and just about knocked my iPad into the water. My stillness worked. I got what I needed—a name. Andy was the name. He was the "boyfriend" my mom and grandmother were talking about. He was the reason Uncle Hubert killed Aunt Tilly. He was the clue I needed to complete the puzzle. Now, I just needed to get the reporter lady to talk to me again so she could get this information to the police. I wanted to make sure Uncle Hubert got what he deserved—a life sentence in prison, or maybe worse?

34

GHOST CAT

THERE IS NOTHING LIKE the pure joy of an animal story to make you put aside all the serious things you are worrying about. The day after I returned from my whirlwind visit to Pennsylvania, Janie hit me with another story that I would put into the you-can't-make-it-up category.

"So, the cat is dead, right? But his ghost, or her ghost, sorry, not sure if it's a boy or a girl, is haunting the house. So, one night the guy, Walter, Walter Mambo, love the name, he hears the ghost-cat skitter across his bedspread and then feels him or her land on his legs like he or she always used to do when he or she was alive. He wakes up suddenly, looks for the cat, doesn't see anything, but he smells smoke. His friggin' house in on fire, like serious, burning-down-the-house fire. He gets out just in time and he says the ghost cat saved his life. How about that for a killer story?"

"How about that?" I say, stunned, as I stir my lukewarm coffee on the kitchen island and wonder how I got here, here in this moment, here in this job, here in a kitchen in North Carolina one day after seeing the house where my mother was murdered. Perched on the countertop in between a wire fruit bowl and a scented candle is the black-and-white photo of myself and my mother that Zack Brumson had insisted I take with me when I left his office. Miranda and Blake had gotten a huge kick out of it. There were very few pictures of me before I went to live with Belle. I was never sure what happened to them. I assumed she felt like it would be too painful for me to have them. But I would have liked the opportunity to make that decision for myself. Because Belle only took pictures on special occasions, like most people before smartphones, I had little photographic evidence of my upbringing. The twins sometimes joked that I had never really been a little girl, that I was born an adult.

"So, Buster will meet you there, okay?" Janie said with a smile in her voice. I pictured her again twisting one of her long blonde curls nervously as she waited for my reply. I could never really get upset with Janie. She always had good intentions. Her energy was part of her passion for rallying a dozen grumpy reporters every single day, many of them who had excuses as to why they couldn't, or wouldn't, do something. It was a tough job, and I admired her tenacity even if I didn't always fully embrace my story assignments.

"I'm in. Ghost cat. This will be a first." I knew it would be a nice distraction from Tilly's case and Roger and all the other insane stuff that was ping-ponging around in my brain like a song or a jingle from a commercial that you couldn't get out of your head as it played in a loop over and over again.

When I hung up with Janie, I picked up the photo of me and my mom and studied it more closely. I smoothed my thumb over her image as if I might be able to will her to life, to make her climb right out of the photo and put her arms around me. The truth was, I barely remembered her. There were just small glimpses of being raised by her, small memories that floated in and out of my consciousness with no warning and no clear reason for me remembering them. I had a memory of listening to the musical version of *Rapunzel* on my cassette player as I tried to go to sleep one night, hearing kids outside playing whiffle ball, the bat cracking against the big plastic ball. The sun had not set yet, and I remember feeling jealous that I was not outside, but instead confined to my bedroom as it must have been past my bedtime. My mother came in and sat on the edge of the bed and brushed the hair away from my eyes, the now-setting sunlight radiating through her red hair, making her look like an angel, just like Zack Brumson described her.

But something had always bothered me about that memory—suddenly, I realized what it was. I remained in the nursery at my parents' house until my mother's murder. My big girl room, the one I was remembering, was at Belle's house where I lived *after* my mother died. *She couldn't have been there.* It must have been a dream. I was mixing up memories and dreams, or was I? Maybe I had more in common with Walter Mambo than I thought.

Walter Mambo was a small, fragile looking Black man with sad eyes and thick Coke-bottle glasses with heavy brown frames. When he shook my hand, he held it between both of his hands and held onto it longer than necessary. I quickly realized from this gesture that Walter was a spiritual man. He believed you could judge people's true nature by the energy in their handshake. He told me I passed the test. I was relieved.

Walter also told me that his wife of forty-two years, Agnes, had recently died of cancer. He said Agnes was his whole world, and Monet was her cat. So, when Agnes died, he felt closest to her when Monet was near him or *on* him, her long gray legs outstretched, barely brushing his feet, or thighs, or arms, wherever she chose to lie in his bed. And once she was there, he would never move for fear he might wake her, and she might leave his side.

"Cats are like that," Walter said with a small smile beginning to form at the corners of his trembling lips. We were at his sister's house, sitting on the steps of her front porch. Buster had already put a microphone on him and set up the shot. Walter seemed comfortable here, sitting on these old stone steps. So, we stayed. "They don't like for humans to tell them what to do. That's how they see even the tiniest nudge here or there. They will run away if you disrupt them."

"Monet is a great name, where did that come from?"

"Art lover, my beautiful lady was. She went to France when she was in her twenties, with a rich aunt. I've never been there. Never been much of anywhere, to tell you the truth. But she visited

Monet's house, they made it into a museum or something, back in 1980. She could never get it out of her head. In fact, that's why we have a yellow kitchen. Monet's house had a yellow kitchen, and she had to have it. So, every cat we've ever had was named Monet."

"How many?" I asked with genuine interest. My curiosity was the reason I was perfectly suited to be a journalist. I was interested in people and their stories. Most of the time, I was more interested in them than I was about the facts. I had to remind myself to pay attention to the facts most days. But in my opinion, every single person I had ever met had an important story to tell. And I just felt lucky to have a job where I got to share their stories with the world, especially when it came to someone as kind and sincere as Walter Mambo. I probably could have sat on those stone steps all day long listening to the melodic quality of his soft, rhythmic voice as it lulled me into an almost meditative state. *Listen, always listen,* I reminded myself. It was the interrupting that ruined an interview, the ego part of our brains that felt the need to interject instead of letting the story unfold.

"Let me think, I think the last one was Monet 5 if I'm not mistaken. Yes, 5. Course, we never used the number in their names, didn't want them to feel bad like they were not as important as the one before. We had a couple overlap, which got confusing at times, Monet 2 and 3, for example. But I've got to tell you, I took a real liking to 5. I'm sure it had to do with Agnes passing away and all, but I also felt like maybe a bit of Agnes stayed behind in that cat. I would talk to her, and she would cock her head, perk her ears up, and look at me like she knew exactly what I was talking about. I know I sound like a nutty old man, but I've walked through a few fires in my lifetime, and I got a sense about things like this."

"So, Monet was a girl?"

"Yep, this one was, not all of them." Walter chuckled and slapped his own knee with his right hand. He was wearing faded jeans cinched tightly around his small waist with a red canvas belt. I wondered if he had lost weight since Agnes's death. I was amazed that he was in such good spirits despite his house burning down. "She was a good girl, stayed by my side all the time after Agnes died.

Hated to put her down last week. But she had lived a good long life, fourteen years. She had complications from diabetes and the vet said it was the human thing to do. So, I figured she knew best, and I went along with it. But I wasn't happy about it, not one bit. Came home and cried like a baby. Felt like I was losing Agnes all over again."

I knew he meant "humane," but his calling it "human" made sense too and made me like Walter even more. Sometimes I asked people to restate things when they misspoke, but in this case, what he said was too beautiful and perfect to redo.

"So, the fire, the house, tell me about that," I said gently, hoping our casual conversation leading up to this moment had earned me the right to ask about what he had just been through—*a* trip through *literal* fire.

"It's just a house. Sad to see it go. Lots of memories there, but the important thing is that I got out. I was sound asleep. I mean the kind of sleep you don't wake up from unless something explodes. So, I was real fortunate."

"Tell me again—exactly how did you wake up?" I knew the answer from Janie, but I needed for him to tell me himself, on camera, *his version*, not Janie's.

"It was the wildest thing. I heard a *scratch, scratch, scratch* across the bedspread. Agnes never believed in getting cats declawed, even though the Monets were inside for the most part. She said it went against their true nature as hunters and gatherers. She believed declawing a cat was like castrating a grown man," Walter said, chuckling again and looking up at the sky as if he was communicating directly with Agnes. This time he slapped his other knee to make his point. Somewhere, in the house behind us, through the screen door, I could hear a television playing and muffled conversation. "So, I heard that scratching sound on the bedspread, and then I felt the weight of Monet on my legs. Can't really explain it. It was just that familiar feeling of her plopping down on top of me while I slept. And then we'd stay like that for a better part of the night. But as soon as my brain clicked in, I remembered Monet was gone, *dead*. I had been right there with the vet when we put her down last week, stroking her little gray-and-white-striped head. So, when this happened last night, I sat straight up in bed, wondering what Agnes was trying to say to me through Monet's ghost. That's when I smelled it..."

"Smelled what?" I prompted.

"Smelled smoke, and I looked under my door at the crack and saw light dancing there, flames, smoke starting to pour under the door like the trail of an airplane doing tricks in the sky. I quickly opened my bedroom window and jumped into the bushes. Luckily, Agnes insisted on a one-story house. She said she wasn't going to walk up and down stairs with bad knees when she got old. So that was it; I was safe. I got out thanks to Monet, and I'm pretty sure Agnes had something to do with it too."

With that, Walter reached over again with two hands and put my right hand in between them.

"I can see the look on your face young lady, I know you're suspicious of this story, that this old man may be telling you a fable. But I got nothing to hide and nothing to gain from making it up. *This is the truth.*"

I sat a little uncomfortably for a minute until he pulled his hands away again. There was something about the way his words landed in my ears like poetry that made me want to believe him.

"So, do you think pets and people can really communicate with us after they die?" I asked this as much for myself as I did for the story. I pictured my beautiful red-haired mother sitting on the edge of my big-girl bed at Belle's house, a halo of light encircling her. What did she say? I don't remember. I just remembered how she made me feel—safe, loved, able to shut my eyes and go to sleep with the musical sounds of *Rapunzel* dancing through the room and the smack of the whiffle bat hitting the plastic ball in the distance.

"I do, young lady, I do. But until it happens to you, it's hard to be a believer. Makes you special though. My mama would have called it 'touched.' Not everyone can communicate with the other world. It's a real gift, a blessing, a knowing that someone is watching over you from beyond. I got no doubt that Agnes has my back."

I had promised Delilah when I returned from Pennsylvania that we would meet to discuss the situation with Andy. I still didn't know what her deal was. I couldn't figure her out. I wanted to believe her, to connect with her on common ground, as the child of a mother who was murdered, but I wasn't sure I could trust her. There were too many red flags in her behavior, and even more in her words.

If she was having an affair with Andy and she lied to me about it, making up this cover story about being sexually harassed, what would be her motive? And why would she trash him to me and imply that he may have done something to her mother as opposed to Hubert? The only answers I could come up with was that she had been rejected by Andy and was angry at him, *or* that she had created this elaborate cover story to protect her father because she either believed, or *knew*, that he had something to do with Tilly's death.

The strange thing was that my conversation with Andy didn't give me even the slightest hint of this kind of depravity, the kind that would make you repeatedly sexually harass a woman who had no interest in you. I saw nothing unusual in him, just a guy who admitted to me that he screwed up by having an affair with a married woman, his boss's wife of all people, and that he thinks this may have led to her death. He wasn't the first man to fall in love with a married woman, but then going after the woman's daughter, that was something else altogether—*if* Delilah was telling the truth.

My instinct was to protect Delilah, because if she was telling the truth, then we shared the same pain. But at the same time, I had been burned before helping someone when I allowed my emotions to lead. The last time this happened it involved another murder case, and it shook me to my core, undermining all the good intuitions I thought I had about people. It took me a long time to trust my gut again. Just because Delilah was holding up a mirror, reflecting my personal history in her story, didn't mean she was telling the truth.

"Maddie, thank you so much for meeting me," Delilah said, standing up from the table in the small coffee shop. She put her hand out to shake mine. Delilah was a natural beauty—no lipstick, no makeup, little jewelry. She wore a plain black T-shirt and small diamond stud earrings. Her long hair hung loosely over her shoulders, not fixed in any style. She had a cup of untouched tea in front of her. "I'm really sorry for hanging up on you the other night; it all just got to be too much."

"Delilah, I get it. And I'm sorry for dropping so much on your plate without warning. Understand, I want to help you in any way that I can, but we can't go to the police with baseless accusations; we have to go with solid facts. And I think there may be more to this story that you're not telling me."

I tried to choose my words very carefully. I didn't want to scare her away. At the same time, I felt sure she was hiding something from me. Things were not adding up about her story, and it didn't gel with the versions from either Hubert or Andy.

"What is it, Maddie, what more is there? What are you saying?" Her words stung. She had gone from zero to sixty, civil to defensive in seconds.

"It's not easy to have this conversation, Delilah. I'm just still really confused about your dad saying you and Andy had an affair, and then Andy denying having anything going on with you. I'm just trying to get to the truth."

"The truth? You want the truth? *I'm not sure you would know the truth* if it was sitting in your lap."

I was losing her quickly, but my head was full of all the pieces that didn't fit together. Hubert told me he fired Andy for having an affair with his daughter. There was no mention of his wife. Andy told me he was fired because he wanted to be business partners with Hubert, and Hubert was having none of it. Delilah told me Andy sexually harassed her and she told her mother who made sure he got fired. It was like a chain necklace full of small tight knots that not even a straight pin could untangle. I just wanted to be convinced that *one person* was telling me the truth. I was hoping that person would be Delilah, but she wasn't giving me any confidence.

"So, why would you believe that asshole over me?" Delilah asked defensively pushing away from the table and her untouched tea as if I were a poisonous snake that might lunge across the top and bite her.

"I went to see him once, and he asked to see me once. The first time, he was extremely angry and defensive, said a lot of mean things about your father, as you can imagine. We were at the front door of his house. It was a short encounter. Then, the second time, he asked to meet with me. He was very apologetic about how he acted the first time."

"That's how he is, a charmer. He sucks people in with his charm, and then he turns ugly," Delilah said with a snort and crossed her arms staring down into her untouched tea as if it might contain the answers.

"Look, he asked for the meeting. I'm a journalist; I wanted to hear what he had to say."

"So, go on. What other lies did he tell you?" She was back to being the defiant twenty-year-old I had met at the yoga studio.

"Well, you've seen his posts on Facebook, right? The stuff he posted right after your mom's death? I think he's now taken them down because your dad rightly threatened to sue him, but he basically accused your father of killing your mother. Why would he say something like that?"

"Because he's a nutjob, because I rejected him and then my father fired him. He thinks my family ruined his life. *He* ruined his life. I've seen the posts, so what? They don't mean anything coming from a disgruntled ex-employee."

"Clearly, he was lashing out at your dad, like you said, because Hubert had fired him. But he said his firing didn't have anything to do with you. Andy said Hubert fired him because he wanted a piece of the business, to be partners, and Hubert said no."

"Okay, that part may be true," Delilah said uncrossing her arms and letting them fall to her side like she was suddenly a rag doll. "I don't know what went on between them when it came to business. I just always assumed my mother told my father that Andy was harassing me, and *that's* why he got fired. But I never asked. I didn't want to know. It was something I was not comfortable talking about with my father. We don't have that kind of relationship. My mother was my confidante, well, at least she was most of the time, when we were on good terms. And I knew when I told her, that she would take care of it, somehow, like she always did."

I knew I needed to address the elephant in the middle of the room—Tilly's affair with Andy. It had been hanging in the air between us since I walked in. It was the reason she hung up on me the other night, and now her silence about it was like a dare. She wanted to see if I would be bold enough to bring it up again.

"Well, I mean the biggest thing in the middle of all of this is the fact that Andy says he had an affair with your mother. That's a pretty big deal. If your father is a jealous person, that could have been a trigger."

I stopped at that point and remained quiet in order to give Delilah a moment to process what I was saying. At least she wasn't running out of the coffee shop like I half-expected her to. She looked angry and sick at the same time—she hung her head, covering her face with her hands. She spoke to me in a muffled voice through her fingers.

"How much more am I supposed to take? Look, my parents didn't have a perfect marriage, far from it. I mean my dad was, *is,* a difficult man. There's no doubt about that. But Andy, he's a wolf in sheep's clothing. He approached her when she was weak, vulnerable. That's the only possible explanation."

"In her defense, Delilah, if I may, as a mother myself. I'm sure she was just trying to protect you. She had a lapse in judgment. It was a brief affair as far as I know, ended by her. She probably saw his true colors, and then you came to her with what he was doing to you and her worst fears were confirmed, that he was in fact a predator, someone she needed to protect you from. She became Mama Bear. That's why she made sure he was fired. I don't blame her for not telling you. It was based on her gut instinct to protect you. What good would telling you have done if it was already water under the bridge? Parents have a lot of secrets from their children. It doesn't make them bad people; it just makes them human."

Delilah looked up at me now, her eyes red, her face tear-streaked. She took a deep breath and pulled her hair into a messy bun on the top of her head with a black hairband from her wrist. I waited for her to speak again.

"Look, lady, I don't know who you think you are coming at me with all my family's dirty laundry trying to stir stuff up. I get that you mother was murdered too, and I'm sorry about that. I really am. But I'm not you and you're not me. This is *my* mother we're talking about, and if you're not going to help me than I think I should leave."

She scooted her chair back from the table with a long scraping sound across the wooden floor and stood. I put my hands together in a pleading motion for her to stay, my head nodding at her to sit back down.

"I don't have all the answers. I do think your dad knew about the affair. And I'm trying to get to the bottom of it, just like you are. In the same way it's not fair for Andy to go on Facebook and accuse your father of killing your mother, we can't go half-cocked against Andy. It's not the right thing to do without real evidence to support it."

Delilah's mouth twisted into a frown, as if she had just lost her only ally. She plopped back down in the chair and scooted back up to the table, loudly scraping the hardwood floor again. She took a sip of her tea that was surely cold by now. The frown remained on her face as she looked me directly in the eyes.

"So, what do I do now?"

"Let me think about it. I will talk to my source at the police department and see what's happening with the investigation. I'll fill him in on your story and we'll see if he thinks its relevant. If he does, they may want you to come down to the station for an interview."

"But what if Andy finds out? What then? The more that I think about it, he could be dangerous. Whether or not he had anything to do with my mother's death, he's a pervert, a sexual deviant, *seriously*. I should show you some of his texts. Given all this, I'm not so sure I really want to stick my neck out there."

"Okay, how about this? I tell my cop friend the story without saying who you are, just that I have information that a man who worked at the restaurant, a guy who was fired, was also sexually harassing another employee. We don't have to reveal your identity right now. Just know, that at some point we might."

"Okay, I can handle that," Delilah said nodding and taking another sip of the cold tea. "Can I ask you something?"

"Sure, anything," I said not even thinking about what she might want to ask me. I was just glad that I had told her everything Andy had told me. I felt unburdened. And the more I thought about her explanation regarding what her father said, it made sense. Hubert didn't strike me as the kind of man who understood the intricacies and the control that went into a sustained pattern of sexual harassment. In his mind, when Tilly told him "sexual harassment," he may have assumed it was an actual relationship.

"You never told me who did it. Who killed *your* mother. Do you know? Was anyone ever charged?"

"Yes, he was arrested, charged, tried, convicted and sent to prison for life."

"Who was it? Who killed your mother? If you don't mind me asking? I just need to know because I want to trust somebody, I want to trust you, I really do. But first, you need to tell me this one thing." Delilah said perching expectantly on the edge of her chair awaiting my response. I studied this young woman in front of me. She was in a woman's body, but really, she was just a girl.

I hesitated. I had told very few people my story other than Adam, Louise, and Kojak. It just slipped out with Kojak one day, but we rarely ever spoke of it. Louise knew a little bit, but not everything. She was a good friend; she didn't ask too many questions, just waited for me to talk about things when I was ready.

But the last time I told a stranger my story, I got burned. That woman had pretended to need my help getting away from her abusive husband. She pretended to be my friend. She used me because she knew I was vulnerable, that her story would resonate with me and make me want to help her, which I did. But it turned out that she was not the person I thought she was. No, I couldn't trust Delilah with my precious truth. Not yet anyway.

"Nobody. Just a guy, a nobody. A drunk loser, drug user. Shot her in the head and took off. It was a robbery. Petty theft, really. It was all for nothing. No reason."

Even as the words came out of my mouth, I wasn't sure if I was talking about Roger or Clifton.

35

SNAIL MAIL

I RARELY WENT TO THE TELEVISION STATION anymore. For the most part, I worked in the field on my laptop, meeting my photographer at our shoots and going live from the scene instead of at the TV station. I could basically do everything I needed to do on my laptop as long as I had a good Internet signal, so there was little reason to go into the newsroom which had a sneaky way of distracting me and pulling me into a rabbit hole of gossip.

But when I got an email from our newsroom's administrative assistant that my mail folder was overflowing in the mail room, I decided it was time to go in and clean it out. It was part of an antiquated rule left over from the anthrax scares after 9/11 when journalists were getting letters with the white powdery poison inside. As a result, our mail had to be searched and remain in the mail room for us to pick it up afterward. I wasn't sure they were even screening it anymore, but the policy remained in place like so many other rules in companies that people never bother to change even when they didn't make sense anymore.

In their defense, we got so little actual mail now that the world relied mainly on digital communication that it wasn't a big deal to go weeks, sometimes months, without checking it. Most of my snail mail came from prisoners pleading their innocence to me, hoping I would do a story on them that would help set them free.

As I scrolled through the large accordion "NEWS" file that was arranged by a list of employees in alphabetical order looking for my letters, I found a thick stack of mail bound by a rubber band with my name on them. I grabbed the pile and started to pull them out of the rubber band one by one. As I predicted, the majority of the letters were from prisoners. My name and address were written in big, block letters with their inmate numbers and prison addresses written in the top left corners of the envelopes. Also in the file, there were a few postcards telling me about upcoming events for possible coverage that had long come and gone, making me wonder why people didn't just email me instead of wasting money on postage.

There were also a handful of sweet thank-you notes from people I had done stories with and from organizers of events where I had spoken or served as an emcee. I applauded anyone's effort these days to write actual letters. It was a rare treat to get a handwritten thank-you note. Belle had always encouraged me to send handwritten thank-you notes after receiving gifts, but as an adult, the habit had gone by the wayside after Miranda and Blake were born. Ironically, I now required *them* to write thank-you notes for gifts they received, even when I didn't do it myself.

There was one letter in the stack that caught my eye. The address was written in black block letters like the others from inmates, but the penmanship had a childlike quality to it. I scanned the top left-hand corner of the envelope and saw that it was from Penny. What a trip this little girl was. First, she catfished me into thinking I was meeting with an adult, and then she was writing me a letter at the station. While most of the mail was weeks old, Penny's letter was postmarked just the day before. I decided it was Penny's lucky day. She had, after all, helped me get Hubert's cell phone number, so, at the very least, I owed it to her to read her letter.

Dear Mrs. Arnette:

I have some important information to share with you. I didn't want to make the mistake again of

194

pretending to be someone else to try and talk with you. I now know that was a very bad idea. But I hope you understand that my intentions were good.

All I've ever wanted to do was to help you solve my great aunt's murder. Yes, I said the word "murder." I have spent a lot of time studying the situation and I do believe there is evidence that she did not take her own life. I base this not only on the facts that I have learned through good detective work, but also on things I have overheard my mother, my aunt, and my grandmother talking about.

Again, you might think eavesdropping, like pretending to be an adult online, is not a very moral thing to do. And in most circumstances, I would probably agree. But I think even you would agree that in the course of a murder investigation sometimes rules have to be broken in order to get to the truth.

So, this brings me to the reason for writing this letter. I won't say that I have solved the case, far from it. But I've been able to secure a strong piece of information that I think may help. I have been listening to the adults talk about Tilly having a romantic relationship outside her marriage—an affair. Well, I've been listening really closely over the last few days to see if I could get the name of the man she was having this relationship with, and I finally got it. His name was Andy. I have no idea who Andy is. I will try to listen harder and see if I can get more clues. But the more I learn, the more I think my great aunt having an affair gives Uncle Hubert a strong motive for murder. That's just my two cents. I'm hoping you can find this Andy person and he can help you set the record straight and figure out what happened to Aunt Tilly.

The ball is in your court now (this is something my dad says all the time). I hope you can use this information to help the police solve the case. I don't need any credit for helping behind the scenes, just in case you were wondering. For me, it's all about doing the right thing (even if I had to do a few wrong things to get here).

Please keep my identity confidential as I don't want to get in trouble with my mother or grandmother!

Yours Truly,

Penny (aka "Nancy Drew")

I refolded Penny's letter and put it back in the envelope. Obviously, she didn't tell me anything I didn't already know, but what I did learn from her letter was that the wagons were circling. The family was buzzing with theories about who killed Tilly. They didn't accept the official ruling that it was a suicide. In my experience, when families started to bang the pots and pans in these situations, the police eventually had no choice but to pay attention. It was only a matter of time before an angry family member or friend would go on television and demand that police reopen the case and find out what *really* happened to Tilly. I had seen this many times over the years. If Hubert didn't do it—and I was still not convinced that he *did* do it—just the fact that there were whispers in his family could get him targeted and hauled in for questioning; the husband was always the most obvious suspect.

I thought about the eleven-year-old girl who fashioned herself as a junior detective. It was so odd that she was interested in Nancy Drew. It was such a dated reference, but certainly a good one. I pictured myself at her age, a shy girl, my mother dead, my father in prison. I was living with my grandmother. I never would have had the courage to do what this little girl did—to reach out to a television news reporter and try to help her solve a murder case.

No, unlike Penny, I was not born with a courageous spirit. I grew into it bit by bit. But Penny, she was something else, and I had to admit that the more I thought about what she was saying, the more it made sense.

Kojak had always told me that when you were looking at a case, the simplest version was usually the truth, because the truth made sense. It's a theory called "Occam's Razor," a concept that came from a fourteenth century English Franciscan friar who basically said that the simplest explanation was probably the right one. Applying this logic, Hubert was looking pretty guilty to me.

36

CASE REOPENED

I DECIDED IT WAS TIME FOR ME TO SIT DOWN with Kojak and tell
him what I had learned about Tilly's case. He'd been very clear with
me from the beginning that investigators would not take another
look at it if I didn't give them a good reason, some strong evidence
of foul play. I had a thousand reasons for them to reopen the case,
but they were mostly circumstantial. I wasn't sure what it all meant,
but I knew there was some serious dysfunction in this family and in
their relationship to the truth.

Could Tilly have killed herself because of all the crazy stuff that
was going on in her life? Of course, she *could* have. But *did* she? I
didn't think so. There was nothing about the way this woman
operated based on what I had learned about her that made me think
she was emotionally unstable or impulsive in any way. Her obvious
love and fierce desire to protect Delilah were the key elements for
me in the argument against suicide. I didn't think she would leave
her daughter despite the fact that their relationship had been rocky
at times.

I knew this was not enough to sway Kojak. I had to have more.
So, I told him everything. I told him about meeting with Andy
twice, about how Andy said Hubert did it because he learned about
his affair with Tilly. I told him about my meeting with Hubert, how

he said he didn't know who did it, but that he also didn't believe that it was a suicide and had hired a private investigator.

I also told him that Andy had been accused of sexually harassing a waitress, and that's what some people thought got him fired, *not* this argument over the business partnership with Hubert as Andy had indicated to me. Because I had promised her anonymity, I didn't mention Delilah's name, even though her relationship to all of the players was very relevant. But I couldn't go back on my word. This was complicated, because my continuing suspicions about Delilah and her possible involvement in her mother's death were part of the big picture. I wished I had not made the promise, but I did. I told Kojak I could not give him her name until I got her permission.

Kojak sat quietly for a minute when I finished my monologue. I had spoken at a breakneck pace as not to leave anything out and not give him room to cut me off. I pictured the wheels spinning in his detective brain, doing the same thing I was doing, trying to figure out who was telling the truth and what it meant to the case. We were sitting on a bench again at Benton Road Park. This was starting to become a habit, but it felt like a good habit to be sitting here in pleasant silence with him, and a good place to meet on a warm early spring day, out in the open with bikers and joggers whizzing by in both directions paying us no mind.

"So, what about the note?" Kojak said after at least of minute of us sitting quietly on the bench with the story between us, staring off into the distance, the wheels in our respective brains churning furiously.

"I'm glad you asked me that. The note was the thing I couldn't get my head around from the very beginning. But as we've already discussed, I don't think it was a suicide note at all. I think Hubert might have found it on her computer and just assumed it was one because it fit the narrative. It fit the investigators' narrative, too. He gave you the computer, right?"

"I can't remember. I'd have to ask the field team, go back and look at the file. But that sounds right to me. I mean he pretty much gave us the go-ahead to search everything including the house and the computer."

"Maybe he wanted you to think it was a suicide note."

"Go on."

"Well, when you go through it, line by line it doesn't sound like a goodbye note to the world at all. In fact, it sounds like it's coming from a very strong woman. It sounds to me like an I'm-done-with-you note. Like she is walking away from someone after finding out something horrible about that person."

I pulled up the copy I had saved on my phone.

"It wasn't really an admission. It was just four simple words. You couldn't help yourself. My questions put you on the defensive.

'What's it to you?'

They came on the heels of my inquiry, indirect, but subtle words with a subtext that we both understood to be an accusation. It wasn't what you did, it was about what it symbolized—the darkness of a person who I didn't know, didn't want to know.

'You know what you did,' I said. To my surprise, I said it without anger, or even despair. It just came out in that moment. I hadn't planned to say it, but there it was, out in the open. And once it was out there, you only had two choices, lie or confess."

"She's obviously confronting someone about something," I said looking up from my phone after what was a fairly dramatic reading on my part.

"Okay, so who did she write it to?"

"Well, that's the quandary. It could be to Hubert; surely, he's done a bunch of really bad stuff based on what people have been saying about him around town. Or, it could have been to Andy. In the note, when she says, "I know what you did," Tilly could have been referring to his sexual harassment of her daughter. It makes total sense that this would change her view of him forever. Or it could be someone else that's not on my radar. Heck, it could even be a woman. She never uses male pronouns in the note."

"Good catch, kid. Anyone ever tell you that you could have been a detective?"

"What really confuses me if the note was meant for Andy is that Tilly apparently broke up with Andy months before this stuff with Delilah. At least I think that's how it went down. But maybe the door was still open a little crack, and when this happened, this thing with Delilah, she wanted him to know she was closing it *for good*. But here's the thing. She ends strong. This is not the letter of a woman departing the world. This is the letter of a woman finding herself again after being sucked into someone else's world. She feels like she's been fooled, that she trusted the wrong person, risked everything, and now this disgusting thing happens. Again, if we presume it is Andy, he goes after the light of her life, her one true love, her daughter. She's telling him she refuses to be fooled by him anymore."

I pulled up the screenshot and continued to read:

What's it to you?

The flippant way you said it, your inflection, made me realize that you were not the person I had fantasized about in my dreams. You were a stranger to me, a vain interloper preying on my vulnerable spirit. How could I be so wrong about a person? I've been beating myself up every single day since that moment, wondering where I went off course.

No, you didn't do it to me. Frankly, it had little to do with me. But your admission finally made me see the real you. It also did something else, something brilliant. It set me free.

-Tilly

"Death is not freedom, or at least I don't think it is, not in this case. I think she's glad to be done with the jerk, whoever he *or she* is. And here's another possibility—that she never meant to send the note. You know, how you write an ugly email response to someone just because it makes you feel good, and then you delete it before you send it? I mean it was on her computer; there was no evidence it was ever sent, right? I would be interested in finding out what Hubert thinks about the note, who he thinks it's about."

"Me too. You've got a point, kid. Good work. Now, we just need to figure out how to put this all together in a way that my team can sort out. The letter doesn't make it any clearer who may have offed her. It actually stirs the pot a bit."

"Right, and I don't pretend to have the answer, but I figured if I told you everything, you could at least get the ball rolling with the investigators. The one thing I know for sure is that this was not a suicide."

"I agree; now we just have to prove it. Switching gears for a minute, how did your meeting with Zack go?"

I could feel a little redness creeping up my neck as he said the name "Zack." I wasn't sure what it meant, but I pushed it away. I sat with the loaded question for a moment. I knew that he wanted me to say—that I was confident Zack would get to the bottom of who killed my mother, and then I could just set it aside for now and wait for the answer. Deep down I think what he really wanted to know was how my meeting with Roger went. This was just a backdoor way of asking me that question. A man whizzed by us on a racing bike in full cycling gear. He was so close I could feel the rush of air brush across my face. We both looked up, momentarily distracted.

"Do they have to do that?" Kojak asked, his hands raised in two tight fists. "I mean, come on. Who's dressed like that exercising in the middle of the day anyway? Doesn't anybody work anymore, or is it just poor shmucks like me, the public servants of the world?"

"Hey, I work too! And pretty hard if I may add."

"Okay, now changing the subject. Did my man Zack give you any info?"

"Well, he said he definitely found a connection between Roger and Clifton. He just wasn't exactly sure what it meant, kind of like we don't know what this Hubert, Andy, Delilah stuff has to do with Tilly's death."

"But he seemed to be working on it, right?"

"He did. I was actually quite impressed by his dedication and tenacity. He even pulled out the old file boxes and went through them. He gave me a photo of me and my mother that I've never seen before."

"Oh, kid," Kojak said with sympathy in his words. He put a hand around my shoulders and gave me a little squeeze. "I know that wasn't easy."

"It really wasn't as hard as I thought it would be. It felt good to see an image of me and my mom that was positive, much better than all the newspaper photos I saw of her in my grandmother's attic. For the first time, I could truly see the love she had for me. It was weirdly reassuring, especially now that I'm a mother myself."

"You got all that from a photograph?" He pulled his arm away and clapped his hands together in mock applause.

"Yes, I did. The hard part was not meeting with Zack. It was meeting with Roger," I said, giving in to his burning desire to know.

"Okay, well I didn't want to straight up ask about that. I was waiting for you to tell me."

"It was so weird to see him after all these years. I mean, he's really aged. He looks frail, like a feeble old man, not how I remembered him at all. I mean, of course I haven't seen him in thirty years, so I guess that was to be expected. It's amazing to think I was the twins' age the last time I saw him."

"And what did you talk about?"

"Not much. He wanted to know why I hadn't read his letters. He told me that everything I needed to know was in the letters. He said it was complicated. He did admit to knowing Clifton, but that's as far as we got. The guard ended the visit quickly and Roger yelled for me to come back the next day."

"And did you? Go back the next day?"

"No, I didn't. I just didn't think I could handle it. It wasn't like I felt threatened or felt like I was in the presence of evil. It was just the opposite. It was just so emotionally draining. I didn't think I could see him twice in twenty-four hours. It was so bizarre. This stranger—he radiated love toward me. Seriously, it was like a force field trying to draw me in. He was so happy to see me and wanted so badly for us to start over and have a relationship again. I honestly felt sorry for him that he thought it might be possible after all these years for us to reconnect as father and daughter."

"But I'm hearing something else in your voice; somehow he got to you?"

"He did. I didn't want to let him in. But it was hard, *impossible* really. Here I was a grown woman feeling like a little girl again who just wanted the comfort of her daddy. And he made me feel that way. Even though I barely remember him. It wasn't what he said, it was how he looked at me with pure love, sincere love. It was just too much. I mean, is it possible to love your child *and* kill her mother? I don't know. It was all I could do not to run out of that prison. I cried in the car for a few minutes and then I bucked up."

"You always do," Kojak said with his trademark sideways grin. "And you know, depending on what Zack finds, you need to consider the possibility that your dad may be innocent. I don't like to throw other cops' investigations under the bus, but forty years ago things were different. People made mistakes. Hell, people make mistakes now. But back then we didn't have fancy tools like the DNA magic we have now. I'm not saying he *is* or *isn't* guilty, but it's just something you need to prepare yourself for, for what he finds."

"Okay. I got it. I just want to stop thinking about this right now. I'm officially shelving it. We've got a murder case to solve. What's the next step?"

37

SOLACE

I WAS TRYING TO LEARN HOW to put everything aside and focus on the kids when I got home from work each night. It wasn't easy. One minute I was discussing the details of a murder case, the next minute I was expected to understand the intricacies of middle school math. Adam had always been my buffer at home, giving me the time and space to decompress after a stressful day before I jumped into mommy duties.

But I was finally learning how to do this all by myself, without Adam as my firewall. On this night, I was truly glad to be home with my children. I left Tilly and Roger at the door the second I walked into the house and saw Miranda and Blake sitting at the kitchen island, perched on stools in front of their laptops. We talked about summer plans. They both wanted to go to a sleepaway camp in Maine. There was a boy's camp and a girl's camp right across the lake from one another in a little town called Sebago—Camp Pinetops. A lot of their classmates from school attended the camp, and more importantly, Adam had gone to the camp as a boy. He had talked to them about it ad nauseum for years, so much, I was sure they were sick of hearing his memories and would never want to go there. But I was wrong. Miranda excitedly clicked through the website showing me all the activities they had, including canoeing, archery, zip-lining, sports, drama, music, and art.

Miranda wanted to go because her closest girlfriends were going, and she had heard about the dances that were held with the boy's camp every other weekend. This intrigued her almost as much as ziplining did.

Blake said he wanted to go because they had a classical piano program that his music teacher at school told him he would enjoy. He also liked the idea of trying new things like kayaking and rock climbing. In reality I knew that he wanted to go because it would make him feel closer to Adam, to walk on the same ground his father had walked on, to swim in the same lake, to sleep in the same cabins. As much as his social anxiety threatened to hold him back, his will to reconnect with a place that represented a piece of Adam was even stronger.

"Okay, so how long do you guys want to go for? They have two-week sessions all the way up to eight-week sessions. And what's really cool is that if you stick with it, in a couple of years you can eventually be counselors."

Blake looked at me wide-eyed as we scrolled through the details of the camp and the application on Miranda's laptop. We were all sitting at the kitchen island, one twin on either side of me, both leaning in close to see the screen. Things were starting to feel more normal again. I realized that my stress over Roger had put a wedge between me and my family, and I had to concentrate on letting go of that negative energy to be fully present as a parent.

"Tell me again how Daddy loved it," Blake said, needing reassurance from me about his ability to overcome his fear of going to camp, a fear not shared by his overconfident sister.

"Your dad said it was the best time of his life. They had campfires and told ghost stories. They went on treasure hunts. They used to sneak out in the canoes at night and go visit the girls across the lake."

"That sounds really dangerous," Blake said breathlessly. Miranda reached behind me and swatted him on the top of his head.

"Oh my God. You're such a baby!" She cried.

"Miranda," I said in my sternest voice as I turned my body and put my hand on her chin, tilting her little defiant face up to mine. "Why do you have to do that to him? He's *not* a baby. He's just making an observation. It *is* dangerous for boys to take out canoes on a dark lake at night. Why can't you just let him be?"

She sat quietly and then pulled her face away from my hand, crossing her arms in front of her and looking down at her lap.

"I need you to apologize to him."

"I'm sorry," she said through gritted teeth.

"You need to mean it, or at least *sound* like you mean it. And look at him when you say it."

"I'm sorry," she said with less anger, but no more sincerity. I figured this feeble apology would have to do in the moment. With everything I had on my plate, I had no more bandwidth to handle this emotional tug-of-war between my kids. That's how it always was with parenting—one minute, I felt like I had it under control, the next minute, I felt like a total failure, second-guessing everything I said and did. I gave up. I closed the laptop and shooed them off to bed, telling them we would resume the camp conversation tomorrow.

The silence in the kitchen was blissful. I loved my children to my core, but nothing sent my blood pressure up more than the two of them fighting. To be fair, it was usually Miranda who started it, making fun of her brother, pushing his buttons in a way that only a sibling truly knows how to do. Not having had a brother or a sister, this relationship was foreign to me, and it was not something I deeply understood. Adam, who had an older brother, Brian, told me that I needed to let them work it out, that Blake would never develop a tougher exterior if I fought his battles for him. Adam said Brian was relentless, picking on him constantly, until one day Adam punched Brian right between the eyes. He told me Brian never made fun of him again. While I would never advocate violence, Blake owed Miranda some serious pushback on her bullying.

I poured myself a cold glass of Pinot Grigio. This was something I rarely did on a work night, but I felt like I earned it. I had seen my convict father for the first time in decades, was trying to navigate a complicated case that might turn out to be a murder and had to referee two strong-willed children. Of all the items on my list, I felt like parenting part was the hardest, especially parenting *alone*. I never knew at any given moment if I was doing the right thing or if something I did or said would scar them for life. I picture Miranda on a therapist's couch as a young woman talking about the time her mother scolded her in the kitchen and grabbed her by her chin.

As I sipped the chilled wine and felt a warm feeling of relaxation come over my body, I absentmindedly sorted through the pile of mail Candace had left on the counter. There wasn't much, just a few bills, advertisements, catalogues, mostly junk mail. But then I saw *it*, the familiar block handwriting with the inmate number in the corner of the envelope. It was the only mail from a prisoner that came to my home instead of my office. It was postmarked two days ago. Roger must have sent it immediately after our visit.

I held it up to the light and examined it, as if I might be able to read it through the envelope. What restraint I had showed all these years in not opening and reading his letters. Who did that? What did that say about me? It would have been one thing for me not to read them as a girl, but you would think as an adult I would have wanted to go back through them, to see what he had been saying all these years. The truth was, until now, I didn't have *any* desire to read them. I so was sure they were all lies and would only bring me more heartache than I had already experienced. But now, *I was curious.* What could Roger possibly have to say to me so soon after our meeting? I knew he had more to tell me, that's why he begged me to come back the next day. So, maybe this letter *was the more.*

I stood up and steadied myself at the counter. I could hear the distant sound of one of the twins in the shower. Someone was playing music from his or her phone. I could hear the tinny stylings of a pop song bouncing off the ceiling. I poured myself another glass of wine and decided it was time for me to know the truth. I ripped open Roger's letter and sat back down to read it after taking another big sip of liquid courage.

Dear Maddie,

I can't tell you how much it meant for you to come visit me this week. I have tried to keep up with you over the years, following your television career the best I could from inside the confines of the prison walls, but it wasn't the same as seeing you in person.

You have grown into a beautiful woman, inside and out. I know you are very accomplished, and I am so very proud of you. I also know you are a great mother. How do I know? I can just tell. This will sound corny, but you have a positive energy about you and a genuine aura of integrity. I know this may not ring true to you, coming from me after all these years, but I am so grateful to God that you turned out to be the wonderful person you clearly are despite the tragedy you experienced.

I'm only sorry we didn't get a chance to visit longer. I have limited visitation time as I've just recently gotten out of solitary confinement and am working to earn back my privileges. You may wonder why I was in trouble in the first place. Well, I'll tell you. I had contraband—a cell phone. The guards smuggle them in for us and we pay them in various ways— drugs, cigarettes, money. You see, we have no Internet in prison, so a cell phone is the only way we can truly see what is happening outside the prison walls. It's a lifeline to the outside world. Just the thought of being able to Google something, to ask any question you want and get an answer, is so miraculous to me. I can't say that I am sorry for doing that, even though it was against the rules. But anyway, I digress.

The thing I most wanted to tell you that I never got to say was how sorry I am that your husband,

Adam, died. I read about it online, on my cell phone. And I know that must have been the biggest blow in your life. After what you went through as a child, losing your mother, it doesn't seem very fair that God would take away your husband, too. But as you probably know by now, the universe is anything but fair.

I know you have not read my letters all these years, so I have no confidence that you will read this one. I've decided this will be my last one. I can't make you have a relationship with me. I see that now, as clear as the slivers of the blue sky peeking through the top of my window in my cell at this very moment. The look on your face when you visited me at the prison, well, it was a combination of pity and disdain. I don't want to make you feel either of these things. You deserve to have a happy life, free of your convicted felon father.

But I would be remiss if I didn't tell you one more time what happened. It's in the other letters, in pieces, but I will tell you again as simply as possible. Here, in this letter, my last letter, I will tell you the brief version of the unvarnished truth, and you can do with it what you want.

I want to be clear that I make no excuses for my role in your mother's death, or how I handled everything. Given the circumstances I am about to tell you, I am guilty for your mother losing her life and I am where I deserve to be, but I want you to know, I never laid a hand on her. I didn't kill your mother...

I put the letter down. I folded it up, placed it back in the envelope, and shoved it in the fruit basket in the middle of the island beneath the oranges and the apples. What the hell? He didn't do it but he's *guilty?* What kind of game is he playing? As much as I wanted to know more, my brain was a foggy mess, thick with confusion, lies, half-truths, and wine. I realized I wasn't in the right frame of mind to accept what Roger was about to tell me in his letter. I had read enough for now. While curiosity gnawed at my gut, the familiar feeling of outrage toward Roger pushed it away. I would not be seduced by his deceit.

"Mom!" Miranda yelled from the top of the stairs. "Blake used all the hot water. How am I supposed to take a shower now? He's just like a girl. He spends twenty minutes in there listening to his music. It's not fair!"

I sat in the kitchen thinking about all the things that weren't fair in life—my mother being murdered, Adam dying, Tilly dying. The list of really big things was so endless that I didn't feel very sympathetic about Miranda's first world problem at the moment. But I knew that if I didn't handle it right away, she would explode, and that would ruin everyone's night, *including mine.*

"Coming," I yelled back, not knowing exactly what I was going to do about it. I couldn't magically fill up the hot water heater again. It would take about an hour. I told Adam years ago that we needed a more modern system. He had laughed and said it just wasn't a priority, that houses were money pits and that we had to pick and choose which hole to put our money in. So, we chose the remodeled kitchen hole, the screened-in porch hole, the hardwood floors hole, the updated bathrooms hole, and unfortunately, *not* the hot water heater hole. I was regretting this now.

As I climbed the stairs to Miranda's room, I started thinking about all the things we let go in life while prioritizing others, how these decisions were often made on the fly, on a whim, not based on well thought-out, critical consideration. Somehow, I had never prioritized moving past my mother's death. Sure, I *thought* I had dealt with it, moved past it, learned to cope, but in reality I hadn't done any of these things. I had carried it around with me my entire life like a bowling ball that weighed me down everywhere I went. Yet, I refused to part with it. And when life got hard, that bowling ball got even heavier, affecting my ability to control my emotions and make good decisions. Why had I been so stubborn when Adam encouraged me to go to counseling, to get it out, to deal with it? I told him I didn't need counseling because I had him. *I was wrong.*

I idealized Adam after his death, which is a natural thing to do when someone you love dies. I recognized it in the way I retold stories about him, leaving out the bad parts and augmenting the good parts. But Adam was a fixer—for better or for worse— he wanted to fix me, to make me whole. And what I had really needed from Adam was empathy, someone to listen to me and to understand my pain. Looking back now, I realized that he had never honestly been that person for me. Emotional insight was not his thing, and now, I was paying the price for never having talked in any depth about the very thing that defined my whole life, that set me on this path of looking for justice for other people, people like Tilly, as a way of healing myself.

"Miranda," I called as I reached the landing at the top of the stairs. I heard the shower running and her singing off-key to a Taylor Swift song.

"She was wrong," Blake said stomping down the hall in my direction. His wet hair wrapped in a towel turban on top of his head. He wore a blue fuzzy robe and flip-flops. "The hot water came back. I didn't take it all. Why are girls so mean?"

With that, Blake buried his turban in my stomach and wrapped his arms around my waist. I held him in the dimly lit hallway, swaying unconsciously to the music coming from the bathroom. I wished I had the answers to all their questions. I also wished I had the answers to mine.

38

SOCIAL CUES

KOJAK WAS IGNORING ME. I knew it had only been a day, and he assured me they were reopening Tilly's case, but I wanted to know exactly what was going on. It was killing me not knowing. I texted him a few times, and he told me to be patient. But patience wasn't something easily located in my toolbox.

One of the talents I did have in my toolbox was being a good online researcher. The first place I always went to learn more about someone that I was investigating was to their social media accounts. I discovered that most people gave themselves away in their posts, even if they didn't intend to. You could learn a lot about a person by what he or she posted, especially from their photos. The very act of posting made people vulnerable to scrutiny, good and bad, and the more vulnerable they were, the more feedback they got. And feedback equals love, right? Or, at least, that's what people believe.

So, while I was sitting in front of my computer, allegedly looking for new content for "Amazing Animal Tales," I decided to peek at Andy Parnell's social media.

I knew he was divorced and had a young daughter. As I scrolled through his pictures, it looked like his account was mostly set to private. But there were a few photos of his goldendoodle, Chestnut, the dog I had seen at his cabin the day I was there, and a few photos of his daughter, Emmy. In most of the pictures he was kneeling beside her with his arms protectively wrapped around Emmy's tiny waist. She had a head full of brown curls, a face full of freckles and a sweet, gap-toothed smile. In several of the photos Chestnut lay at their feet. They looked like an all-American happy family. A man, his daughter, and his dog. The only thing missing was his wife.

I dug a little bit deeper, going as far back as I could in Andy's account. Men weren't very good about scrubbing their exes from their social media. They either didn't know how to do it, were too lazy to do it, or they simply didn't care. Finally, after scrolling all the way back to 2009, I found what I was looking for—his ex-wife. Her name was Liz Parnell. The photo was slightly grainy, probably taken on an early version of a smart phone, or maybe on a real camera and then screenshotted. They were sitting in the bed of a red pickup truck with the tailgate open. She was tanned, with long brown curls like Emmy's, a round face, and smiling blue eyes. She also had the same smattering of freckles as her daughter. She wore jean cutoff shorts, a plain white T-shirt, and cowboy boots. Her legs were casually draped over Andy's. He looked pretty much the same then as he did now, handsome in a dangerous way, only a little younger and slightly thinner. They were both beaming in the photo—in love and proud of it.

I then clicked on Liz Parnell's name and went to her page. I wasn't sure exactly what I would find, but I knew I was likely to find some insight. In my line of work it wasn't unusual for criminals to out themselves online—like the drug dealer who had a photo of himself holding a fanned stack of $100 bills in his hand, or the gang member who made gang symbols with his hands and showed off his gang tattoo. But as far as I knew Liz Parnell was no criminal. I expected the clues I was looking for to be far more subtle.

Her page was also set to private for the most part. I knew I was only seeing a fraction of her posts because most of them were much older, and there were big gaps in the timeline. But one thing I did notice was a fundraiser she was promoting for the local domestic violence shelter. As I scrolled down through the post, which was about two years old, something caught my eye. It was buried in the third paragraph.

It read:

> Survivors of domestic violence need to stick together and help one another. I am a survivor of emotional abuse, and without the help of this organization I would not have been able to get out safely and get back on my feet, to regain the confidence that I now have as a woman who believes I deserve to be treated with respect in all aspects of my life.

I looked closely at the date. The post was from 2016. She had to be talking about Andy. Emmy looked to be about five or six years old today, which meant in 2016 she would have been two or three. I decided I needed to talk to Liz to learn more about Andy. Maybe the police would think about reaching out to her, but maybe not. If I learned something from her that I thought was relevant to the case, I would tell Kojak. I clicked on messaging and sent her a quick note. Sometimes, this felt like a fishing expedition, but since no one had home phones anymore, and it wasn't that easy to find someone's cell phone number, this tended to be the easiest and fastest way to reach people.

> Liz, my name is Maddie Arnette. I'm a television reporter for Channel 8 News. Lately, I've been looking into a case that involves the death of a woman your ex-husband, Andy, used to work for, at her husband's restaurant. I was just wondering if we could chat, off-the-record. I'm trying to learn more about the people who worked for her restaurant and see if they might have any insight into what happened.

I knew this was a risky move. What if Liz and Andy were friends now? They were clearly co-parenting. Maybe they had put all their bad stuff behind them, and she would immediately contact him when she got my note. It was a risk, but it was one that I was willing to take for Tilly's sake. I reread the note before hitting send, making sure it didn't sound too accusatory, just curious.

Then, as an afterthought, I clicked on Liz's friend list assuming it would also be set to private. Surprisingly, it was wide open. Not surprisingly, Andy was *not* on her friend list. Then, as a lark, I tried Tilly's name, and up popped up the beautiful profile photo of Tilly, her unmistakable dark hair, porcelain skin, and ruby red lips staring back at me as my brain did somersaults trying to figure out exactly what this meant. Sure, a lot of people were *casual* friends on Facebook—but friending the new lover of your abusive ex? It all seemed a little weird. I filed this note for later, thinking how I needed to remember to talk it through with Kojak.

Then, I decided to take a look at Delilah's social media again. Unlike Andy and Liz, Delilah's page was wide open, which didn't surprise me for a young woman. Although, based upon the fact that she had accused Andy of stalking her, it seemed like she would be a little bit more conscious of protecting her privacy.

Delilah's photos were typical of most twentysomethings—beauty shots of herself in sunglasses holding a coffee cup with the natural light at just the right angle bathing her face in an angelic glow, shots of intricate yoga poses, deep quotes from poets about life's universal truths. Around the time of her mother's death, she had posted nostalgic family photos of herself, Tilly, and Hubert throughout the years. She wrote several glowing tributes to her mother that were full of emotion and grief. Her banner above her profile picture was a neon sign that read "SHINE" in hot pink lights against what appeared to be a dark desert backdrop. Her profile photo was a picture of her perched on a rock, wearing hiking clothes, her long, dark hair blowing in every direction as she looked up at the blue sky that contained a few thin, feathery white clouds.

It occurred to me that Delilah, like me, was an only child, and not just an only child, but an only daughter. I thought of how fiercely she had defended Hubert to me when we met at the yoga class, and how her suspicions about Andy served only to remove the blame from her father *and from her*. I wondered if I had been older when my mother was killed if I would have immediately jumped to Roger's defense instead of turning against him in my adolescence, too immature and petulant to understand the possible nuances of the situation. I pushed the thought aside and kept scrolling.

Nothing unusual stood out to me about Delilah's page. She was a typical young woman doing typical young-person things online— baring her soul, sharing deceivingly candid photos only when she looked her best, and trying to sound wiser than her age by quoting dead poets.

But then I refreshed the page one more time and something caught my eye. She had just posted a series of photos from an outing with friends from the night before that only popped up when I reloaded the page. It looked like they were at a bar. Everyone was gathered around a table, holding up drinks, toasting one another, their free arms draped over the shoulders of the people next to them. There was a familiarity among the group, a genuine fondness for being together. In the background, it looked like a typical crowded bar with people tightly packed on a lit-up dance floor while a band played behind them.

The caption beneath the photos read: "My first night out with my besties since my mom passed. I am lucky to have such good friends to help me get through this. I don't know what I would do without you guys. Love you so much!"

In each photo, Delilah was with different combinations of friends, sometimes just two; in others she was with three or four people. They were mostly women, but there were a few men as well. They all looked slightly buzzed, faces red, hair askew, smiles too wide. They appeared to be Delilah's age. I assumed they were friends from school or work.

There were about twelve photos, and I studied each one intently, not knowing exactly what I was looking for, but knowing there was a chance I would find something interesting. While I didn't understand Delilah hosting this raucous celebration so soon after her mother's death, I also knew that people grieved in different ways. How would I have reacted if my mother had been killed when I was twenty instead of when I was three? I didn't know; I couldn't know. I was not going to judge Delilah for the way she chose to manage her grief. Unless maybe it really wasn't grief at all. Could it be relief? Could their relationship have deteriorated to the point that she wanted her mother dead?

As I flipped through the photos for a third time, I was about to give up finding anything insightful or out of the ordinary when I spotted *him*. He was in the background of one of the photos where Delilah stood between two of her girlfriends. Their heads were tilted together, beer bottles raised in the air in front of them, their mouths parted in what looked like mid-song. Behind them, a little to the right, on the edge of the dance floor was a familiar face. *It was Andy.* He was standing maybe fifteen feet behind the women. He was also holding a beer and looking directly at the camera. He had a huge, knowing smile on his face, like he had a secret that he wasn't about to share.

I clicked on the photo and zoomed in with my fingers, trying to determine whether he was *with* the group, or whether he was just there, an unwanted predator lurking in the background. Either way, it was no coincidence.

There were only two explanations: Delilah was lying to me, and she and Andy really were a couple, which then cast doubt on everything she had told me, and even put her in line to have some part in her mother's death. The other possibility was that Andy was stalking her, that he had never stopped harassing her, and this was just another one of his sick attempts to try and connect with her. But the boldness and casualness of his gaze in the background of the photo led me toward the former conclusion. Had Delilah invited him there?

At that moment, I heard the familiar "ping" of a message arriving on my Facebook page. I clicked on the icon and saw that Liz Parnell had gotten back to me.

"I'd be happy to talk to you," it read. "But you need to keep my name out of it. I've had enough trouble with him, and we have a daughter together. We share custody. I can't get publicly involved. Call me."

I quickly scribbled down the number in my notebook. Then I saved the photo of Andy in the background of Delilah's big night. I would have to get back to that later. I wasn't exactly sure what it meant, but I knew that it was *important*. It was something I would also share with Kojak when the time was right, even though he didn't seem to be sharing too much with me at the moment.

⸺

"Liz, hi, this is Maddie Arnette. Thanks for taking my call."

"No problem. But again, you *can't* use my name. I just can't get involved, for Emmy's sake. She loves her dad, and he's actually a really good father considering what a shitty husband he was. He loves her. We've gotten to a civil place where we are co-parenting pretty well. I just can't let anything disrupt that."

"I totally get it. I'm just looking for background stuff. I will keep your name out of it. One hundred percent. You have my word."

"Thank you. I appreciate that. I've been watching you for years. I really admire your work. That's why I agreed to talk to you."

"Thanks so much. That means a lot to me. Like I said, I won't let you down. I guess I'll dive right in. Do you have any idea why Andy was fired by Hubert Dawson?"

"He really didn't get into it too much with me, but he said it had something to do with wanting a share of the business and Hubert wasn't having any of that. Hubert is a pretty, how shall I say it? He's not a very diplomatic guy. It's his way or the highway. When Emmy was born, he wouldn't even give Andy a day off. Made him come right back to work the next day after being up with me at the hospital all night long. Said we'd be fine without him, *that a man's place was at work.*"

"So, they kind of had a difficult relationship."

"You could say that. I mean it wasn't always that way. When Hubert first hired Andy, he was young, never had a head chef job before, just line assistants at chain restaurants like Hooters and Applebee's. This was a chance for him to really build something of his own. Hubert basically let him take over the menu, and with every location they added, Andy got to tweak it, update it, and make it his own. He's actually a very talented cook. But I think Hubert felt like he gave him too much power, like he was getting too big for his britches, and you need to understand: *It was Hubert's kingdom.*

He didn't like someone else getting all the attention. And Andy was definitely getting attention. He won some awards for his ribs, they featured him in the newspaper, on the local news, and in a couple of online food blogs."

I pondered this balance of power between these two men who both appeared to be classic narcissists. I could see how the shifts in their business and their roles created mounting tension between them. Most men were not good at sharing the spotlight, and they were equally as inept at sharing power. Imagine them sharing a woman like Tilly? Hubert and Andy seemed to me to be the kind of men who sucked all the air out of a room when they entered.

I decided I had to go for it and ask Liz *the money question.* Even if she was offended by it, I might learn something from her reaction.

"This might sound indelicate, but did you know that Andy had an affair with Hubert's wife, Tilly?"

"Oh, that's a fair question. It was after we separated. Now, don't get me wrong. He is a true-blue womanizer; there was always a woman on the side before we parted ways. But the thing with Tilly, it came later. And to tell you the truth, I think he met his match in her. She was a little bit older, wiser, beautiful, confident. I think maybe for the first time in his life he was really *in love.* And because of that, he didn't walk all over her like he did with me. And then she dumped him, and he was *devastated.* At first, I thought it was just his pride that was hurt, but then I realized the poor fool thought she was going to leave Hubert for him.

Kind of ironic that I grew into my confidence after I left Andy. I became the woman he saw in Tilly: strong, willful, independent. But it was too late for us, so I guess that's why he was drawn to her. She was something else, something special. I have to admit. You couldn't be around her and not be impressed."

"How did you know all this? Did he tell you about it?"

"Not directly, but we had this old iPad when we were together. I totally forgot about it. Shoved it in a closet. Powered it up one day and realized the messages on the iPad were connected to his iPhone. I tried not to read them—I really did. I would open it up and just glance at a few and then slam it shut and put it in a drawer. To tell you the truth, they made me pretty mad. I wasn't jealous so to speak, but just confused as to why we couldn't make it work, but he could with *her* even though I understood how amazing she was.

I tried to stop snooping, but I could hear that damn thing pinging, telling me there was a new message, and I was like, *What's the harm in reading just one more?* So, I kept reading. After a while, I couldn't control myself. As soon as I dropped Emmy off at school, I would run home and pull it out of the drawer, curl up in my big armchair in the den with a cup of coffee and read all about their love affair. I was kind of living vicariously through them—thinking about the love affair he and I should have had that never materialized. But I also understood it in a way because Tilly was the whole package— beautiful, smart, confident. I knew what I was doing was wrong, but it was like I was someone else. I *had* to know what was happening between them."

"I get it. The temptation was too great not to look. I don't think very many people wouldn't have looked. It sounds like it was pretty compelling."

"Oh, it was. Andy fashions himself a charmer. And I guess whatever he's got does work on some women—*a lot of women,* actually. I was surprised it worked on Tilly, though. She was so much smarter than all the hoochie mamas he cheated on me with. But I guess maybe it was real love on both their parts. I honestly think she was the brains behind the restaurants and Hubert was just the face of it with the big megaphone trying to get attention and bossing everyone around. From what I understood, his staff doesn't care for him much, but they loved Tilly. She was kind and fair. And I wasn't around her too much, but when I was, she had this really incredible quality that made you feel like you mattered, like in that moment you were the *only* person who mattered."

"Okay, this is going to sound kind of weird, but did you ever know Andy to be out of line with women at work, to make unwanted advances or send inappropriate texts? Not Tilly, but any other women."

"You mean like sexual harassment? That sounds like something he might do."

I was afraid of giving up Delilah's identity, but I wanted to get down to the core of who this guy was, and I knew Liz was the best person to take me there. But I still couldn't do it. I couldn't break my promise to Delilah even if I wasn't completely convinced of her credibility. I decided to keep her name confidential, but at the same time see what Liz knew.

"Yes, exactly, like sexual harassment."

"Here's the thing. Andy wouldn't have seen it that way. He has such a big ego that if a woman looks in his direction, he thinks she likes him and wants to have sex with him. So, in his mind, it wouldn't have been harassment. He probably really believed the women he did this to liked him. He can be subtle too. So, if he opened with: "You look nice today," and the woman responds "Yes," he thinks he's got an in, that she's on board with it. And then he starts talking dirty. That's how he operates, but I guarantee you he'd put his hands on a stack of Bibles and swear on Emmy's life he wasn't sexually harassing anyone."

"Pardon me, but that's really screwed up."

"You're telling me. He messed with my head *for years.* Made me think I was stupid, that I couldn't survive without him, that no one would want me. It's amazing that I stayed with him as long as I did. He tried to get back with me a few times after he left. I think he was tired of sleeping on friends' couches; that's why he eventually moved to Verdine's cabin. But I rejected him just like he had slowly rejected me with his words all those years. Once Tilly came into his life, that all stopped. After that, he only contacted me about things having to do with Emmy."

"Did he ever hurt you?"

"Physically, no. He had a temper. He got mad and said awful things, but mostly he just emotionally abused me. He cut me off from my family and friends, talked trash about them until they didn't want to come around anymore. And we shared a car, a car that he drove every single day, so I had to walk anywhere I wanted to go. I had no money other than what he gave me: fifty dollars a week. Can you imagine that? It was a real shit-show. I was young and foolish when we first got together. I was pretty much right out of high school. *I was so in love.* But after I had Emmy, I knew I couldn't raise a child in that environment. I didn't want her to grow up thinking this was how women deserved to be treated."

There was something about the way she said "I was so in love" that made me pause. I wasn't convinced that love was gone. In fact, despite the way he had treated her, it sounded to me like she might have taken him back if Tilly hadn't gotten in the way. It also sounded like Andy wasn't the only one smitten with Tilly. Liz also seemed to be a big fan.

"So, he just let you go?"

"Not really. Like everything else with Andy, I knew it had to be *his* idea. So, I waited until he was head over heels with another one of his waitresses, and I told him that I wanted more children. I stopped taking care of myself, stopped showering, gained some weight, and really let myself go. I did it on purpose to make him not want me. But I was also pretty depressed by that point and didn't have the energy to do anything when it came to my appearance. *It worked.* One day he told me we were over, told me to get out and take Emmy with me, that he didn't want to be tied down. Little did he know I had my bags packed already in the trunk of the car. I went straight to my parents' house in the country. Believe it or not, he never looked back. We hired a mediator to handle the divorce. There really weren't any assets, I didn't want anything of his, and my parents were helping me out financially, helping me get back on my feet. All he wanted was time with Emmy. I was surprised by this, but she was becoming a person, a little girl who communicated with him and called him 'Daddy,' and I guess he did have something inside of him, some love for her that he never showed to me. So, that's where we are today. We split custody, although I have primary physical custody, and for the most part he leaves me alone. Since we each have her fifty percent of the time, there's no child support. I didn't ask him for alimony. I don't need his money. I started my own business with my parents' help, bought my own house, my own car. It all worked out. I mean, I wish things had been different. I still believe in marriage, that kids should be raised by two parents, but sometimes love just isn't enough. And even if I had wanted to try and work things out with him, I could never have competed with Tilly."

"Wow, that sounds like it was a tough journey. I'm so glad you got out and landed on your feet. You've been so helpful. I really appreciate your insight and the background. Let me ask you one more thing. You know how Tilly died, right?"

"Yes, awful. I heard she shot herself in her driveway in broad daylight. So sad. You just never know what is going on in someone's life that drives them to such despair. I guess maybe the breakup with Andy hit her harder than she realized. Maybe if she couldn't live her life authentically, the way she really wanted to live it, then it just wasn't worth it, all the pain. You know?"

"Well, some people believe she didn't."

"Didn't what?"

"Didn't kill herself, that maybe she was *murdered*."

"Wow, that's really out there. Who would want to do something like that? I mean, like I said, everybody loved her from what I understood. I think people around here just like to wag their tongues. It was suicide, alright. That's what the police ruled it. Wait, are you asking me this because you think Andy had something to do with it?"

I wasn't sure why I was asking her. By the way Liz told her story, *she* had more of a motive to kill Tilly than just about anyone else. In Liz's mind Tilly had taken away everything from her—the man she loved, the father of her child.

Liz's voice bordered on hysterical like I had duped her into going down this road which was not my intention at all. Clearly, she still had a lot of feelings for Andy. Him possibly being involved in a murder was not something she was prepared to believe.

"No, not at all. I just want to get your take on the situation. Do you think Andy is capable of something like that? Of violence?"

"Andy? No way. He's all bark. Never laid a hand on me. I can't imagine him hurting Tilly after the way he talked to her in those texts. Even when they broke up, he just begged her to take him back, not a cross word. He wouldn't hurt a fly. Seriously, I wouldn't let my daughter *near* him if I thought he was capable of physical violence. No way. Now, Hubert, on the other hand, he's another story. I wouldn't put *anything* past that man. But I still think you're going down the wrong path. People around here think suicide is a sin; that's why they don't want to believe it and are running their mouths about some bullshit that makes no sense. Suicide is a tragedy for everyone involved. We should have compassion for the victim and her family."

She sounded to me like a woman who was trying to talk herself into something. I knew that tone because it was the same one I had used in my life many times. I had convinced myself Roger killed my mother; nothing seemed capable of changing my mind—not even cold, hard facts. I realized that we all created our own beliefs about people and situations to allow us to carry on, and sometimes our constructs were mere fantasies. I didn't know for sure in this moment who killed my mother or Tilly, but I knew that I needed to get to the bottom of both cases in order to live freely with truth, *not fantasy*, as my guide.

Could Liz Parnell be covering up for her ex, the man she still loved? I looked at the photograph of them again in the back of the pickup truck. They were young, innocent, naïve, in love. Or, I wondered, could she be protecting *herself*?

39

GRAY MATTERS

I COULDN'T GET THE CONVERSATION WITH LIZ out of my head. It was like she was describing two completely different people when she talked about Andy. On one hand, he had been a controlling, isolating, emotionally abusive husband and a womanizer who demeaned her throughout their marriage. On the other hand, he had been head-over-heels in love with Tilly and appeared to be a devoted and engaged father to Emmy. Her positive comments about him and their early loved lingered in the air above my head, begging me to go down another road. Was it possible that Liz had it out for Tilly, that Tilly had dashed her one hope of working things out with the husband that she still seemed to be in love with?

My experiences as a journalist over the years taught me that people were never black-and-white, but were instead full of gray areas that blurred together. Yet, I was still surprised by someone like Andy who carried such contradictions, and I was also surprised by Liz's apparent unrequited love for her ex, despite the way she said he had treated her.

I was sitting on my porch drinking coffee, waiting for Janie to text me with the day's assignment when my phone rang. I assumed it was either Janie or Kojak. I had texted him right after I did the deep dive into Delilah's and Andy's social media accounts to tell him what I had learned. But purposely, I didn't tell him *everything*. I just teased him a little to make sure he would have to call me to learn the rest.

Got some news after doing social media research.
Delilah and Andy may not be adversaries after all.
Also talked to Andy's ex, interesting stuff there.

I was stunned he had not called me right away given the gravitas of my message. That was not like him. I assumed he must be working on something much more important to be ignoring me considering the bait I had sent him in the text.

So, when I looked down at the phone and saw that it was Andy calling, I was more than surprised. I immediately wondered if I had been double-crossed by Liz. Did she run to him and tell him everything about our conversation? How was I going to explain my snooping to this man who had been nothing but kind and candid at our last meeting? I didn't think Liz would do that based on my preliminary assessment of her. But I didn't have a lot of time to process this thought. It was either pick up Andy's call, or let it go to voicemail.

"Maddie Arnette here."

"Maddie, it's Andy, Andy Parnell from the restaurant. Well, used to be from the restaurant. You know what I mean. Keep forgetting that's my *old life*."

"Hey Andy. What can I do for you?" I said, trying to sound as casual as possible, as if Liz had not just laid bare his entire adult life to me, complete with his major character flaws.

"Well, something very weird is going on. I don't want to talk about it over the phone, but let's just say I think Hubert and Delilah are ganging up against me. *Setting me up.*"

"In what way?" My thoughts were now racing, trying to decipher what he was telling me.

"Like telling lies about me and stuff, to the police. The police came to see me about Tilly. Apparently, I was right. She might not have killed herself. That's what they implied, at least. I guess they saw those Facebook posts I made, the really stupid ones, and it made them start looking at the case in a different light. Anyway, I really need to see you. Can we meet?"

I remembered Louise's stern warning about meeting Andy by myself the last time, the warning I had ignored. This time, considering his real intentions might be raking me over the coals for my probing of Liz, I decided I would not meet with him alone again. I would take Louise up on her earlier offer and bring her along as my safety net. Andy didn't need to know this.

He and I agreed to meet in an hour at the closest public library on the third floor. It was his choice, and it seemed kind of odd, but I believed nothing could happen in a public place especially with Louise in tow. I texted her right after I got off the phone with Andy, and she enthusiastically agreed to join me with a smile emoji and a few floating hearts plus a kiss. I figured she must have been in the middle of something very tedious when she got my text for her to reply so quickly. And she was—she was making wedding seating arrangements for a couple who had so many family feuds that it was like putting together a five-thousand-piece puzzle. She told me she would be right over.

⌒

"Why the heck did he want to meet here?" Louise said waving her hand at the red brick mid-century library. "I don't remember the last time I was in a library. It's kind of creepy actually."

"Louise, not everyone buys their books on Amazon or downloads audiobooks. Some people still come to the library and check out *real books*. It's not that archaic."

"Whatever," she said, waving me off like I was talking nonsense.

It was the middle of the afternoon, and the library was almost empty, with the exception of a few people using the public computers to access the Internet. I imagined the library was always desolate when almost everything could be read online from home now. Louise was right. Who did come to the library these days?

We rode the elevator to the third floor as Louise bounced back and forth on her toes with nervous energy. I explained to her that she was just there for backup. That she was not to say a word, just to listen discreetly and then rescue me if things got heated.

"I got it," she said with a grin. I had seen that grin before and I knew it meant—*I'll do my best, but I'm not making any promises.* In truth, for all her appearances of being scatterbrained and full of frenetic energy, Louise was very smart and surprisingly capable in a crisis. We had been through a lot together, and I knew I could always count on her.

As we walked to the stacks at the back of the third floor, Louise hummed what sounded like the soundtrack of a scary movie.

"Stop it," I said turning to shush her, but I did it with a smile, and she couldn't help herself. She kept it up. That is, until Andy turned the corner of the aisle and almost ran right into us.

"Oh, hey, it's you," Andy said looking at me, and then over my shoulder. "And you, again." He said nodding in a not-very-friendly way to Louise.

"Yes, this is my friend, Louise. We were having lunch when you called, so she just came along since we were together." I had to stop myself from overexplaining. Clearly, I had brought her because I didn't want to meet a man alone in the back corner of a library. I motioned for Louise to sit at the next table. She slumped away in a mock show of being banished, sat down, and picked up a magazine. I could tell she was doing her best to pretend to be engrossed in an article. But she was a bad actor.

Andy and I sat down at the next table. He looked agitated, anxious, *unhinged.* He kept running his hand through his hair and tapping out a drumbeat on his knee with his other hand. It was making me nervous just looking at him.

"So, what's this about Hubert and Delilah ganging up on you?"

"Well, you know I said all that stuff about him on Facebook. *Pretty bad stuff.*"

"Yep, you accused him of *murder.* I can understand why he may not be very fond of you."

"Right, true. And he wasn't very fond of me before that. I mean the whole failed partnership thing, and the thing with his wife."

"You mean the affair, *that thing.*"

"Yes, that thing," Andy said bowing his head and putting both hands up to his face.

"So, what's going on now, what's happened?"

"Well, there's one more thing I didn't tell you," Andy said dropping his hands and looking up at me. Out of the corner of my eye, I could tell that Louise had stopped turning the pages of the magazine. She was silent and completely riveted by what we were saying. But it didn't matter, Andy was so focused on what he was telling me, he wasn't paying her any mind.

"Okay, go ahead."

"It's really embarrassing, and I guess kind of weird. I just need you to help me. This has all gotten really messed up. I don't know what's going on or who I can trust."

"Okay, well first you have to tell me what it is you didn't tell me."

"So, you know Delilah. We kind of had a thing going after Tilly broke up with me."

"A thing, like an affair?"

"Like a flirtation. We'd been dancing around each other for months. Tilly found out and she was really upset, understandably. So, Delilah, well, she lied to her, she told her I was harassing her because she was afraid to tell her mom the truth. Delilah panicked. She *knew* about my affair with Tilly. I told her the whole thing, and she just thought it would upset her mother so much to think that *we* might be getting together, so she lied, said I liked her and was coming on to her, but she didn't like me back. I'm telling you, it's so twisted. So, that's why I got fired, for real. That's the truth. Tilly went to Hubert and told him I was harassing his daughter, and he canned me. And I was mad, very mad, about the whole thing. I was mad at all of them. I was mad at Tilly for leaving me and then selling me out. I was mad at Hubert for not following through on our partnership deal, and I was mad, *so mad,* at Delilah for throwing me under the bus. So, I did something stupid—I sent Hubert an anonymous note telling him about Tilly's affair with me. I really wanted to hurt him, but what I didn't realize is that I was actually hurting Tilly, that my note would send Hubert over the edge. That's why he killed her, that's why he did it, because of my note. I made up the whole thing about him finding out from an email from the hotel chain. It was really all my fault. So, when the police came to interview me, I just freaked out. I didn't know what to tell them because I look really bad in this whole thing."

Andy buried his head back in his hands and appeared to be crying. His muffled, high-pitched sobs were getting louder and louder. I looked over at Louise who was shaking her head in an I'm-not-buying-this gesture. I was trying to process everything he was saying, especially the part about Delilah *knowing* her mother had an affair with Andy. I thought back to her award-winning performance at our meeting where she acted like *I* was the one who told her about the affair.

"Andy, I hear what you're saying. But you didn't make Hubert *do* anything. If he killed his wife, that's on him. You can't make someone kill a person. Why do you think they're ganging up on you now?"

"Because yesterday, out of the blue, Delilah texts me and says she and some friends are going out to celebrate, that she's trying to get beyond the grief, and she invited me to come. It's weird because we had never gone anywhere together before, just hung out at the restaurant, by ourselves after hours and I don't even know her friends. But *I'm into this girl*, as weird as it sounds, even though I was also in love with her mother. I know it's screwed up, believe me, *I know.*"

He stopped, suddenly, maybe looking for some judgment in my eyes. I kept my face stoic, my eyes expressionless, focused on his face. I was well-trained in this department. He continued.

"So, I get there. And everything's cool. Her friends are nice, we're drinking, cutting up, taking some pictures. And the next thing I know, I'm at the bar getting another round of drinks for everyone and I turn around and see Hubert standing behind me like a brick wall. I practically run into him and spill the beers. He just stands there, staring me down. Finally, he yells over the music: 'What the hell are you doing around my daughter, you piece of crap? You better stay far away from her or you're a dead man.' The next thing I know, he's dragging me out of the bar by the collar of my jean jacket.

I dropped all four beers, they shattered at my feet soaking both of us. This doesn't stop him moving for one second. Just hauls me out the front door of the bar and basically slings me into the parking lot where I rolled a good ten feet in the gravel before I hit the curb."

I noticed a large red mark on Andy's forehead now. He took his hand and raised his hair so I could get a better look at it. As he turned in my direction, I could also see a long red gash that ran down the side of his left cheek. He opened his palms and held them up to me revealing scrapes maybe from hitting the ground or the beer bottles shattering in his hands.

"She *set me up*. I know she did."

"Why would she do that?"

"I don't know. I really don't. But then I get this visit from a detective today who says he wants to talk to me about an allegation that I sexually harassed Delilah Dawson. I tell him that I didn't do it. That it wasn't true. Then he asks me why I was stalking her at the Dancing Barn last night. I'm like dude, you've got to be kidding me. *She invited me there.* He then tells me, that's not what she's saying and that's not what her father is saying. Hubert told the police Delilah called him and told him I was lurking around her and her friends at the bar. That's why they came; they were called.

So, next thing I know the cops start asking me questions about Tilly during this interview, about her death. It's all just really fucked up. I mean, I've done some bad things, I get it. But I certainly didn't *kill* anyone."

I was having trouble taking in everything that Andy was saying. Delilah had seemed sincere when she told me that Andy had sexually harassed her. Yet, I also had an uneasy feeling that Delilah hadn't told me the whole story. And Liz made it seem like it wasn't out of the question that he would do something like that, even if he didn't see it as harassment. But at this point, someone had to be lying. And I had no idea who it was. Clearly, Andy had been in some sort of a scuffle, but was he the *victim* or the *antagonist*? I needed more information to make sense of it all.

Then, my phone rang. I cursed myself for not muting it in the library. I half-expected an old-school librarian with a tight bun and glasses perched on the bridge of her nose to come over and shush me. As I silenced the ringer, I looked at the name on the screen. It was Kojak.

"Andy, excuse me for a second. I have to take this."

I walked away from Andy into one of the aisles of books so that I could have some privacy and not draw attention to the fact that I was answering my phone in the library of all places.

"Where the hell have you been?" I scolded him when I answered.

"Busy solving a murder case, kid. Where are you? Why are you whispering?"

"I'm in the library."

"The library?"

"I know. It's not my normal hangout. But I was meeting someone here. You'll never guess who and what he told me."

"I have no idea. But make it fast. I got news to tell you."

"It's Andy, Andy Parnell. Chef Andy. And he says—"

"You're at the library with *him*? You're there with him *now*?"

"Yes, why?"

"Don't ask any questions. Just do as I tell you. Leave *now*."

I ended the call and ran back down the aisle to get Louise. I had no idea what Kojak knew, or what he was trying to tell me. But I could sense from the intensity of his voice that he felt like I might be in danger. I couldn't believe I had been so stupid to put Louise in this situation. I sprinted out of the stacks and practically ran into the table where she was still sitting. She was no longer pretending to read the magazine. She was scrolling through Facebook on her phone. I barely stopped moving to grab her wrist and jerk her up from the table, pulling her behind me to the stairwell. I didn't want to get trapped in an elevator with Andy.

"Hey, you're hurting me," she screamed in a non-library voice. "Slow down, what's going on?"

I ignored her, grasped her wrist even tighter, and passed the elevator pushing through the exit door to the stairs.

"Where is he, where did he go?" I said, noticing Andy was nowhere to be found when I returned from my call with Kojak.

"The crying dude? He bolted right after you left to take that call. He's full of crap, by the way. Is that why we're running away from him?"

As we stumbled down the stairs, I didn't have an answer to her question. I had no idea why we were running. I was just doing what Kojak told me to do. And I was scared.

⌒

When we got to the street, the sunlight was so bright I had to let go of Louise's wrist to cup my hands over my eyes and look in both directions to make sure Andy was not there. The street was empty with the exception of a few cars moving slowly past the library. Louise stood on the sidewalk looking at me wild-eyed while she rubbed her sore wrist with the opposite hand. I looked down at my phone and saw there was text from Kojak.

> 911! Hubert is after Andy. Looking for him right now, has a gun. Not sure what he's capable of. Get out now. You don't want to be there if Hubert finds him.

Just when I thought things couldn't get any more complicated. I still couldn't believe the anger between these two men had escalated into something out of the Wild Wild West. Who goes after someone with a gun at a library? Was this for real? Or was this all just Hubert blowing smoke and the police being cautious because they didn't know what he might be capable of?

"I'm sorry, Louise, for scaring you. I didn't have a choice. I'll explain later. I've got to go. Do you mind catching an Uber?"

"Girl, you are going to owe me something fierce. First, I wingwoman that meeting with the grown man crybaby, then you drag me down three flights of stairs and turn my wrist into sausage. Now, I've got to find my own ride home? You're something else," she said hugging me and then giving me a wink to let me know she was kidding. "Don't know what you're mixed up in this time, friend. But please be careful. Love you. Call me later—*or else*."

As I watched Louise sashay down the block, her blonde bob catching the sunlight as she skipped a little to some unknown beat, I, too, wondered what I was mixed up in. And then I noticed someone else, a woman standing on the sidewalk staring at me. She paid no attention to Louise as she passed. She just kept her gaze fixed on me. It took me a second to recognize her from her profile picture on Facebook. It was Liz Parnell. Apparently, my text thread with Andy must have come up on her iPad and she followed us. But why? As soon as I spotted her, she ducked backward into an alley and vanished, making me wonder if I had really seen her at all.

40

DAY OF RECKONING

I'M A BIG BELIEVER that all significant days in life start out as ordinary days. When they become significant, you always look back at how they began and think, *If I only knew when I got out of bed this morning how it was all going to turn out, I might have stayed in bed.*

I had escaped Janie's grasp for one day, but then she called me after the library incident and told me she had me set up on a story bright and early the next morning. As much as I wanted to race over to the police station, plant myself in Kojak's office, and demand he tell me what was going on, I knew that I had to do my job first. Without the job, there were no tennis or piano lessons, no house, no summer camp in Maine. I was the breadwinner now and getting distracted from that mission was not an option.

The story Janie set me up with was about a blind, drug-and-bomb-sniffing German shepherd. Noki worked for a private company that handled searches for contraband at big events like concerts and conventions. While most working dogs specialized in one category or the other, Noki was the exception, excelling at both. He had apparently developed a very well-defined sense of smell after he lost his sight when a burglar broke into the family home and threw rubbing alcohol in his eyes to disable him. Noki's owner just happened to be a police officer, and when he found out from the vet that Noki was permanently blind, he was determined to give his faithful companion a bigger purpose in life. Since he worked in the vice unit of his police department, he got permission to train Noki to search for drugs. Eventually, he realized that Noki also had the ability to sniff out explosive devices after he found a homemade bomb in a teenager's room during a drug search. Noki's owner, Tom, eventually started a private company using Noki and other dogs with disabilities with keen senses of smell to conduct these searches.

When I pulled up to Noki's house, Tom came out to greet me. Noki followed him obediently onto the porch and sat ramrod straight at his side. My mind was going in a million different directions, but I willed myself to focus out of respect for Tom and Noki. Work was my therapy. I knew at this moment that this story was the perfect distraction from everything else that was going on in my life.

"So, I thought we would do a mock search first. I've hidden some things to simulate drugs in the house and you and your cameraman can just follow us around and get whatever video you need."

Buster had just pulled up in the driveway behind me, and I was glad he didn't hear Tom call him a "cameraman." The preferred term was "photographer" or "photojournalist," because they did much more than just point a camera and shoot, but regular people didn't know that. Tom wasn't trying to be disrespectful; he just didn't know what the appropriate term was.

"Hey there," Buster said, nodding at Tom. His hands were full of gear, so he nodded his head and his right hand with the tripod in tow at Tom. "I'm ready whenever you are. Just give me a sec to set up and I'll just follow you around while you do your thing."

I sat on the couch in Tom's den while Buster followed Noki and Tom around the house as he alerted for the mock bag of drugs. While I wanted to tag along, I felt like it might be too distracting for Noki, and Buster wouldn't get the video he needed. Plus, the house was modest with small hallways and narrow doors.

I kept looking at my phone, waiting for Kojak to text me with some news, but the more I stared at it, the more anxious I got. I scrolled through my email—it was the usual assortment of emails to the broader newsroom about stories we were working on or policy changes, there were my subscriptions to different news services, emails from the twins' school and from the summer camp they were planning on attending. The deposit was due. They needed medical forms filled out. There was a list of rules parents and campers needed to read and sign, and a survey for cabin assignments and food requirements, as well as a packing list. I sighed as I thought about how life had become so much more complicated since we held the world with all its stress on this tiny computer in our hands.

There was also the usual assortment of hate mail. Large and small perceived wrongs perpetrated by me and the station were documented and sent to me personally, *in detail.* From my hairstyle to a word choice to their imagination that I had some greater agenda other than feeding my family, they found a myriad of things to gripe about. Many of the emails were personally insulting, often threatening, and bordered on obscene, using colorful language to make their points. Back in the day, before email, viewers would have had to write a letter, put it in an envelope, find a stamp, and mail it. No one would take the time to do that today. It would be way too much work. Lucky for them, and unlucky for us, with a few quick keystrokes anyone could spew their vitriol at us. Knowing I sometimes had a tart tongue and often didn't use good judgment when responding to hate, I deleted them and then blocked the senders from further communications with me. It was for my own sanity, and it was a system that seemed to work.

"Okay, we're going to do the search for explosives now," Tom said cheerfully as he and Noki came back into the living room, interrupting my brief hate-mail-blocking binge.

"How did he do?" I said, looking up and putting my phone down on my lap to give the duo my full attention.

"Great. He found everything that I hid. And I think your cameraman got the shots he needed. I tried to go slowly, to give him time to get ahead of me and capture everything we were doing."

"We got plenty," Buster said, trailing behind Tom with his camera now down at his side. "We can do the explosive stuff and then set up for the interview. We're going to do that outside, right?"

"Yes," Tom said. "I hid it under my truck. You can come along on this one since we're outdoors. Just stand back a little bit so you don't spook him," he said waving for me to get up and follow them outside.

Buster set his camera on the tripod in the driveway about ten feet from the truck. I stood behind him as Tom and Noki came out of the house. Tom was giving commands as they got close to the truck. Buster had put a wireless mic on Tom, and he was listening through his headphones to make sure he could clearly hear what Tom was saying to Noki. As Tom got close to the truck, Noki stuck his nose under the right front passenger side tire and made an alert sign with his paw on the ground to show that he had found something. Tom pulled out a plastic wrapped package with wires protruding from it—something that was obviously meant to simulate a homemade bomb.

"So, we go to coliseums, amphitheaters, convention centers, anywhere our clients are holding major events, and we take Noki and our other dogs. We have nine dogs in total. We check the bathrooms, the vendors' kiosks, the seating area, the stage, every possible hiding place."

"Do you ever find anything?"

"Well, I can't tell you about specific cases because that would violate my clients' privacy and cause alarm at a particular venue, but yes, we do find drugs hidden and forgotten by patrons and sometimes, more rarely, explosives."

"Homemade explosives?"

"Most of the time. Unfortunately, there's way too much information on the Internet telling people how to build bombs. It's insane. And it's not that hard. Most of them are not very sophisticated and would only do limited damage to people in the immediate vicinity. But that's bad enough and our clients want to make sure their venues and their events are safe and free from anything like this," Tom said holding up the fake bomb in his right hand for emphasis.

"Why would someone do something like that?"

"Hard to say. If I knew the answer to that I'd be out of business most likely. The longer I do this work, and having a background in police work, I just think people seem to be getting angrier and angrier. It's like the littlest things can set them off, and they're looking for a way to retaliate, even if it means hurting innocent people."

"And, I guess you have to take them all seriously."

"Absolutely. First rule in violence prevention is always if someone threatens harm, operate like they're going to follow through. Society is like a powder keg these days, with people ready to blow. It's kind of scary, if you ask me. But that's why dogs like Noki are so important in creating the safest possible environment when you bring thousands of people together in one place. At least safe from this kind of violence. You can't stop every bad thing from happening in a crowd. That would be *impossible*."

As Tom continued to talk about Noki, his special training, how his olfactory senses were stronger because he was blind, my mind started to connect the bomb-makers with the hate-mail writers. He was so right about the bubbling anger beneath the surface of almost every interaction these days. Why was everyone so angry? What would it take to change that? Something major, I thought, something global, like a reset button on society that made us rethink everything we thought was important. It happened for a little while after 9/11, but how quickly we had forgotten those lessons of kindness, compassion, and helping others.

When we finished the interview, Buster and I shot a taped lead-in to the story with me kneeling down, petting Noki, who stood at rigid attention by my side with the help of Tom's commands coming from just outside the camera's view. If I knew anything about our viewers, it was that they loved seeing dogs on television. We could probably just play a thirty-minute video of dogs and it would get higher ratings than a newscast.

Finally, Tom released Noki from his military stance with the word "free," and I was able to sit on the ground and play with him for a few minutes while Buster packed up his gear.

"When will this story air?" Tom asked.

"Probably tomorrow at five. I'll text you. And then it will be online, too. I can send you the link so you can share it."

"Sounds great, thanks for everything," Tom said, giving me a hardy handshake while Noki nuzzled my legs several times as I stood.

"Bye, Noki," I said vigorously rubbing his head as his ears perked up and his tail wagged rapidly revealing his obvious delight. Why couldn't people be like dogs? Open, friendly, accepting, full of love for anyone who showed them love?

As I got into my car and started backing down the driveway, I realized I hadn't looked at my phone for at least twenty minutes. *That had to be a record.* When I got into the street, I pulled up to the curb, put the car in park and glanced down to make sure there were no urgent messages. There were seventeen emails and three texts. One text was from Janie about when the story would air. One text was from Miranda reminding me to make her a doctor's appointment for the camp health form. One was from Kojak. It read: "Big news! Call me ASAP."

I called Kojak as soon as I pulled out of Tom's neighborhood and onto the highway. I knew if I had sat there in front of his house talking on the phone, Tom would wonder what I was doing.

"So, give it to me. What's the big news?"

"Well, we think we may be getting close to charging your buddy with murder. Occam's razor strikes again; it's the simplest answer."

"My buddy, who's my buddy? You know I hate it when you use that term."

"Hubert, the shitty husband. He certainly showed his true colors the other night when he threw that guy, Andy, his former cook, out of the bar on his ass. We talked to him already, Andy. He's pretty beat up and shaken by the whole thing. And then, yesterday, Hubert was flashing his gun around at the restaurant, telling everyone he was going to look for Andy, and that if he found the bastard, he was a dead man because of the situation with his daughter. We got half a dozen witnesses who saw that. That's why I told you to get the hell away from Andy yesterday. I didn't know if this Hubert guy was blowing smoke or was for real. I didn't want you caught in the crossfire. This guy Hubert has got real anger issues, jealously issues, control issues, you name it. He perfectly fits the profile of a wife-killer. Plus, that towel on the driveway thing, well it's always bothered me. But I finally figured it out."

"It is weird. So, what's the deal?"

"So, everyone we talked to said Hubert was a frigging nut about his house—keeping things a certain way. OCD on steroids. And specifically, he had a thing about his driveway. Got it redone like every other year, repainted. He was a freak about keeping it perfect. Didn't want his wife and daughter to walk on it in street shoes. They had to wear slippers to the car and put their shoes on once they got inside the car."

"He put the towel down to keep from staining the driveway with her blood? Now, that's pretty bizarre."

"Yep. But he couldn't help himself. And he's such a control freak he didn't think it would tip anyone off. Apparently, the daughter, Delilah, had a towel hung in the garage that she used to do yoga on the driveway, so he must have just grabbed it. Believe it or not, he's agreed to come back for a more detailed interview. He's coming in willingly. Says he's got nothing to hide. But he is bringing a lawyer. Don't blame him. I would, too. This doesn't look good for him. And even though he comes across as a brute redneck, he's a businessman. He understands the optics of this situation."

I sat with what Kojak was telling me for a moment. It had seemed clear to me that Hubert was the obvious suspect from the beginning. A controlling, emotionally abusive husband with anger and jealousy issues finds out his wife is cheating on him *and* that the same guy is coming on to his daughter. It was textbook husband-killing-wife scenario, the perfect storm.

"And Delilah, the daughter. We're bringing her in, too. I'm not saying she was *involved* or anything, but I'm pretty sure she was covering up for her father after the fact, that she figured it out. And now, she's trying to protect him."

"You can't blame her for that. That would be a natural instinct to protect her father. You're not going to charge her?"

I suddenly felt protective of Delilah, thinking about what she had been through. As irrational as it sounded, I could understand her need to defend her father. He was all she had left. Maybe if I had stood up for Roger, he wouldn't have sat in prison for nearly four decades for a crime he may, *or may not*, have committed.

"Right, but you can't protect a murderer, if he is, in fact, guilty. So, we're going to leverage her for everything we can. If she knows *anything* and is willing to turn state's evidence, she won't be charged. But if she refuses to play ball, well, she could be looking at an accessory charge. And I'm not so sure she's been straight with us through this whole thing anyway. She's been throwing the Andy guy under the bus pretty hard, but it looks to me like there may have been some hanky-panky going on there between them."

That's when I told him everything—that *Delilah* was the woman who told me she was sexually harassed by Andy, that it wasn't just some random employee. I also told him about what I found on social media, about the picture of Andy at the bar. How it looked to me like he was there enjoying her company, *not* stalking her. I also told him how Andy told me she had invited him to the bar and then made a big show of calling her dad to have him thrown out—that it looked like Andy had been set up.

I stopped short about telling him about what I had learned from my conversation with Liz Parnell. For some reason, I still wasn't sure how she fit into all of this yet and wasn't ready to show my hand. She was a piece of the puzzle that didn't make any sense right now. I still couldn't shake the image of her staring at me on the street near the library. What in the world was she doing following Andy? When I reached down into my purse to get my car keys and looked back up, she was gone, *vanished*. Liz was further proof that there were a lot of people in this strange case that had secrets, things to hide, and motives to want Tilly Dawson dead.

41

AND IT ALL COMES DOWN TO THIS

As SOON AS I GOT HOME, I sat down in front of my computer and immediately went to Liz Parnell's account on Facebook again. She had 247 photos in her gallery, but there was one in particular I was looking for. Since our conversation, Liz had friended me so I could now see everything on her page that was once semi-private.

I was looking for a photo that was taken after Emmy had attended a birthday party a year or so ago. I remembered seeing several photos of the party with kids in the pool tossing around a large beach ball. There were also some photos of them standing around a picnic table poolside singing next to a large, white frosted birthday cake with Disney Princesses embossed on the top surrounded by lit sparkly pink candles.

But there was one specific photo I was looking for where the mothers and daughters were all lined up. Everyone was in bathing suits, but most of the mothers, including Liz, had wrapped towels around their bodies as not to appear in the photos scantily clad for the world to see. In my opinion, they all looked like attractive women who should have no shame about appearing in a bathing suit on camera, but I also understood how our culture shamed women into believing they weren't beautiful.

After scrolling through dozens of photos, I finally found it. I had seen it after a cursory review of Liz's account once she friended me, but at the time it meant nothing. The eight mothers were behind their daughters, one hand on their shoulders, one hand holding on to their towels for dear life lest they drop and reveal their bathing suits. I zoomed in on the photo and I could see the designs and colors of each towel. Liz Parnell was wearing a pink-and-white-checked towel. I screenshotted the photo and called Kojak.

"Where's the towel?"

"The what?"

"The towel from the driveway. The towel under Tilly's head."

"In a bag in the evidence room, soaked in blood, *her* blood. What else do you need to know about it? I told you we think it came from the garage. It's like a Target brand towel, nothing unusual about it."

"Listen to me. You need to get it out and examine it. I'm going to text you a photo. You'll understand why after you see it."

"Okay, kid. It may take an hour or so. Got to jump through some chain-of-evidence hoops and fill out some paperwork to make that happen. But go ahead and send me the photo." Despite his agreement to do so, he sounded fed up with my insistence on pulling the towel out of evidence.

As soon as I hung up with Kojak, I texted Liz and asked her if she had a minute to chat. I was a little hesitant to call her after the stalking incident from the day before, but I decided it was necessary to go right to the source. I would not mention the strange sighting of her at the library because I wasn't sure that she realized I had seen her. She texted me back immediately saying she was available to talk. She called me right away.

"Hey there. Can you hear me? I'm in the car on my Bluetooth on the way to an appointment. What's up? Is this about Andy getting attacked by Hubert?"

"No, I mean, *maybe*. I'm not sure what it's about, yet."

"Okay, well that sounds kind of cryptic. I knew Hubert would go off and show everyone what he was capable of at some point. I'm not saying Andy didn't deserve it—sleeping with Hubert's wife and then going after his daughter and all. He kind of made his own bed. But still, that Hubert is a piece of work. Thinks he can do anything he wants to in this town."

I was so caught off guard by her ambush, that it made me think I had made a big mistake in calling her. It seemed like she was willing to defend Andy at any cost, even if it meant defaming Hubert, who was quite possibly an innocent man—not innocent of *everything*, but quite possibly innocent of his wife's alleged murder.

"So, Liz, this is going to sound odd. But I need to ask you a quick question. Do you remember Emmy going to a birthday party, a pool party about a year ago? You posted some photos of it on Facebook."

"Sure, it was her friend Tenley's party. It was so cute, Disney Princess theme. They all had so much fun splashing around in the water. Why do you ask?"

"I will explain when I can. But just stay with me for a moment. Do you remember what you were wearing, I mean, not *wearing*, but what towel you had with you? I know it's a real long shot."

"I mean, I have a bunch of beach towels. If you tell me what bathing suit I had on, that might help. I'm kind of a geek. I like to bring a towel that matches with my suit."

I quickly scrolled back to the photo on my laptop. I could only see the top of the suit because of the way she was holding the towel, but the straps on her bathing suit appeared to be pink.

"Pink, a pink bathing suit, I think."

"Okay, well, and I can't say for sure, but I do have this really soft pink-and-white-checked towel that I may have brought with me. Although, I haven't seen it in a long while."

"So, the towel, do you know what happened to it?"

"Well, as I recall, Andy picked up Emmy from the party because it was his night to have her and I think I may have wrapped her in it to go home because hers was soaking wet. She was cranky, so I just gave her mine. He's supposed to wash everything when he has her and then send it home in a bag. But Verdine's washer is not the best. It's always busted, or at least that's what he tells me, so a lot of the time he doesn't send the stuff home, or he sends it home dirty."

"So, the towel, what about that? Did he ever send it home with her?"

"No, no, I don't think so. The last time I saw it, it was in his car. He always had a towel on the back seat next to the booster seat, a towel for his dog Chestnut to sit on. I think I even said something about it, asked him if he couldn't just use an old towel for the dog so I could have my towel back. He basically just blew me off, as usual, and it wasn't something I wanted to pick a fight about."

"When was this, when you saw the towel in his car?"

"I don't know, maybe two months ago? That's when I last noticed it. But most of the time I don't go up to the car. He brings her to the door."

"When was the last time you went to the car to get her out?"

"I actually know *that* for sure. It was about ten days ago. She had a fever and told Andy she wanted me to come to the car and get her and help her to the door while he carried her bag."

"Did you see the towel then?"

"No, as a matter of fact I noticed that Chestnut was sitting on a red plaid blanket that looked a lot more comfortable than the beach towel, even though it was a pretty sweet towel. I was about to say something smartass to him like, "*Can I have my towel back now?*" But she was so sick, felt really awful, it wasn't the right moment to start something with Andy. So, I just let it go. What's this all about? What does this towel have to do with anything?"

"I don't know right now. Just keep this between us. I promise I will fill you in when I can. One more question—it sounds like a pretty standard towel, was there anything unusual about it that might make it stand out?"

"Not really, I mean I think I got it at Target like hundreds of thousands of other people. Let me think. No, not that I can recall. Well, there might be one small thing. I mean I'm not sure when it happened, but Chestnut is a chewer. Andy never did anything to train that damn dog, chews everything—shoes, socks, Emmy's toys, underwear. I did notice when I saw the towel in his car one time that it looked like Chestnut had chewed the hell out of the corner of the towel, chewed it right off. That's the other reason I didn't ask for it back, figured I didn't want it all messed up like that.

You've got me curious. This doesn't have anything to do with Tilly, does it?"

Suddenly, Liz's voice had morphed from casual and helpful into a sharper tone.

"I'm not sure. I really don't know at this point. I just have a hunch about something. But I don't want to speak out of turn. Let me do a little more research on the situation, and I promise I'll get back to you. But please, don't breathe a word of this conversation to anyone."

"Will do, but don't forget to call me back when you know something," she said firmly. "Promise me."

"I will, I promise."

As I hung up with Liz, I felt like I had just made a terrible mistake. If Liz told Andy what I had asked her about, things could go downhill very quickly. Clearly, it looked like she would do anything to protect him. And then I had a chilling feeling, what if Andy *did* give her the towel back. Or, what if he never took it in the first place and the towel had been in Liz's possession the entire time. This could only mean one thing: *Liz,* not Andy, might be behind Tilly's death.

I was just getting ready to call Kojak back when my doorbell rang. I pulled up the Ring doorbell view on my phone and saw Andy Parnell standing on my front steps. He was looking right into the viewfinder, directly at me through the doorbell's video system. My car was in the driveway. He knew I was home. My only option to get away was to go out the back door through my screened-in porch and cut through the woods to another neighborhood, but he could be around the back of the house in just a few seconds. I had to buy some time. I texted him and said I was on a Zoom call in my home office and would be out in a minute. Then, I started moving toward the back door as I pulled up the Ring app on my phone and waited a few seconds before speaking.

"Andy, what a surprise. What are you doing here? How did you know where I lived?"

"Voter registration records. You're not that hard to find. No one is. I want to finish the conversation we started yesterday. I want you to hear me out about Hubert, about what he and his *crazy* daughter are doing to me."

"Andy, I understand. But my house is not the place for us to meet. Can you go to the coffee shop down the street and I will meet you there? It's just a mile away, take a left at the top of my street and it's down on the left."

I did want to hear him out but coming to my house like this unannounced was not appropriate and it made me very uncomfortable. So far, despite what others had said about him, he had been nothing but kind to me, with the exception of our first abrupt meeting. And I was still willing to give him the benefit of the doubt, but *not here, not alone.*

As I spoke to him, I quickly ditched my heels and pulled on my sneakers in the hallway preparing to make a run for it. Hopefully, he would get the hint and just go away. But I wasn't taking any chances. Luckily, I had on pants, not a skirt. I watched the screen on my phone carefully to make sure he was still on the front steps as I quietly opened the back door from the porch and started to descend the wooden steps into the yard. I kept one eye on the phone and the other eye on the edge of the woods and the trail that I would begin speed-walking down as soon as I reached it. I was trying to make as little noise as possible as I tiptoed down the steps. If I was wrong about him being here for an untoward reason, and I hoped I was, I didn't want to embarrass him or myself by acting like a fool, like a scared little girl running away through the woods.

And then, I got my answer as he responded forcefully through the phone.

"No, I'm not going to a coffee shop. I want to speak with you right now in person, here. You need to hear me out. You need to make this right. The police will listen to you."

I could hear the desperation in his uneven voice. It sounded like he was struggling to control himself, but he was failing. I had just reached the edge of the path, I looked down at the video and the frame was empty. He was gone, either back to his car, or he figured out what was going on and he was coming around the side of the house to find me. It would only take him a few seconds to get to the edge of the trail. My fast walk morphed into a jog and then into a sprint.

Suddenly, I heard him, his heavy boots cutting through the brush, crunching the gravel along the trail, his panting, the sound of him calling to me from a distance. My ankles between the bottoms of my pants and the tops of my sneakers were getting scraped and bloody from passing through a tunnel of pricker bushes that had grown over the path. I knew I had to get off the trail and run through the woods. He was a big man. It would be hard for him to navigate the trees and the brush. Plus, he didn't know the area like I did. Adam and I had lived here since before the twins were born. I had spent many hours with them when they were little on nature hikes in these woods, chasing them, playfully, telling them it was time to come home for dinner.

I ditched the path and dove into the thickness, pushing away branches and bushes as I went. My sleeves were torn, I could feel blood dripping down my arms, but I kept going. I could still hear him in the distance yelling, but I was widening the gap between us. I didn't have time to stop and dial 911, but I could open the screen with my thumbprint and hit a recent call number. I hit Kojak's number.

"Kojak, it's me, I'm running in the woods behind my house," I panted, trying not to be too loud.

"Slow down, kid, I can't understand you. Why are you calling me while you're running?"

"Running away, running away."

This got his attention. My voice was urgent. He wasn't used to hearing that tone.

"Running away from what? From who?"

"From *Andy, Andy Parnell.* He came to my house. He's angry. He's after me. I'm heading in the direction of Glendale. Need police."

"On it, and I'm on my way. It's going to be okay, kid, I promise."

I wanted to believe him. I really did, but as I pushed through the branches, I heard Andy's yells getting closer to me. I could now hear what he was saying clearly.

"You women are all the same. You can't be trusted. All you want to do is bring men down."

Those were the last words I heard before I fell. My shoe caught on a rock, sending me into the air. It felt like it was happening in slow motion. I landed with a thump at the foot of a tree, my head hit the bark with such force that I saw stars, then I felt more blood trickling down my face which was planted in the mud at the base of the tree. In the distance, I thought I heard sirens wailing, but I couldn't be sure. At first, I felt relieved. Then I turned my head slightly, through bloody tears and I could just make out a person standing over me. I wanted so badly for it to be Kojak. But I saw a full head of dark hair and realized it was Andy.

I knew how this was going to turn out. He jerked me up from the ground, my whole body battered, bloody and aching, and shoved me into a sitting position with the tree behind me to prop up my weary body. That's when I saw the pistol in his right hand. The sirens were getting closer. I hadn't imagined them. I estimated Glendale was probably just another third of a mile from where we were. But the woods were so dense, there was no way anyone could see us. There was no way anyone could get to us in time if Andy decided to kill me, to put a single bullet in my head like I now presumed he had done to Tilly.

Andy brushed the hair out of my eyes and forced me to look up at him. He was still fuzzy through my thick tears, but I could see the look on his face now. It was one of pure anger and disgust.

"You women think you can treat men any way you want. First, there was my bitch wife, Liz, talking back to me, letting herself go after having a baby, not wanting to do what she had to do to make me happy. Then there was Tilly, dumping me for nothing, for that old bastard that treated her like shit, disposing of me in a text like I was some loser, some piece of trash. And then, the worst of all, their devil spawn of a daughter who led me on for months with no payoff, and then she calls her crazy-ass father to attack me. You're all the same. Evil, undermining, sent here to ruin my life. The only good female in my life is Emmy. And I will make sure she understands how to respect a man."

I was going in and out of consciousness as he talked, trying to listen, trying to form any response that might keep him at bay, keep him from hurting me, or worse, *killing me*. I hoped in that moment I was worth a lot more to him alive, that he would think he could use me as a hostage or a human shield if the police found us.

Suddenly, I thought about the police. Where were they? The sirens had stopped. Where was my phone? It wasn't in my hand anymore. Had I dropped it? I remembered yelling into it to Kojak, telling him where I was. Had I hung up the call? I didn't think so, which meant if the phone was nearby, he might be hearing the entire conversation. Somehow, I had to let Kojak know where we were in case he was still listening.

I must have hit my head hard, because I could feel a large bump beginning to form on my forehead, and my brain was fuzzy, tired, zigzagging in and out of disconnected thoughts. I was fighting the urge to sleep.

"Listen, bitch," Andy said, placing the barrel of the gun under my chin and using it to lift up my face to look at his. "You're going to make this right for me. You're going to tell them I didn't do anything wrong. I didn't hurt anybody. Hubert is the bad one, and so is his asshole daughter. I'm the good guy. I'm the one who got the short end of the stick."

Even in my injured state, I could understand enough of what he was saying to be incredulous. How in the world could he say *he was the good guy* when he was holding a gun to my head? His denial was so beyond anything connected to reality. I almost wanted to laugh. But I stayed silent, trying to think of anything I might say to appease him.

"Okay. I will tell them that. Just please don't hurt me. I have two kids. My husband died. I'm all they've got."

He got quiet for a minute, and I thought maybe I had won him over. I was congratulating myself silently when I felt him slap me across the face with the back of his free hand.

"Do you think I give a shit about your kids? I have my own daughter to worry about."

And with my eyes closed, I braced for another blow to my face. But it didn't come. Suddenly, my hearing seemed to be elevated. I could hear every bird chirping, the wind slicing through the brush, a fly buzzing, Andy pacing in dried leaves in front of me. Like Noki's sense of smell, my hearing suddenly became bionic. Somewhere, not too far away, I heard the almost imperceptible sounds of feet crunching through the brush. I focused on it, as Andy paced, and talked gibberish under his breath. He obviously wasn't hearing what I was hearing.

I didn't care to understand what he was saying. I simply focused all my energy on the sounds of the feet as they got closer to us. I decided I needed to say something to him, to distract him, to keep him from noticing what I was hearing.

"You're right, Andy. You need to think about Emmy. That's why you can't hurt me. You'll just end up in prison. And then, you'll be no good to her."

"Sweetheart," he said, spinning around to look at me, holding the gun high up in the air this time. I had opened my eyes just a crack. "Do you not think I'm already going to prison for Tilly's murder? *That's inevitable.* And the amazing thing is that I was the only one who really loved her. That asshole of a husband, he didn't love her, treated her like crap. If she wasn't going to be with me, I had to protect her from spending the rest of her life with that shithead. And you know, when she found out about the Delilah thing, which was *nothing*, by the way. Just some fun, just a crush. Tilly really lost it over that whole thing. Made me feel like I was a monster. I'm just a man, just a red-blooded, regular man. *Not* a monster."

The letter, I thought, suddenly. The letter wasn't a suicide note after all. Just like I told Kojak. The letter was from Tilly to Andy after she found out about Delilah. It was the last straw for her. She was disgusted with herself for having the affair in the first place, and then she was even more disgusted when she found out he was coming after her daughter. It was all making sense now. And yes, *Andy was a monster,* despite what he was telling me.

"Get up," Andy said, suddenly jerking me off the ground. I knew I wouldn't be able to walk. I was dead weight to him, and he was annoyed. "We're going to move!"

Even now, it's hard for me to parse what happened next. There was a loud boom. It was probably the loudest sound I had ever heard that close to my ears, *louder than fireworks.* Everything went silent, as if the boom had temporarily blocked all sound, and then we were both falling to the ground. Andy let go of me, and we both fell backward. I hit the soft ground this time instead of the tree, but the pain from everything else made it feel like I was hitting a concrete floor.

I opened my eyes for a few seconds expecting to see Kojak there with his gun pointed at Andy, but instead, I saw a woman, a woman with brown curls and freckles. As the tears in my eyes suddenly drained, making everything clearer, I could see that it was Liz Parnell standing there with a gun pointed directly at Andy. Even in my foggy state I recognized her again from her picture on Facebook. I also recognized the look on her face—that of a woman resigned to getting revenge on the man who had wronged her.

And then there was lots of noise, commotion, commands being yelled, the sounds of sirens again in the distance, static from two-way radios, feet crunching through the underbrush. I felt hands beneath my skull, something soft being shoved under me to prop up my head, and then a familiar voice that filled me with hope. But it was not Liz's voice; it was a man's voice.

"Kid, it's okay. I'm here now. It's going to be all right. You are safe. We got the bastard; we got him in cuffs."

42

BLINDED

ANDY SURVIVED BEING SHOT by his ex-wife. The bullet just missed his heart. I learned later from Kojak that Liz had been following him when I spoke with her on the phone about the towel. My inquiries had sent up so many red flags, that despite her longtime love for him, she had realized he might be dangerous and wanted to find out for herself. That's why she followed him to the library the day before. She had the iPad that was still connected to his text messages that she used to track his whereabouts.

When she saw my text about being on a Zoom call, she knew he was up to no good, so she parked her car down the street and followed him as he walked around my house into the woods. Since her divorce, she had gotten a handgun for self-protection in her home. She went to the range on a regular basis, and she knew how to use it.

I was right about the phone. Kojak *was* listening to our entire conversation in the woods. They tracked me through Friend Finder. I had put the app on the twins' phones so they could always know where I was, and vice versa. Kojak called the school and asked the principal to get Miranda's phone and access the app and walk him through where I was. Once we stopped, the police surrounded the area and quietly crept through the woods until they could see us.

They were holding back, not wanting to spook Andy. And that's when Liz came out of nowhere, out of the bushes and shot him. Liz was questioned, but not charged with anything as her actions were clearly in the defense of another person who was in lethal danger. Personally, I knew her motives for shooting him were much more complicated than that, but in the end, she saved my life. I owed her a great debt, as did my children.

Just before my call to Kojak, he had gotten the towel from the evidence room and saw the pink and white checked pattern. But he didn't know what to make of it. All I had sent him was a photo of Liz wrapped in the towel with no explanation. He did recognize Emmy from earlier photos I had sent him of Andy, Emmy, and Chestnut and assumed she was with her mother in the photo. But he didn't know if my text was aimed at putting Liz in the hot seat or Andy. Frankly, at the moment I sent it I didn't know either.

After more examination, Liz's story checked out. The corner of the towel had been chewed by a dog, and there were dog hairs on the towel. Police got a search warrant for Andy's cabin and they were able to match the hairs to Chestnut's hair found in the home.

Hubert and Delilah were still interviewed because they would clearly be witnesses against Andy if the case ever went to trial. Hubert surmised that Andy, who knew Hubert very well, had put the towel on the driveway to frame him for the murder. Everyone knew how fastidious Hubert was, and it appeared Andy thought the towel would be a nice detail to include. He assumed because it was a generic towel that could be purchased almost anywhere that it could not be traced. He didn't consider the fact that his own dog would quite possibly send him to prison.

Hubert denied ever knowing about Andy's affair with Tilly despite Andy's assertion that he did. He reiterated that he fired Andy because of what he thought was an inappropriate relationship between Andy and Delilah. He said Tilly had brought it to his attention. Now that he knew about the affair with his wife, Hubert was doubly angry, not so much at Tilly, but at Andy for what he had done to his family. He even admitted to investigators that he was never a very good husband, and he could understand why his wife would have looked for affection in the arms of another man. But *that* man? This he could not understand.

Despite what Andy had said, Delilah denied ever returning Andy's affections. She said he made the whole thing up. That he was obsessed with her, and that he came to the bar the other night because he saw her post about planning to go there with her friends. She said when she saw him, she got scared and called her father.

Kojak called Candace for me and asked her to stay with the kids, telling them I had had a fall while running and hit my head, and that I needed to be in the hospital overnight as a precaution. *It wasn't a total lie*—I did have a fall plus two broken ribs, a huge bump on my forehead, five stiches in my scalp and enough scrapes and cuts on the rest of my body to make it look like I had rolled down a rocky embankment with no clothes on. Yet, with the exception of a slight concussion, there were no injuries that the doctors were very concerned about.

There was one call I needed to make myself.

"Liz, it's me. I'm so sorry I didn't call you right away. I just wanted to thank you. It sounds so feeble, just hearing the words come out of my mouth. But I can never repay you for what you did. *You saved my life.*"

"Maddie, it's okay. I'm just so glad you're okay. That he didn't hurt you. You don't owe me anything. I'm just thankful I followed my gut and *followed him.* I'm relieved I was there to stop him. I just can't believe I didn't see it coming. It's like I ignored all the signs. What kind of a mother am I to let my daughter spend weekends with that horrible excuse for a human being?"

"Liz, you can't beat yourself up. You loved him. You had a child together. He emotionally abused you, controlled you. You were blinded to his true nature. It's not your fault."

Liz was quiet on the other end of the line. I thought maybe I had lost her for a moment, that she had hung up.

"I guess you're right. I just wish there was a way to know if people were good or bad, some definitive test we could put them through so we would know for sure and not have to be blindsided like this."

I thought of Roger in this moment. I wished there were a test that I could give him so that I would know for sure whether he was good or evil, or maybe even just somewhere in between like most people. *Gray,* not black or white.

"Liz, unfortunately there is no test," I said wincing at the pain from my broken ribs. "We can only go by our guts, and sometimes, our guts are wrong."

EPILOGUE

AFTER I WAS RELEASED FROM THE HOSPITAL, my news director told me to take a few days off, to heal and spend time with the kids. The case had obviously turned into a huge news story. Keri Hue, the crime reporter who had taken over my old beat, came to the house to interview me with Buster. There were so many twists and turns, but I tried to tell them what happened in the most linear fashion possible. In truth, Keri really just wanted me to talk about my time in the woods with Andy and how I made it out alive.

They tried to interview Liz, but she declined. I decided I would do it for both of us and be the firewall that would shelter her from the limelight she was obviously shunning. I didn't blame her.

I wasn't concerned about talking because the prosecutor had already spoken with Andy's public defender who assured her that there was no way they were taking this case to trial—that it would definitely end in a negotiated plea, that the evidence against Andy was too overwhelming and the state would be seeking the death penalty if it went to trial. After all, Kojak had heard him confess through my cell phone as it lay on the ground in the brush near me during my brief encounter with Andy. Andy wasn't about to risk going to trial and getting the death penalty. He would take a deal for life in prison.

Still, I didn't tell Keri everything. Having been on her side of the camera thousands of times, I knew exactly what she was looking for.

"So, that moment, the moment you heard the 'boom' and fell, did you know what happened? Did you think you might be shot?"

"I wasn't sure. I didn't know where the sound came from. But as soon as we hit the ground, I heard all the commotion and I knew the police were there. I was going to be okay."

"I guess you owe your life to Liz Parnell. That had to be a huge relief," young Keri said with a little too much enthusiasm. I saw Buster rolling his eyes behind the camera, which was over her left shoulder.

"Yes, yes it was. And I do owe her a huge debt of gratitude. I am so lucky she was there. But it's still very traumatic for me. Imagine being on the edge of a cliff and almost falling, but at the last minute someone pulls you back and keeps you from falling. Sure, you're grateful. It was a near miss. Still, you never forget that moment of staring down into the abyss and being about to fall. That's what escaping death is like. It's like this great gift tempered by the memory of almost dying. It's really hard to explain. But I will never forget the feeling, *never*."

Keri looked at me momentarily stunned by the great sound bite I had just given her. Buster even looked stunned, and he was rarely stunned. There was nothing more I needed to say.

"Here you go, kid," Kojak said as he handed me a manila envelope. I looked at the return address, it was from Detective Zack Brumson with the Pennsylvania State Police. "I haven't opened it, even though he sent it to me. I figured whatever is inside is really for you to know and tell me if you want."

I thought about Roger's letter, his cagey confession that he didn't kill my mother, but that he still felt *responsible* in some way. With everything that had been going on with Tilly's case, I hadn't stopped to think about whether or not Roger was telling the truth. But maybe the truth was inside this large envelope from Zack. Maybe

Zack's truth and Roger's truth would be the same, or maybe, I would find out that Roger was lying. I wasn't sure which one would be worse.

"Kid, you don't have to open it now. Just wait until you're ready. Do it when you feel like you can handle it."

"I'm not sure I'll ever be ready to handle it."

"That's okay, too, there's no rule that says you need to get caught up in this thing. It's part of your past. You're the one who wanted to know because you thought it might help you heal, but if it's not important anymore, or you don't think it will help, or you're just not ready, then put it away. There's no rush. He's not going anywhere."

I reached across and put my hand on Kojak's. He had been more of a father to me than a Roger ever had. Not ever having a real father, I wasn't sure what a father was supposed to be like, but I imagined it was like this—someone who supported you, loved you unconditionally, and wanted what was best for you.

"Thanks. I appreciate your advice, and I think I'm going to take it. I'm going to put it away in my closet with all the letters from him I've never read and save it for a rainy day, save it for when I'm really *ready*. I've got a lot on my plate right now, a lot of healing to do. I don't need to add this to the immediate pile."

"So, what's next?"

"Taking a little time off, and then back to the grind. But I'm thinking about taking an extended vacation this summer, a sabbatical. The kids will be at camp in Maine; I thought I might go to the beach and write. I need some time and space to be creative. It's hard to find that space between work and parenting these days."

"And don't forget being chased though the woods by a homicidal maniac. All joking aside, that sounds great, kid, I think you should do that."

"It will be a nice respite. I think I can swing it. There's a podcast I've been thinking of working on about this old murder case that happened in the seventies that I read about. It sounds really fascinating. I've already done a little poking around to see who I might be able to interview."

"That sounds like *work*, not a sabbatical."

"It's all relative; whatever gives you joy, right?"

And with that, I tucked the envelope under my arm, picked up my to-go coffee cup and headed out of the cafe after giving Kojak a friendly squeeze on the shoulder. As the door swung open and I walked into the bright sunlight, I realized the world would always look different to me now after what I had been through. But maybe that wasn't such a bad thing. Surviving almost-death seemed like it could be a superpower. Now, I just had to figure out how to use it for good instead of evil.

NO WAKE ZONE

Maddie Arnette Series, Book #3

THERE WAS SOMETHING ABOUT THE WAY MY PADDLE BROKE through the water, like it was slicing through a layer of glass. I could see my reflection on the smooth surface as the sun rose in the distance, casting a reddish-orange glow on the horizon. Around my paddleboard, round amber jellyfish swirled and bobbed, their long white amorphous tentacles trailing behind them down into the murkiness just below the surface.

Paddling on the Intracoastal Waterway was calm and comforting. Docks jutted out within reach in front of massive waterfront homes if I ran into trouble—like needing to get out of storms that came up quickly in this part of North Carolina. Even in the early morning, recreational boats heading out to sea for a day of fishing traveled slowly in the no wake zone.

The only sounds were my paddle pulling back the water with a tiny *woosh*, and then brushing against my board with a shallow scraping noise. Boats tied up at the docks along the waterway bobbed up and down as I passed, straining against their lines, greeting me with their subtle groans against their entanglements.

I looked up at the sky and saw my favorite gray pelican perched in a nest atop a channel marker, looking down at me like she was smiling. I obviously didn't know for sure if she were the same bird I saw every morning, or even if she was a *she*, but I made up stories about her and her travels along the coast. She nodded as I passed, bidding me good morning. Sometimes, I pretended she was my mother, Patty, long dead, reincarnated as this magnificent bird to watch over me. In that vein I often spoke to her—giving her an update on my current life situation.

"Top of the morning, Mom. Vacation is going great. Yes, I'm still doing a little work, a little writing. But getting away from the fray has been good for me."

"*Fray*" was an incredible understatement. I had narrowly escaped death investigating my last murder case. I briefly ended up with a gun to my head in the woods before I was rescued. As a result, my boss had encouraged me to take a little break. Which I agreed to do. But I assumed that if my mother had, in fact, come back as a bird, she already knew all this. I didn't need to explain the whole thing to her.

To my left, the tide was low, and the marshes with their black oyster beds were uncovered, looking naked and unkempt with masses of green grass sprouting from the dark mounds. One step into their lushness would end in a severe cut to the foot as pieces of sharp shells littered the black, mucky sand.

Occasionally, I would see a blue heron in the marsh, standing at attention, looking royal, perched on a sandbar. At the slight sound of my oar breaking through the water, the heron would take off, its massive blue wings like a small airplane just skimming the surface as it ascended into the sky in a powerful display of nature's untouchable beauty.

All was right in the world when I was on my paddleboard. I left the troubles of the previous months behind me. I was healing both physically and emotionally. I was feeling strong again. While my kids were not with me, they were safe and having fun at summer camp, a new experience for all of us, this independence which felt at once sudden and also just right.

It felt like a new season of my life was truly beginning—as an intrepid news reporter who had traded crime for stories that made people smile, as a widow and a single mother determined to be strong for my family. I certainly didn't have *everything* under control, but things were finally coming into focus for me, a more authentic life was within my grasp now. I just had to paddle a little harder to get there.

When my paddle caught on something in the water, I thought it might be a tangle of seagrass. I had seen huge piles of the stuff floating like barges down the waterway over the years. But I also knew that while seagrass might snag my paddle, it wouldn't feel like I was hitting something solid. This was different; this was *not* seagrass.

Slowly, I pulled my oar backward to turn the board around so I could retrace my steps and look at what I had hit. I knew it could be a dolphin or a shark, so I quickly scanned for a fin. A shark fin moves back and forth along the surface; a dolphin's fin goes up and down. I had learned this years ago when I first began paddle boarding. If you were lucky enough to see a dolphin, you followed it and watched its graceful dance to the surface, into the air, and then down again. If you saw a shark, you got yourself calmly to the closest dock.

It also wasn't uncommon to see a stingray lounging in shallow water near the marsh, tipping one small part of its pointed body up, breaking the surface like a fin. Sometimes they even jumped sideways out of the water in a magnificent arc through the air with a stream cascading behind them like a waterfall.

But there were no fins on the water that I could see. As I cautiously approached the spot where I had felt the thud, I did see *something*. I saw red and white flashes of material fluttering just beneath the surface. As I got closer, I realized I was seeing clothing—red shorts and a white shirt, probably something someone dropped off a boat by accident. *Two strokes, three strokes, four strokes.* I was finally back at the spot of the thud.

I looked down into the water and realized it was not a pile of discarded clothing. It was a discarded person. The body of what appeared to be a young man was floating on his back just beneath the surface, arms and legs splayed like a starfish, dark eyes wide open, staring back at me, begging me to help him. But it was clearly too late for help. His face was slack, sallow, and marred only by a single brown mole on his right cheek.

Suddenly, I heard a loud scream slice across the water and bounce off the sides of the houses along the seawall, reverberating back across the surface to me. I looked around to see where it might be coming from. Then I realized it was coming from *me*. I was the one screaming.

Available Spring 2022

ABOUT THE AUTHOR

AMANDA LAMB is a television reporter with three decades of experience. She covers the crime beat for an award-winning NBC affiliate in the southeast.

Amanda is the author of numerous books, including true crime stories, memoirs, children's books, and the popular *Maddie Arnette* novels.

Amanda makes her home in North Carolina with her husband, two daughters, and her poodle, Dolly Parton.

Connect with Amanda:
www.alambauthor.com
Twitter @alamb
Instagram @wral_amanda_lamb
Facebook:/wralAmandaLamb

IF YOU LIKED *LIES THAT BIND*
you'll love these books
Dead Last by Amanda Lamb

When Suzanne Parker falls to the pavement in front of Maddie during the Oak City Marathon in her small North Carolina city, Maddie assumes it's an accident. But then Suzanne whispers words that make Maddie's skin go cold and sends her crime-fighting antenna into high gear—"my husband is trying to kill me."

The Nicole Graves Mysteries by Nancy Boyarsky

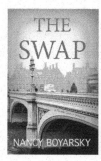 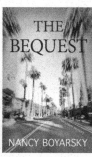 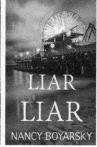 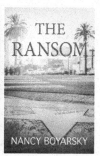

The *Nicole Graves Mysteries* have been compared to the mysteries of Mary Higgins Clark and praised for contributing to the "women-driven mystery field with panache" (*Foreword Reviews*) as well as for their "hold-onto-the-bar roller coaster" plots (*RT Book Reviews*). *Kirkus Reviews* concluded, "Boyarsky's weightless complications expertly combine menace with bling, making the heroine's adventures both nightmarish and dreamy."